TRANSPLANT

DEBORAH SIMINOU

Wild & Precious Life Press
Newport Beach, California

This is a work of fiction. Names, characters, places, and incidents portrayed in this book either are the products of the author's imagination or are used fictitiously. Any resemblance to actual persons, living or dead, businesses, companies, events, or locales is entirely coincidental.

Cover design by Miblart
Interior design by Taryn Nergaard

Library of Congress Control Number: 2025922944
eBook ISBN: 979-8-9931438-0-4
Paperback ISBN: 979-8-9931438-1-1
Hardcover ISBN: 979-8-9931438-2-8

This book is dedicated to the mothers
and loved ones of the missing.
May they find peace.

"The U.S.-Mexican border *'es una herida abierta'* (open
wound) where the Third World grates against the first and
bleeds. And before a scab forms it hemorrhages again, the
lifeblood of two worlds merging to form a third country—a
border culture. Borders are set up to define the places that
are safe and unsafe, to distinguish *us* from *them*."

— *Borderlands/La Frontera: The New Mestiza*
by Gloria Anzaldúa

1

The jarring movements of the truck startled Livia out of sleep. Her body ached as though someone had beaten her with a rubber hose. The dark air in the space was sweltering and reeked of exhaust and body odor. Her head pounded, and her mouth felt as dry as the sand of the Mexican desert where she was born.

Panic filled her as she tried to orient herself in the dim light. She could make out that she was in the back of a rickety truck. Despite the narrow air vents along the walls, she struggled to breathe. A faint glow came from a cell phone screen held by a young man—no, a boy—his back against the wall of the truck bed, wearing only a stained "wife-beater" undershirt. Sweat beaded on his dark forehead, and the damp peach fuzz on his upper lip hardly concealed his rotted teeth. The boy wouldn't meet Livia's eyes.

She tried to sit up but found someone had strapped her to some kind of gurney. She tilted her head and winced as a sharp pain shot through her neck. On the floor of the truck beside the boy, Livia noticed a semi-automatic rifle, its metal glinting in the faint light. She gasped when she spotted the IV in her arm, its cold tape pressing against her clammy skin.

An IV? Did I have an accident? she thought. *But why would an ambulance have an armed guard? This is something else. Something worse.*

She struggled against the restraints, trying not to draw his attention.

Trying not to scream.

The truck lurched on the uneven road, flinging Livia's body from side to side. Her forearms and shins felt bruised from where the straps and buckles dug into her skin. She swallowed nervously and looked at the boy. Even to her eighteen-year-old eyes, he looked so young next to the gun.

"*¿Dónde estoy?* Where am I?" Her words came out hoarse, barely above a whisper.

The boy stiffened but didn't answer. She tried again, louder this time.

"Who are you? Where are we going?"

He stole a glance at the closed doors at the back of the truck, then back to his phone. Finally, in a shaky voice he whispered, "Shh. I'm not supposed to talk to you. Stay calm. We'll be there soon."

Livia's heart raced. *There? Where was "there"?*

She thought back to the last thing she remembered from the night before but came up blank. Instead, the image of her daughters, Valentina and Ximena, flashed in her mind like a lifeline. Back in the village, her mom was looking after them, and Livia regularly sent them money. Their father had gone north to work in Kansas, and the last she heard, he had started a new family there. She pictured her *princesas* with their big brown eyes and long lashes, the way she held them both on her lap and breathed in the scent of their hair, trying to make it last until her next visit. She had promised to give them a better life, to shield them from the same desperation that she had faced.

Who will protect them if I don't come back?

Tears stung her eyes as she imagined the fate awaiting her when the truck at last stopped rumbling. Each possibility felt worse than the previous one. Sold to a brothel? Raped and left for dead? Perhaps she'd join the tens of thousands of *desapareci-dos*—Mexico's missing, faceless victims of the country's shadowy wars, their families desperately waiting for them to come home.

The rough straps dug into her skin as she struggled. Her voice broke as she pleaded in a whisper, "Why? Why me? I'm begging you, I have children." She tried again. "Would you treat your sister this way? What would your *mamá* think?"

The boy flinched and looked away, his face a battlefield of guilt and duty. He squeezed his eyes shut and crossed himself quickly, mumbling a prayer under his breath.

"You don't have to do this!" she pleaded.

"Be quiet!" he hissed. "If they hear you talking..." His voice cracked. He wiped the sweat from his brow and muttered a prayer under his breath.

Livia didn't encounter young people often. For the past year, she'd been living at a truck stop along the well-traveled highway running parallel to the U.S. border. It was a place that buzzed with its usual grim routine, a place where no matter how often Livia showered, she could never scrub the desert grit from her skin. The dry winds had turned her face, arms, and legs into something reptilian. She was still a teenager herself but felt ancient. At least the girls who worked and lived in the trailer there looked out for one another and shared a camaraderie, all of them rowing hard in the same rickety boat.

Now she remembered, blinking hard into the dark. Hours before, she had stood in her room, staring at the dirty gray ragged lace curtains hung where a previous inhabitant had dared pretend there was a window, let alone any kind of view worth framing. How her bunkmate had warned her about the driver of the purple and red truck.

"Keep your distance," she'd said. "He's always hopped up on *pericos.* You don't want to see what he's like when he gets too rough."

Livia had nodded, but there were no guarantees in her line of work. She'd jumped down from the upper bunk and landed on the flimsy floor of the trailer, closed her eyes, and taken a deep calming breath of air. As usual, it had smelled of diesel fumes and grilled *salchichas* and done little to steel her for the evening's work. She'd slid into her neon pink miniskirt, adjusted her tank top to show enough of her red bra straps, combed out her bangs, and applied her makeup with precision. Her reflection stared back at her, painted and unrecognizable. She wasn't Livia anymore—just another "lot lizard," as the truckers scornfully called them.

The night had started like any other. Grimy men with cigarettes and loud voices leaned out of their cabs, negotiating prices with girls who kept their smiles tight and their eyes wary. Livia remembered climbing into the cab of a semi, hoping to be in bed by 3 a.m. The truck was green, she remembered. Not purple and red. It was supposed to be safe.

But something had still gone terribly wrong.

Finally, the truck screeched to an abrupt halt, throwing both Livia and the gurney forward against the restraints.

"*¡Ya llegamos!* We're here." the driver barked from the cab, his voice muffled but sharp.

The boy scrambled to his feet, his small hands gripping the oversized rifle. He hesitated, glancing at Livia. For a fleeting moment, she thought he might let her go. But then he turned away, yanking the doors open to blinding sunlight.

"Let's move her," the driver growled, jumping into the back. She felt hands — rough, impersonal, lifting her. A bandana obscured his face, but his cold eyes told Livia everything she needed to know.

The boy snuck a quick glance at her one last time, his lips parting as if to speak. Then he grabbed the gurney and wheeled her out into the glaring heat.

Livia squinted against the sudden burst of sunlight. She felt herself being placed into what looked to her like a real ambulance this time, its faded red cross under a fresh coat of white paint. Two men dressed as paramedics moved in tandem, one driving while the other climbed into the back. The younger man leaned over her, his voice surprisingly gentle.

"Relax, *mija*," he said as he adjusted her IV. "It'll be over soon." A cold sensation rushed through her veins. The morphine dulled her pain and pulled her into the abyss despite her best efforts to stay conscious.

Just before everything faded into blackness, her mind raced.

Think! You can't let it end like this! Not for Valentina and Ximena. As the rear doors of the ambulance slammed shut, one thought burned in her mind: *Survive. For them.*

2

Francisco Obregón, or "Paco" to those who dared to call him a friend, stalked the edge of his property like a restless *pantera*, his boots grinding the well-trodden dirt path underfoot. He gazed out at the smattering of homes in the valley and the brown hills sheltering them on either side. He finally stood still and crossed his arms over his chest and, like a king on the turrets of his castle, surveyed his domain below.

Behind him loomed the immense and well-guarded hacienda where he lived with his wife Blanca and their three daughters Lola, Esperanza, and Teresa. Built in the style of *narco arquitectura,* its glittering gold accents, oversized arches, and overstated design made a statement about the owner's wealth and power.

Inside, preparations for his eldest daughter's *quinceañera* party hummed like a well-oiled machine.

Next weekend, Francisco's eldest daughter Lola would take her place as a princess, draped in a yellow ball gown that was as ostentatious as the hacienda. Francisco imagined the moment he would take her hand for the father-daughter dance, while his friends and family admired her and his rivals envied him.

A well-coiffed young party planner trailed behind him,

clipboard in hand, her impractical high heels digging into the dirt as she struggled to keep up. Every time he glanced her way, she seemed more nervous, eyeing the tattoos crawling up his muscular arms, shrinking away from the scar slicing a jagged line beneath his right eye. He knew his presence was commanding, and he liked it that way.

"I want my *princesa's* party to be perfect," Francisco said. "Money is no object. I want Lola's party to be unforgettable. After all, a girl only turns fifteen once, and her coming of age party should be something special."

The planner nodded in agreement, scribbling notes on her clipboard. "Of course, *señor.* We've planned a wall of roses here," she said, gesturing to the right, "and artificial cherry trees with twinkling lights around each table."

Francisco's lips twitched into a smile. The extravagance and the beauty of the celebration were a carefully orchestrated message. A show of force.

He spun away and looked back towards the hills in the distance. He marveled at how different this was from his own childhood in the countryside. His peasant farmer parents could not afford to throw a *quinceañera* for his own sisters. Memories flickered unbidden: a dirt-floored house, his father's bowed head, the sound of his older sister María's broken sobs as blood stained her torn dress, and little Francisco swatting angrily at a black moth fluttering near the oil lamp. He'd been only seven, too young to fully grasp what was happening. But he'd understood enough.

"The mayor said that nobody would believe me," Maria had sobbed. "That I'm a simple girl and a whore. He told me, 'I play cards with the police chief. It will be your word against mine, and who do you think he will believe? Me or trash like you?'"

Francisco had felt so powerless then. Even his father, a grown-up, had been unable to do anything to protect his family or get justice for his daughter. He'd felt so ashamed of his father and full of rage for feeling powerless. Now, he'd seen to it that nobody would dare lay a finger on his own daughters. His lovely wife would never work her fingers to the bone cleaning houses like his mother had. He had everything his father had not: power, wealth, and respect.

He adjusted the black fist-shaped stone amulet, the *mano de azabache,* hanging from a leather strap on his neck that he had been wearing since childhood. His mother, a devout Catholic-plus—following Catholic rituals while also hedging her bets with pre-Columbian superstitions passed down from her mother and grandmother—had fastened the talisman around his neck decades ago to ward off the jealousy of others. It hadn't failed him yet.

Francisco glanced back at the party planner, locking his eyes onto hers like a predator tracking its prey. "Make sure everything is flawless," he said, his tone brooking no argument. "The decor must be exquisite," he told her. "This is a night for kings."

The only thing that gave Francisco pause was the ever-present risk that one of the partygoers might fix the evil eye of envy on his daughter when she was the center of attention. Francisco rubbed the amulet three times with the right hand and three times with the left, as he did in times of stress.

He entered the house into his lavish living room where Lola was in her formal dress, practicing her dance. She looked up at him with wide eyes.

"*Papá,* do I look okay? The dress feels so heavy."

"*Princesa,* you look perfect. As beautiful as your mother on our wedding day." He took her by the hand and guided her through the dance, gazing at her tenderly. Then he proceeded to his office, where his expression hardened as he pulled out his phone and called Marcelo López.

"Marcelo, it's Francisco. I will come to the clinic tomorrow to discuss our collaboration there. I expect you will have some news for me about our progress."

"Of course, *jefe*. We are expecting a delivery, so you will be able to review our operations firsthand."

Excellent timing, Francisco thought. He did not like to trust important details to others more than necessary. His daughter wasn't the only one who'd never forget this week.

It was the start of a grand new phase for them both.

3

uby tightened her grip on the steering wheel of the golf cart as she approached the ferry dock and saw that the boat from Long Beach had already docked and the passengers were disembarking. Feeling the early morning breeze, she zipped up her purple windbreaker, then pulled her visor a little lower over her frizzy blonde curls and took a deep breath of the salty ocean air. She didn't relax until she saw Andy's familiar figure standing with a duffel bag slung over his shoulder, waving enthusiastically like a man who had just won a running race.

Andy Frederick learned early how to take care of himself. Most mornings, before the sun had fully risen, when his mom and brother were still asleep, he was already paddling out through the Huntington Beach breakers. The water was cold, the air too, but none of that mattered to him. The ocean was a key part of Andy's day, and nothing could keep him from it.

By the time he got home, shaking sand from his hair, his mom was already gone—double shifts at the diner, trying to keep food on the table. The note she left on the counter was the same most days: *Make sure your brother eats. I love you.*

Andy grabbed the peanut butter and jelly, slathering them onto Wonder Bread and cutting the sandwich in half. "Hey, kid, don't forget your lunchbox!" he told his little brother as Andy saw him walk into the kitchen rubbing his eyes, his sun-bleached hair sticking up at all angles.

During the long summer days at the beach that Andy lived for, his baby brother trailed behind him and his friends, trying to keep up. Before long, his brother was catching waves with the best of them, even the guys much older than he was.

At school, Andy felt like a square peg in a round hole. Letters seemed to jump around on the page. Teachers called him lazy, but he wasn't. As much as he tried to concentrate, he just couldn't make sense of it all. But in the water, that was always a different story. He joined the swim team, and the years of surfing had made him strong and fast. He knew with his academic record, college was not an option.

The summer after high school, Andy tried out to be a Huntington Beach lifeguard. The try-outs were brutal and competitive—long-distance swims, rescues, and endurance drills, but Andy thrived. The second he pulled on the red trunks and ran across the sand with a rescue buoy in hand, he knew that was where he was supposed to be. He couldn't believe he would actually get paid to spend the day at the beach.

Andy had a healthy respect for the ocean. As a surfer, powerful waves had pulled him under many times, nearly drowning him in the process. As a lifeguard, he saw the way a riptide could pull a kid out to sea in seconds. How a brief lapse of attention could mean he might miss someone being dragged under the water silently.

The same instinct to be near the water carried him into the U.S. Coast Guard. Andy was a natural, and he loved the structure and thrived in the camaraderie of the organization and the feeling that he was doing something important.

"Hey, babe," he said, wrapping Ruby in a bear hug as she stepped out of the cart to greet him. The scent of his body wash lingered as he planted a big kiss on her lips. She felt silly thinking it, a full-grown woman and a feminist to boot, but she sensed a flutter of warmth in her chest in Andy's arms. He was in his late thirties but maintained his swimmer's physique because of his active lifestyle and his job with the Coast Guard, and when he put his arms around her, she felt small and safe.

"I'm starving. Let's hit the Pancake House," he suggested, grinning widely. "I would kill for a cup of coffee." Ruby noted that Andy's unguarded expression was so different from her own carefully maintained composure.

"Great minds think alike. Jump in!"

Last month, for her thirty-second birthday, Andy had given her a card with a swashbuckling pirate on the front. To her surprise, the inside of the card contained lines from a poem by William Arthur Ward about how a person may try to avoid suffering and sorrow by not taking risks.

He knew she preferred to be comfortable and cocooned on *terra firma,* and she'd tried not to wonder if the poem was a gentle rebuke, its last line a challenge to throw caution to the wind and join him:

Only a person who risks is free.

As they drove to the restaurant, Ruby looked out at Lovers Cove next to the ferry dock, a marine protected area where snorkelers could feed the fish and tourists could view them while staying dry on the glass-bottom boat tours. Lovers Cove always reminded her of summers spent here as a child, before everything had unraveled. She blinked the memory away.

They shared a plate of pancakes with strawberries and whipped cream with a side of scrambled eggs as they caught up on the week they had been apart. Andy reached for a strawberry and spoon-fed it to Ruby. In her heart of hearts, she liked it but good-naturedly reprimanded him. "You're such a goofball. I'm not a baby!"

"I know," he teased, "but I like to take care of you. Is there anything wrong with that?"

Ruby loved his easy affection, but a voice in her head reminded her to be cautious. Her last relationship had started the same way, all tenderness and adoration—until the cracks showed. Nick's sharp words and cruelty still echoed in her mind, and the humiliation of his revenge haunted her.

Ruby felt lucky to have met Andy in line at a restaurant in Long Beach on one of her trips back to the mainland to see her mom. He was a breath of fresh air after Nick, but as sweet and loving as Andy treated her, she felt gun-shy. She was happy that Andy was divorced and had no plans to remarry anytime soon. Andy had told her that his ex-wife Mandy had felt lonely with him being constantly at sea for work, but instead of taking up pickleball or joining a book club, Mandy had been Netflix and chilling with her boss, who was also married with children.

"Where did you take the girls last weekend?" she asked, changing the subject. "The Aquarium? A Taylor Swift concert?"

"Haha, not this time. We hung out at my place, and I grilled up some hamburgers and then we watched a movie together. I made them turn their phones off. I want to spend quality time with them to make up for the lack of quantity now."

She admired the way the divorce turned Andy and his ex into amicable co-parents. They cooperated to manage the girls' schedules, and he generally put his girls' needs first.

"How was your week?"

"I was working on Dr. Fisher's books all week," Ruby recounted. "It took me days to recreate the financials since their hard drive crashed. Can you imagine not having a backup in this day and age?"

He shook his head. "On the plus side, more hours for you to log."

After two years of working in public accounting, Ruby had been able to "punch her ticket" as a CPA and set up her own business. She worked on clients that *she* chose, for only the number of hours per week that she wanted to. Ruby had been working remotely from her mom's private-gated community condo in Avalon on Catalina Island since the beginning of the pandemic. She could work from anywhere with Wi-Fi, so why not here in paradise?

"I guess so. How was your week?"

"Pretty uneventful. We saw two pods of dolphins. You would have liked that. We also had to go out and rescue a sailboat and its crew who lost their motors. But we also caught a sport fishing boat operating in a Marine Protected Area. These people couldn't care less about overfishing or environmental degradation. It's disgusting."

"Well, it's good that you caught them. I know how you feel about the ocean." But even as she listened intently to his stories, part of her held back. When he reached for her hand, she let him take it, but her grip was loose, tentative.

"Up for some snorkeling today? I brought my gear and some for you."

"I don't know, Andy." She pulled her hand away. "I do love the water, but it's so cold this time of year. And I know you think my shark phobia is ridiculous, but..."

"Yeah, even with the lame special effects, the Jaws movie scarred many people for life. Are you sure that's all it is though? Does this have anything to do with your dad's accident?"

Ruby thought about his question. As much as she loved her home on Catalina Island, it came with feelings of nostalgia and pain in equal measure. Every summer weekend, Ruby's family used their cabin cruiser to go to Avalon, which was still a sleepy town before cruise ships started stopping there. She and her siblings wandered like feral children, snorkeling, fishing off the boat, watching movies in the Art Deco theater on the first floor of the Casino, buying candy at Leo's Drugs and hiking up to Wrigley Mansion, stomping to warn away any concealed rattlesnakes.

At night, they hunkered down in their sleeping bags inside the boat and listened to books on tape as a family.

The family's trips to Catalina Island came to an abrupt halt before Ruby started middle school. Her dad died one July day while scuba diving in the dive park in Avalon Harbor. A Los Angeles County Sheriff's Deputy had singled her out from the group of teenagers waiting for the ferry back to the mainland after a three-week biking trip and asked her to accompany him to a waiting van. She saw her family looking tearfully out at her. The sudden loss made Ruby feel like a frolicking deer abruptly brought down by a hunter's bullet.

Now, when Andy spoke again, his voice was gentle. "Maybe facing your fears would be the best way to honor your dad's memory."

She wished it were that simple. Trusting the water. Trusting people. She didn't know if she was built for it anymore.

"I'm sorry," she told Andy now. "I'm just not ready. But I'll think about it, okay?"

Andy didn't pressure her further. He never did. But still, his birthday card flashed in her mind. The free-spirited pirate who deserved a woman bold enough to hop aboard with him. And that line at the end of the poem inside.

Only a person who risks is free.

Sunday evening, with her bare feet propped up on the balcony railing and a glass of Pinot noir in her hand, Ruby looked out as the sun set over the Pacific Ocean and took in a deep cleansing breath of salty ocean air, listening to the waves lapping against the beach. After many summer weekends on the boat, her parents had come to love Avalon so much that they invested in the condo where Ruby now lived, thinking they might retire there one day. Of course, Man plans and God laughs.

She'd had an amazing weekend with Andy, full of long walks to the Descanso Beach Club and fancy dinners grilled together at home and enjoyed sitting on the balcony facing the wide expanse of the ocean. And he'd said all the right things when he left about wishing they had more time together. Though a part of her felt the same way, another part enjoyed having a warm, kind and handsome man in her bed who would return to his own routines in the morning. By the time he left, the introvert in her was ready to rest and regroup.

Ruby was thinking about how grateful she felt to be living in such a beautiful place when she peered over and saw her neighbor Jaime, a mature Ricky Martin doppelgänger who shared the long balcony, sitting in his own deck chair nursing a beer.

"Hey, Jaime. How was your weekend? How's Robert?"

"He couldn't make it out this weekend, too much work. Had to stay at home in Torrance. Hopefully, he'll make it here next weekend."

"Andy was asking about him. Plus, he missed Robert's famous margaritas at Happy Hour. How are you doing?"

"No complaints here. I'm living the dream!"

When the condos where they both lived were initially developed in the spot where seaplanes used to land to deliver mail and the hillside was razed, many islanders thought the project blighted the environment and clashed with the town's culture. But to Ruby, the development reminded her of a Greek island resort, far enough from downtown Avalon to afford some privacy and quiet but close enough to eat at a nice restaurant or pick up her work mail from the post office.

The slower pace of island life suited her and also helped her manage her multiple sclerosis. Ruby's condition had first presented itself just after she'd graduated from college. Following the diagnosis, Ruby wondered if anyone would ever love her now because of her "flaws". From the very start, Ruby had committed to doing everything in her power to manage her symptoms. She incorporated meditation and light exercise into her routine and adopted a healthy diet, but stress impacted her condition more than anything. Leaving the CPA firm—and Nick—went a long way towards living a more Zen-like existence. She often sat there and looked at the ocean, feeling relieved at the twenty-five miles between her and Nick.

Ruby's corgi Abacus jumped in her lap, and she scratched his chin. Ruby had rescued him from a shelter after his adorable face, and even more adorable personality, captivated her. Abacus's fervor and unconditional love had become a comfort to Ruby, and she often had frequent conversations with the dog. They may have been one-sided, but they were honest, and he was a steadfast companion who enthusiastically wagged his tail at everything she said. At night, when she'd lay awake in bed thinking of the gentle patience in Andy's voice, Nick's voice was often there too, sharp and cutting, lingering like a smoke that refused to clear. But Abacus would curl his long warm body at her side, and she'd breathe a little easier.

"He's a good boy," Jaime said, chuckling at the dog.

"The best guy a girl could wish for."

4

Marcelo López had already showered and dressed for work. He sat at the kitchen table with a mug of steaming coffee, which he held with both hands. His wife Marisol sat across the table from him, her dark hair falling in waves around her shoulders, sipping her own coffee. Their housekeeper tiptoed around the kitchen, frying eggs and chopping fruit as she did every morning.

"It's going to be a busy day today," Marcelo muttered, the weight of his words settling between them. His green eyes were sharp, but his voice carried a hint of worry. "A busload of *gavachos* is coming in, and the *jefe* will be in town. I might not make it back for dinner."

Marisol smiled faintly. "It's okay, *amor*. My sister's coming over. We'll be fine. Have a good day at work."

Marcelo leaned in and kissed her cheek as he did every morning. He had known her since high school, and even now, after all the years of marriage and children, he still had no buyer's remorse. Marcelo tucked his purple dress shirt into his slacks and headed outside, where he found his driver waiting for him in a black sedan. Marcelo slid into the backseat, leaning his head against the cool leather.

He never forgot how far he had come. The gleaming high-rise apartment he had bought for his family would have once been unthinkable. Let alone the private school tuition for his kids. A *driver.* He allowed himself a moment of pride as the car glided through the streets.

Marcelo had toiled to climb the ladder, taking each opportunity, cutting each corner. His parents had provided for him—his mother, a nurse, and his father, a clerk at the Department of Transportation. But their life had been solidly middle class. Marcelo never wanted to scrape. And now he didn't have to.

The *New Me Clínica Médica* was a sleek, modern building tucked off Boulevard General Rodolfo Sánchez Taboada in the Zona Río in downtown Tijuana, a modern area with shops, restaurants, nightlife, and medical tourism. Ricardo, Marcelo's ever-faithful office manager, was already at his desk flipping through the day's schedule. He had been with Marcelo since they first met at the warehouse where they had worked together years ago. His decision to ride Marcelo's coattails turned out to be a prescient move as Marcelo's career trajectory had been nothing short of atmospheric over the years. Ricardo had been Marcelo's "work wife," organizing Marcelo's life and meeting his every need before Marcelo himself even knew that he had one. Now Marcelo relied on him for the daily operations of the clinic.

Marcelo nodded a quick hello at him. "What do we have today?"

Ricardo glanced up, his face unreadable. "Upstairs, we have three neck lifts, four facelifts, and five tummy tucks."

"And downstairs?"

"Three kidneys."

"Muy bien." Marcelo rubbed his hands together in anticipation.

"We have an important visitor coming, so no mistakes. *No la jodes!* Don't fuck around, got it?"

Ricardo nodded and hurried off to prepare for the day's surgeries. Marcelo felt a sense of satisfaction at the control he wielded over everything in his clinic — the precise scheduling, the calm efficiency, the business growing with every new client.

But as he glanced out the windows of the clinic that morning, his stomach tightened as a gnawing thought pestered him, the same one he had every day.

Sure, business was booming. He and his family had everything they'd ever wanted. But was it worth it?

5

A sudden pothole jarred the ambulance, moving Livia in and out of consciousness. Each vibration rattled her fragile body, and each bump sent sharp jolts of pain. Through her feverish haze, she caught glimpses of passing shadows outside the narrow, frosted windows at the sides of the ambulance. The air inside the ambulance felt suffocating.

The ambulance rolled into the dim parking structure of the *New Me Clínica Médica* and pulled up to the rear basement door of the clinic. The ambulance driver and a waiting male orderly thrust open the vehicle's doors, and she squinted against the bright sunlight as they rolled her gurney onto the pavement and then into the building.

The sudden cold of the clinic's air pushed Livia further into semi-awareness. Her damp mini-skirt and tank top clung to her, and her body trembled. The bright overhead lights were blinding and disorienting.

She tried to move, but her limbs felt like they belonged to someone else. As they pushed her gurney past rows of beds, she saw several people with pale faces, all of them unconscious.

Somewhere nearby, a deep voice echoed off the tiled walls.

"The demand is there," a man with a purple dress shirt was telling the other man with a scar below his right eye, gesturing toward the patients. "We could triple our capacity if the supply chain were right. North of the border, the doctors are eager to send us clients."

It was obvious that the man with the scar was in command. He stood erect as his serious face swept the room until his eyes landed on Livia's. He froze, his expression shifting ever so slightly. Livia stirred, blinking through her terror and fatigue, wordlessly imploring him to help her.

She could only imagine how she must look, trembling, vulnerable, still wearing her neon pink miniskirt. But that softening in his eyes. Maybe she reminded him of someone.

Please, she thought. *Let me remind you of someone. Someone who matters.*

The man's face turned red, and a glimmer of agitation flashed across it.

Then he clenched his fists and turned back to the man with the purple shirt.

"*Dicho y hecho,*" the man in command said, and though his voice was colder now, the other man nodded approvingly. "Leave the supply to me."

6

The day of the party was finally here. Blanca, Esperanza, and Teresa swarmed around Lola in her bright orange bedroom, chattering. Francisco strode into the room and sat down on Lola's intricately carved wooden bed with the green velvet headboard, clearing away some of the decorative textile throw pillows to make room for himself. He saw Lola's reflection in the mirror over her dressing table and smiled at how lovely his daughter looked, how grown up. He felt content, knowing that his *princesas* were happy, that he could provide this life for them.

"*Papá,* can you help me with my tiara?"

"Of course, *mi vida,*" Francisco crossed to the dressing table, glancing out of Lola's bedroom window to the backyard below where the elaborate party arrangements were being set up. In the distance, his security guards walked the perimeter of the hacienda with rifles slung over their torsos.

"*Papá,* aren't you happy? You keep looking out the window."

Francisco forced a smile. "I was just thinking about how beautiful you look."

"Will you dance with me later?"

"Of course I will!" he nodded, but again his eyes drifted to the guards outside.

Francisco hadn't expected how apprehensive he'd feel about the enormity of the event. He had so many family members and friends coming, as well as his colleagues in La Familia and their wives and children. He also invited some of his rivals so that they could see that he was the king of his castle. Cartels implicitly agreed family events were neutral territory. Still, he reached for his amulet, caressing the smooth stone.

"Come," he said, setting the tiara on his daughter's head. "Our guests are about to arrive."

As they headed downstairs to greet their guests, a crowd was already forming. He spotted Don Emiliano from Sinaloa. *I need to keep an eye on him,* Francisco thought, excusing himself from his wife to speak with him. Emiliano was an aggressive man, a man with pretensions. Francisco needed him to know that he better not get any ideas.

"Don Emiliano." Francisco looked him in the eye. He placed his left hand on Emiliano's shoulder, signaling that he was the alpha male. "Thank you for coming. I hope you and your wife will enjoy yourselves."

"Thank you for hosting us." Emiliano glanced over at Lola and then back at Francisco. "It's a beautiful celebration, Francisco. A real testament to family. Let's hope nothing spoils it."

With a surge of adrenaline, Francisco gripped Emiliano's arm, his voice a low growl. "If you so much as breathe in her direction, I'll bury you myself."

"Take it easy," Emiliano laughed dismissively. "I meant nothing by it. It's just that she is so stunning. It's hard to protect such a precious treasure. She will have many suitors."

Francisco slowed his breathing and looked away. He fingered

the talisman around his neck. He wouldn't let anything spoil this evening. Emiliano was goading him to get him to react. He refused to give the man the satisfaction. But the exchange had left him feeling shaken, and his head throbbed.

"Why don't you go get yourself a drink and enjoy the evening?"

"Thanks, Francisco. I will."

As Emiliano walked away, Blanca walked quickly to her husband's side.

"You look angry. Is everything okay, *mi amor?*"

"Yes, but I don't trust Emiliano. He's a sneaky bastard."

"But what did he say to you?"

Francisco relayed Emiliano's words to Blanca, and she turned pale. "Do you think she's in danger?" she stammered. "I hate the people in your business. I hate it is such a dangerous life. Oh, Paco!"

"Come here," he said, pulling her face to his. "I have everything under control."

"But what if something happens to Lola? Or to you? Every time you walk out the door, I worry that something bad will happen to you!"

They had had so many versions of the same argument over the years, and Francisco responded with the same refrain. "Everything I do is for you and the girls. You think I want this life? It's what I had to do!"

"What if we leave it all behind?" Blanca begged. "We have money outside the country. We could leave. We could survive with less."

"I refuse to run away like a dog with its tail between its legs. I have worked hard for this family, to give you and the girls everything you could ask for in this life. I will not throw it all away! You need to trust me."

That night, although Francisco felt exhausted from the day's events, he lay in bed still unsettled, listening to Blanca's light snoring. Suddenly, he heard a rooster's crow echo across the valley. That was an omen of death, he knew, and it chilled him to the bone.

7

After she put the kids to bed, María Elena Pérez sat hunched over the desk in her small home office. She typed on her laptop, feeling angrier and more determined with each sentence. She was nearly finished with the article, and she knew it would displease those in power. But this was the truth, and she would write it for anyone brave enough to read it.

A photo of her father as a young man hung on the wall beside her, notebook in hand, his face lit with the same determination she felt now. Journalism ran in her blood. She could still hear her father's voice, warning her when she revealed her career plans: *"María, the truth is a dangerous thing here."*

María brushed his warning aside as she worked, the house quiet and dark except for the colorful Talavera lamp on her desk. She had chosen the journalist life with intention, the way she'd chosen every word she typed. She knew Mexico was one of the most dangerous countries in the world for journalists. Law enforcement was no help because public officials committed half of all attacks on journalists, and they blamed organized crime for everything. Outside, she heard the revving of a motorcycle passing by. She winced, listening intently, but to her relief heard the noise fade into the distance. She chided herself for being paranoid and so easily distracted from her task.

Her phone dinged. She glanced at the screen and saw another message from an unknown number.

"Stop this story, or we'll stop you."

Her chest tightened, but she set the phone aside. It wasn't the first threat she'd received, and it wouldn't be the last. She wrote about the twenty-five thousand people who had disappeared in her home state and the discovery of mass graves. She researched Mexico's Dirty War which mirrored those in Chile, Argentina, and Guatemala in the 1970s and 80s in which the secret police and the military tortured thousands of young dissidents and made them disappear, burying their bodies in clandestine graves or tossing them out of airplanes into the ocean. After all, no body, no crime. She wrote to bring attention to the fact that various cartels adopted the Dirty War tactics, causing the mass disappearances happening right now in Mexico. She reviewed the article she was writing and selected the most representative photos she had taken of the grieving mothers she had interviewed, their hands gripping photographs of their missing children.

These stories needed to be told.

After a night of fitful sleep, María sat at the kitchen table with her two young children. She put her worries out of her mind and gave the children her undivided attention. Her daughter smiled and showed her latest drawing to her mother, expecting praise. María let herself relax, the laughter shielding her, if only for a moment, from the very real dangers she was facing.

Then her phone dinged again. This time, the photo captured her children outside their school earlier that day.

Her hands shook as she gripped the cell phone.

"We know where they are."

Her daughter looked up, concern in her eyes. "*Mamá,* are you okay?"

María forced a smile. "I'm fine, *mi amor.*"

Her heart said otherwise.

The next morning, María stood outside a courthouse, clutching a folder of legal documents. Bogus lawsuits were used as a tool, intended to exhaust her. A reporter from another outlet approached her.

"María, do you ever think about stopping?" he asked. "I'm sure you're in their crosshairs. They'll never leave you alone while you're shining a light on their sins. It's not safe!"

María straightened her shoulders. "If I stop, who will tell their stories?"

He didn't answer.

That night, María wrote another exposé, this one about some crimes of La Familia. She believed in her heart that freedom of the press was vital because it provided citizens with the information that they needed to hold their leaders accountable. She also believed that what happens to journalists in Mexico should be a cautionary tale for other countries. María stayed up late, long after her children had gone to bed, and put the finishing touches on her work. Afterward, she sat back, staring at the screen, and took several deep breaths to calm herself.

The silence of the house felt heavier than usual.

Two weeks later, she was driving home late at night after gathering evidence for a story when a black SUV appeared in her rearview mirror. Her eyes moved back and forth between the road and the car behind her. At first, she wasn't sure that she was being followed but then noted that every turn she made, the other vehicle did as well.

The realization that it wasn't all in her mind made her heart beat faster in her chest. Without thinking, she gripped the steering wheel tighter. Then it happened. The SUV accelerated, slamming into the rear bumper of her car. She felt the force of the impact in her bones, and her head ping-ponged sharply forward and back.

She pulled over to steady herself, waiting for the worst, but no one got out of the SUV. It sat there watching her for a moment, its headlights blazing into her rearview mirror, and then it sped off.

When she got home, her hands shook so much that it was difficult for her to put the key into the lock. The house was silent as she had sent her children to her sister's house for the night. She sensed the emptiness and lack of the usual toddler energy and felt a visceral longing for them.

She didn't sleep that night.

Days later, María's front door stood wide open. Her neighbors called her name with a sense of dread and peeked in through the open door. Inside, the house was in disarray, and furniture was overturned.

María's lifeless body lay on the kitchen floor, her face bruised and battered. Her laptop and phone were missing, but her purse and other valuables were still on her desk.

The neighbors whispered among themselves. They had seen this before.

"Those poor children! Do you think it was a robbery?" one asked.

"No," another whispered. "Everyone knows what this was."

The authorities looked at it differently. According to the official statement, this was a burglary gone wrong, totally unrelated to María's work as a journalist. No arrests were ever made, and her murder went unsolved.

But her words and her truth remained. The articles she wrote and the truths she uncovered would never disappear.

8

Francisco took a long drag on his cigarette and looked out the window onto the spacious backyard of the hacienda with satisfaction. He exhaled and brought his gaze back to the men facing him expectantly from across the other side of his imposing desk, a tile crucifix hanging on the wall behind him.

The maid entered through the office door silently to make sure that her *patrón* needed nothing more from her. She glanced at the men assembled in the room, then at Francisco. He nodded his chin at her toward the door, and she walked out, closing it behind her.

The office was silent as the lieutenants settled into their colorful hand-painted country-style wooden chairs arranged in a semicircle. They sat up straight like schoolboys in front of a strict teacher, their glasses of tequila untouched. The men knew better than to relax in Francisco's presence and, anyway, it could be taken by him as a sign of disrespect.

"Let's get started," Francisco said, his voice low but commanding. He looked at each of his men and then said, "David, begin."

David Sánchez, who had been his best friend since childhood

and was also his first cousin, was now his most trusted lieutenant. Francisco knew that when push came to shove, blood trumped all. He trusted David with his life. When he wanted to talk through an idea or had to deal with a rival cutting in on La Familia's territory, he turned to David. The other lieutenants respected David, and the rank and file feared him. But Francisco commanded fear and respect more than anyone else in the room.

David ran his fingers through his thick hair. "Paco, most of the territories are running smoothly, but Armando's plaza is another story. We've had more seizures than usual, especially with the larger shipments. Something feels off, like someone's been running their mouth."

Francisco drew in a long, steady breath to calm himself, his nostrils flaring. He reached for his cigarette, feeling his head throb. "What about the sweets we have been handing out to the guards and the Chief of Police? They've all been eating from the trough, haven't they?"

David nodded. "Yes, they have. Nothing's changed there. Maybe it's just bad luck."

Francisco took a deep drag from his cigarette, giving himself time to compose his thoughts, the scar on his cheek deepening as he inhaled. He didn't believe in coincidence. Bad luck wasn't random; it was a living, breathing thing. He rubbed the amulet again with his thumb, caressing the smooth stone to calm himself.

Francisco drank superstitions in his mother's milk and was always on the lookout for bad omens. He once cancelled a multi-million-dollar business deal at the last minute because the night before he had seen a large black moth fluttering around the lamp at the front door enter the house, which his mother had told him was a bad omen.

"Keep an eye on it," Francisco told David. "If it's not just bad luck, we'll root out the problem. I won't tolerate betrayal."

David promised he would do so, as Francisco turned his attention toward the next lieutenant. One by one, they gave their reports detailing bribes, shipments, and territories secured. Francisco listened in silence, noting what was said and what was left unsaid.

Francisco had come up through the ranks of La Familia, from foot soldier to lieutenant and now Boss. He still remembered when, as an eight-year-old boy, he first saw a lieutenant with his gold chains and brand-new F-150 truck near his village and told himself that he wanted that success for himself. He wanted little boys to admire him like that when he grew up. Once he began doing odd jobs for cartel associates to earn some pocket change, people around him started looking at him differently. His parents warned him not to get involved with those people, that they were dangerous and not God-fearing. But he liked the feeling that others' fear and respect gave him.

Even at a young age, he knew that it wasn't his destiny to stay on the ranch. His parents believed that hard work and faith would be rewarded. But they were at the mercy of the landlord, of the crops, and of Jesus himself. Francisco refused to bend over and pick strawberries in the blistering sun for the rest of his life like the people in his village.

La Familia recognized that Francisco was clever and resourceful, and he worked hard to move up. As a foot soldier, Francisco had followed orders without question and had become an integral part of the group over the years. He was loyal to his family and La Familia and expected the same from his men. And now he was on top and intended to stay there. No matter what.

When the last man finished speaking, Francisco took another drag on his cigarette and exhaled deeply towards the men. He let the silence stretch, watching his lieutenants squirm under his gaze. When he was ready, he spoke.

"There's another matter," he said, his eyes serious. "The Tijuana venture."

At the mention of Tijuana, the lieutenants looked up with interest. They shifted in their chairs, their expressions guarded.

"I visited a few days ago," Francisco continued. "The operation is already solid and profitable. But there's huge potential for growth." He sat back in his chair and took a gulp of tequila. "We need more donors. I need everyone to spread the word throughout our network that we are offering cash payments for every donor and referral. Convince them it's a safe and easy way to make some quick cash."

The men nodded their understanding, but Francisco thought he saw tension in their shoulders, the way they glanced at each other, but their expressions remained neutral. This venture raised the stakes for all of them.

As the meeting concluded, Francisco dismissed the men with a curt wave of his hand. David lingered, his broad frame casting a long shadow across the room.

"What is it?" Francisco asked, his tone softening slightly.

David stayed back, signaling to his cousin that he had something more to say. Once they had all left, he asked, "Do you trust them, Paco? All of them?"

Francisco's eyes darkened. "Trust is a luxury, *primo*. What I trust are results."

A black moth tapped its wings against the glass of the windowpane.

9

Ruby's mother Janice's longtime and perhaps only friend, Doris, had called Ruby earlier in the day to tell her that an ambulance had taken Janice to the hospital. A few hours later, Ruby hustled into the hospital room, sun-kissed, her blonde hair wild from the boat ride. Her mother was sitting up in the narrow bed, her hospital gown slipping off one shoulder. She tugged it back into place, then adjusted the pillow behind her head with a jerky motion.

"Hi, Mom. How are you feeling?" Ruby asked, her voice a careful, practiced tone.

Janice tilted her head and gave a thin smile. "Oh, you know me. I can't complain."

Ruby's face tightened. *I can't complain? Haha. Her mom did nothing* but *complain.*

Her mom's face was puffier than the last time Ruby saw her, a yellow tinge shadowing her cheeks. She pulled at the hospital gown again, fingers brushing over her neckline, hoping the loose fabric could somehow flatter her. "God, I must look terrible. Do I look terrible?"

Her mom had always been vain, getting Botox and the occasional nip and tuck to keep herself looking youthful. She used to disdain women who "let themselves go". But now she constantly lamented her appearance to Ruby, saying things like, "Will you look at me now? I'm like an Easter Peep marshmallow!" or "Jesus, Mary, and Joseph, I look like an old hag!" Ruby reassured her, saying "You look great for your age. You have a medical condition," but that didn't stop the griping one iota.

"No, Mom," Ruby lied. "You look fine. But really, how are you feeling?"

When in her mom's presence, Ruby struggled to think compassionate thoughts, calling up the loving-kindness meditation phrases for dealing with difficult people to repeat in her head. "May you be happy. May you be peaceful. May you be free from suffering." Ruby had been working on sending compassionate thoughts to her mom for years. She tried not to, knew it was pointless, but she still held a grudge about so many things from her childhood.

After her dad's death, her mom thought of herself first, as she always had. Ruby and her sister and brother were also hurting, but Ruby had to see her mom canoodling with a man ten years her junior in the kitchen of their house with the yellow tiles that her dad had picked out, *before his body was even cold,* she thought resentfully.

Within a year, her mom had remarried a man who on the surface seemed to be genuine, but a short time later he disappeared like a thief in the night. The new husband was, in fact, a thief, and a con man, having emptied their safe of diamonds that her dad, a history buff, had amassed through hard work over the years after reading *The Rise and Fall of the Third Reich,* thinking that they might be needed one day to keep his family safe and alive. *How could she have been so gullible to trust a man that much after such a brief courtship?* Ruby swore to herself that she would never make the same mistake.

Ruby knew her mom was afraid, and she couldn't fault her for that. Her liver had been on a downward spiral for years. When Janice had told Ruby about her initial diagnosis - Wilson's disease - Ruby had never heard of it.

"You see!" her mom had told her indignantly. "I'm not a secret boozer like the doctors accused me of being once they saw the cirrhosis. It's a genetic problem." *Not that Janice had ever been concerned that her offspring might be carriers or have the disease themselves.*

Now, according to Janice, she needed a liver transplant.

"The doctors say I'm going home tonight, but we'll see." Ruby heard the cynicism in her mom's voice. *As if it's my fault that she is sick.* She fought the urge to roll her eyes. *Don't let her get to you. Don't engage* she told herself. She was concerned, though, and her mother did not look healthy at all, her face swollen and tinged yellow.

Ruby wondered again how Doris had been able to put up with her mom all these years. Of course, it was Janice's world and Doris was only living in it, but still.

Ruby pulled up a chair and sat next to Janice's bed. "But really, Mom, how are you feeling?"

"If you want to know the truth, I'm getting really tired of waiting for UNOS to call me," she complained. "You know it's not first-come, first-served. They decide who gets an organ based on how sick a person is, what their survival chances are, and how good the donor-recipient match is. I'm so disappointed that none of you were a good match for me."

Ruby's eyes widened. "I know it's hard to be patient. It's so sad that there are more people waiting than there are organs."

"I don't understand why people can't sell their organs. It would fix everything, wouldn't it? People sell blood and sperm all the time. Why not organs?"

Ruby shook her head, frustration building as she bit back a sigh. "Mom, it's not that simple. You know that. When you give blood, you eat a few crackers, drink a little juice, and you're basically fine. Organ donation is major surgery and a lot riskier than giving blood. If people could sell organs, you know it would be the poor selling and the rich buying."

"You're so idealistic!" Janice said. "It's easy to be idealistic when you're not the one facing the reality of it. If the seller gives consent, who is Big Brother to say what people can or can't do with their own bodies?"

Ruby tried to keep her voice calm and measured. "How would that be ethical, Mom? You'd be taking advantage of people who don't know better."

Janice's lips twisted into a bitter smile. "You've always been a bleeding heart. You're sure you know how the world works. You need to get off your high horse before I die without ever getting the call."

Ruby paused, searching for the words. "Of course I want you to get a new liver, Mom. But the system has to be fair to everyone. America is not like Pakistan where some poor bastard sells a kidney to free himself from slavery or get out of debt but then afterwards he can't work because of his health and he's right back where he started. And a middleman took most of the money from the sale, anyway. How can someone so uneducated even give consent if they don't understand the very real risks of a surgery like that? If organs were for sale, it would always be the most vulnerable people who would get screwed. What about their human dignity? Do you really think it would be right for us to 'plunder peasant parts for profit'?"

Janice's face turned red, her anger building. "I don't see how you can justify not taking a theoretical risk to a total stranger when your flesh and blood is sick and has a real and immediate need. I hope your idealism still holds when I die of liver disease before they call me." Janice turned her face to the wall.

Ruby said her goodbyes and took the elevator to the first floor to exit the hospital. She summoned an Uber to catch the last ferry of the day back to the island from Long Beach. She needed to finish up the Carters' financials, and her mom was stable. *At least physically.*

The night had turned cold, and the wind had picked up. Ruby pulled her sweatshirt out of her backpack and put it on before she stepped out of the Uber in front of the ferry terminal. She then started walking towards its large glass doors. The island was calling her back. The sidewalk was dark and deserted since by now all of the tourists had come back to the mainland. She adjusted the strap of her purse on her shoulder and glanced at her phone. *Thirty minutes until the last ferry.* Her shoulders relaxed, but the feeling was short-lived.

As the driver pulled away, out of the corner of her eye, Ruby saw a man step out of the shadows and walk right towards her. She glanced up, and when her eyes locked with Nick's, her chest tightened. *How did he find me?*

"What are you doing here?" she hissed, her voice low but sharp. She recoiled, her hand fumbling at her side. "You're not supposed to be within a hundred yards of me. There's a restraining order, remember?"

He smirked at her, hands raised in mock surrender, though

his voice was tight and sarcastic. "I remember," Nick said, moving one step closer. But you wouldn't answer my calls. What was I supposed to do? I knew you would visit your mom eventually, and I was right."

"It's over, Nick," she stuttered. "It's been over for a long time. Can't you accept that and move on?" she begged, her voice shrill.

She willed herself to run inside the ferry building for help, but she felt rooted to the spot. Her stomach clenched as she looked around to see if anyone was nearby that could help her but saw no one. Her arms felt weak as her fingers inched toward the side pocket of her backpack.

She remembered the early days of their relationship. He had been the charming guy - bringing her flowers, chocolate, telling her she was beautiful, making her feel special. For the first time in her life, she felt safe enough to open up to someone. *I thought he loved me.*

He had shared with her how when he was a child, his mom never paid attention to him, sat on her butt smoking and watching game shows. How whenever he got upset about something that happened at school or had a fight with a friend, if he showed even the least bit of emotion, his mom would tell him "You're acting like a baby!" or "You're too old for that." At the time, Ruby felt compassion for the sad little boy in him. But then, those memories vanished as her mind spiraled to darker times.

She thought back to their arguments. The way he lost his temper. She could still feel the sting of his nonstop criticism. The cruel comments about her job and her appearance. When she had gained ten pounds as a side effect of her new MS medication, he would look her up and down and say, "Your body fat repulses me." When she would tear up, he would tell her "Don't you want me to be honest with you?" When she would try to defend herself, he would raise the tone of his voice to something approaching shouting and tell her mockingly, "You're too sensitive" or "You don't know how to take a joke." He had broken her little by little, and by the time she had worked up the courage to break up with him two years ago because the relationship was causing her to lose sleep and her MS to flare up, she felt beaten down and unlovable. Ruby had heard so much criticism growing up from her mother that this all felt like familiar but unpleasant territory.

She backed away, her fingers brushing her purse again, but Nick stepped closer, like a predator closing in on its prey. "We belong together, Ruby," he told her. "You know that."

She shook her head, more memories crashing down on her like waves. Her mind flashed back to Nick's rage-filled reaction to her breaking things off. She had to hire an attorney after he humiliated her by posting pictures of her on social media and sending them to her friends and family. She had to file copyright claims to force some websites to remove the image of her breasts. *How could he think that I would ever take him back?*

After the breakup, she wanted to be as far away from Nick as possible. She had moved to an island in order to feel safe. And yet here she was, face to face with him. She looked back on the entire relationship with regret and pain, and the experience reinforced her view that it was better to play it safe. Both here and on the island. *I would rather be alone than leave myself vulnerable again to a person who might not be who they seem to be.*

"No," she told him firmly, her voice trembling. "We don't."

Nick's expression darkened, his eyes filling with anger and

something approaching pure hatred. "You're making a mistake," he said, his voice dangerous.

In one swift movement, Ruby's hand shot up, the pepper spray hissing as it struck Nick in the face. He fell back and wiped the liquid from his burning eyes, which only made it worse.

"You—" he roared into the deserted street, struggling to keep his balance.

Ruby didn't wait to hear the rest. She turned and ran inside the ferry building, her heart beating as if she had run there from her mom's house. Inside, she stumbled and ran to find the security guard. Crying and shaking, she felt adrenaline coursing through her veins, her heart racing. She tried to speak, but no words came. She heard Nick shout, "You'll regret this!" A few moments later, she heard his car peel out from the curb, tires screeching as his salsa-red Toyota sped into the night.

Once the security guard checked that Nick was gone, Ruby went into the bathroom to splash water on her face. The adrenaline hadn't worn off yet. It surged through her, a wave of terror that wouldn't let go. She looked at her face in the mirror. *I should have seen it...How could I have been so blind?* Ruby berated herself.

She didn't feel safe again until the police arrived, taking her statement while she clutched a water bottle, her hands still shaking, the officer's calm demeanor doing little to soothe her. "He violated the restraining order," the officer said, his eyes serious. "We're going to find him."

But Ruby doubted she could believe that. She thought of the island, the distance, the safety it had given her. Every time she dared to return to the mainland to visit her mom, Nick seemed to find her. And every time Nick was rejected, his obsessive behavior intensified. She wanted to get back to her island home — her sanctuary — as soon as she could.

The ferry's engines rumbled to life as Ruby sank into a seat by the window. The dark water sprawled around them.

Even though she was no longer in immediate danger, her body still shook as the adrenaline surged through her veins. She fidgeted with the small tin heart-shaped charm fastened to a white beaded bracelet on her left wrist. Her mind floated back to the trip to Acapulco she had taken with her college roommate after she had left Nick. She had spent days swimming in the Pacific Ocean and then lying on the sandy beach on her towel, letting the sun dry her body, feeling its warmth on her skin. She had felt physically and emotionally drained from the breakup.

Perhaps sensing her sadness, a street vendor took out a box of tiny charms from a tin box, displaying hands, feet, crosses, and animals. But from the chaotic pile, the woman rescued the small heart and held it up to Ruby, pointing at her and speaking in Spanish with passion.

Ruby didn't know what the woman was trying to communicate to her, but she kept repeating the words *"milagro"* and *"corazón."* Ruby's heart felt heavy when she took the charm from the woman, but something deep within her started to stir. Somehow, she felt a bit lighter holding the heart in her palm. Ruby didn't believe that the charm held any magical powers but the symbolism of it spoke to her. Maybe it would help her heal her broken heart through the placebo effect if nothing else.

After Ruby handed her a few pesos, the woman attached the charm to an elastic beaded bracelet, and Ruby slipped it over her wrist. Months had passed, but she still wore it, hoping for a positive and uplifting love.

Ruby stared out at the black night and even blacker ocean as the ferry pulled out into open water and the engines accelerated as the boat sped toward the island. Her island sanctuary loomed closer, but the sense of security it once brought felt out of reach.

I'm not safe anywhere.

10

Ruby took the last few sips of her strawberry and banana smoothie and turned towards her laptop to begin to work. She still felt a bit rattled by yesterday's encounter with Nick at the ferry terminal but was determined to put it out of her mind. The marine layer was still thick over the island, so she reached over to switch on her desk lamp. She could concentrate better with plenty of light. The financial reports from Coastal Surgical Associates were on the screen, and she looked them over again.

Jacklyn Carter's email to her was, as always, meticulously organized. No wonder she was a good office manager for the practice. Ruby opened the reports, her mind already running through the routine checklist: income, expenses, anomalies, and entered everything into the QuickBooks software. She was soothed by the sound of the surf's rhythmic pounding against the rocks. Most of the reports from Coastal Surgical looked standard—insurance reimbursements, payroll, rent, and supply purchases. But when Ruby flipped to the Shipshape Art Gallery's statement, her fingers paused mid-keystroke.

The screen showed a list of incoming bank wires labeled

"consulting fees." One was from an unfamiliar charity—"Second Lives Foundation." The others, outgoing wires, were addressed to medical entities: "Nephrology Specialists of Newport Beach" and "Liver Specialists of Orange County."

Ruby frowned. *Hang on. Why are consulting fees being deposited into the art gallery account?*

"This makes no sense," she muttered, scrolling back through the previous months' records.

She reached for her phone and dialed Jacklyn's cell phone number. It rang twice before Jacklyn picked up, and she sounded as busy as usual.

"Hey, Ruby. Everything okay?"

"Yes, I have some questions about the financials. I noticed something strange in the Shipshape account," Ruby said, looking at the bank statement up on the screen. "These consulting fees from Second Lives Foundation, and then payments out to some medical offices. Can you clarify that?"

"Oh, that." Jacklyn responded. "Dr. Carter joined the scientific advisory board for Second Lives. Those are related to that work."

Ruby paused, considering this information, and then asked her, "But why would the payments go into the art gallery account, not Coastal Surgical? And why would he be paying other doctors directly?"

"I'm really not sure. Kevin would have to answer that." Jacklyn's response was rushed.

"Okay, could you can ask Dr. Carter and then update me?"

"I'll have to get back to you on that. I gotta go now," Jacklyn said and disconnected.

The call ended, but Ruby still felt unsatisfied with that explanation. Her curiosity piqued, she decided to learn more about the "Second Lives Foundation."

According to Google, the Second Lives Foundation supported "organ donation awareness." Ruby noted the mission statement and then downloaded its Form 990, the annual report that non-profits file with the IRS. The Form 990 showed income sources and major expenditures. A significant portion of the Foundation's expenses were listed as grants to "New Me Clínica Médica," a private medical facility in Tijuana.

Ruby rubbed her eyes and thought for a moment. *New Me Clínica Médica?* She searched again, this time focusing on the facility. The search results were limited, but what little she found raised more questions.

She looked back at the bank statement still open on her laptop screen. Dr. Carter's payments from the Second Lives Foundation matched what she'd seen on the Form 990—$200,000 annually in consulting fees. But why funnel them through Shipshape Gallery? And what was the connection to New Me Clínica Médica?

She then opened Coastal Surgical's website, scrolling through Dr. Carter's bio. He was a general surgeon who specialized in general surgery—gallbladders, appendices, and liver resections. He didn't appear to do anything remotely related to organ transplants or plastic surgery.

After researching for the better part of an hour, she felt more confused than ever. The more information she could glean, the less the pieces of the puzzle fit together.

Abacus stirred at her feet, oblivious to her growing unease, and let out a contented sigh. Ruby leaned down, scratching behind his ears, her mind racing.

"What are you up to, Dr. Carter?" she whispered.

Payments from a charity. Wires to doctors. Consulting fees for a gallery. Ruby's stomach churned. Something wasn't right.

‖

The kitchen was quiet now, the gentle sound of the waves lapping on the shore below the only sound as Ruby settled onto the living room sofa, a paperback by Michael Connelly in her lap. She glanced toward the TV, where a true crime documentary was paused on the screen. It was one of her guilty pleasures, though she rarely admitted it. Tonight, though, neither the book nor the TV held her interest.

She looked over at her mosaic workstation, which she had set up in the corner. Sheets of glass in various colors were arranged like a painter's palette in the craft cabinet she bought for this purpose. She could faintly smell glue and grout, a strangely comforting combination. Ruby pulled her hair back into a loose ponytail, rolled up her sleeves, and walked over to sit down at the station.

The project she was working on was a blue and green spiral seashell design, its pattern mimicking the Fibonacci sequence, numbers found in the "golden ratio" of flower petals and other repeating patterns in nature. She donned her protective goggles and started cutting the larger glass sheets into smaller pieces. She scrutinized them to find one of the size or shape that she needed, holding each one up to the light before placing it in the growing design that she sketched out in pencil. She had to work carefully as the glass edges were sharp and uneven, but she liked that. The pieces weren't perfect, and they didn't have to be.

As she worked, her thoughts wandered. The pieces didn't fit together at first, and sometimes she had to cut them into even smaller pieces or into different shapes. But with some patience, the design came together—a mix that would eventually transform into something beautiful. *Perhaps my life is like this mosaic.* She distractedly dabbed glue on the next piece of glass—a little jagged and broken but still full of potential.

The sudden ringing of the phone startled her out of her reverie. Ruby dropped the piece of glass she was holding onto the table. She picked up the phone and smiled when she saw her brother's name on the screen.

"Jack, how's my favorite brother?"

"Your only brother, you mean. Thanks for the sticker books you sent. Charlotte's obsessed with the unicorn one. Sabrina says thanks, too."

"I'm glad she liked it. And sorry again I missed the party. I just came back from the mainland to check on Mom. She was in the hospital, but they already released her."

Jack grunted but made no comment. "Things still hot and heavy with Mr. Baywatch?"

"Haha, very funny," Ruby said, rolling her eyes even though he couldn't see. "Yes, we're still seeing each other. He came to the island last weekend. How's work?"

Jack groaned. "It's fine, except the little shits get worse every year. Actually, it's the parents that really make me question all my life choices."

Ruby laughed. "I'm sure you're a great math teacher, even if your students don't deserve you."

His voice softened as the questions became more personal. "How are *you* doing? Is your MS still under control?"

"I'm okay," she said, leaning back in her chair. "Cool weather helps. My symptoms get worse in the heat. Work has been steady. I'm not retiring anytime soon, but it's enough. Catalina's quiet, mostly."

"Did you make it back into the water yet?" Jack asked hopefully.

Ruby's smile faded. She stared at her mosaic, her fingers trailing over the half-finished design. "No, not yet. I've been going to the jetty where the accident happened just to sit and take some deep breaths. I don't know if it's important anymore. I'm comfortable where I am."

"But are you *happy?*" Jack pressed her.

"Comfortable can be happy," she replied. "Besides, those juvenile great white sightings aren't exactly inviting."

She looked up at the *Jaws* poster on her living room wall showing a swimmer oblivious to the monster beneath her swimming up toward her. Ruby shuddered. *I really need to redecorate.* The babysitter who let her watch that movie when she was nine years old should be paying for her therapy. Her gaze wandered to other posters: The silent film Treasure Island shot on Catalina, and a lone bison in profile with the words "Catalina Island" in bold letters underneath, a reminder of the wild animals brought to the island for Zane Grey's western film and still roaming the interior.

Jack's voice broke into her thoughts. "You're just making excuses. How can you live on an island and not swim? You need some exposure therapy, Ruby. It'd be good for you."

"What if I don't want to be exposed?"

"Ruby," he said, softer this time, "it's time."

She sighed, rubbing her eyes. "Jack, don't push me."

"Okay, fine," he relented.

"How's Sabrina? Is she still working day shift? I heard the nurses at her hospital might strike."

"I'm glad she's not working nights. Otherwise, she'd be too tired to have sex with me!" Jack's laugh was as obnoxious as ever.

"TMI!" Ruby groaned.

"And how's our dear, sweet sister doing?" Jack asked, mischief in his voice.

"Which one? Anastasia or Drizella?" Ruby quipped, referring to Cinderella's stepsisters.

Jack laughed. "You're bad. But seriously, have you seen her?"

"I haven't seen her lately or really even talked to her," Ruby admitted. "I see her online posts. That's enough for me."

"And Mom?" Jack asked, humor gone from his voice.

"She's back home. You should visit her," Ruby said, more sharply than she intended.

"I value my mental health, thanks. You're a saint for talking to her daily."

"She's sick, Jack. She needs a liver transplant."

"No wonder. In Eastern cultures, the liver's the seat of the soul. Hers must be rotten."

"Jack, you're incorrigible," Ruby said, though she couldn't suppress a giggle. "Seriously, call her."

"I'll think about it," he muttered, but Ruby knew better.

12

Francisco paced the length of his office, looking up at the crucifix on the wall. When his cell phone rang, he heard David clear his throat and then blurt out the words.

"*Primo,* we have a situation."

Francisco stopped in his tracks and gripped the phone harder. "What kind of situation?"

"They seized another shipment. It was a big one, worth four million dollars. Armando says it was one of our most reliable routes."

Francisco reached up to stroke the black stone of his amulet, but it did little to calm his nerves. He said nothing.

David continued. "Armando thinks that someone is feeding intel to the authorities. That it was an inside job."

Suddenly, the room felt stiflingly hot. "How sure are you about Armando? He's been running that plaza for years, but I guess loyalty has its limits."

La Familia had been the undisputed owner of the plaza along the Tijuana border city for several years. There was an unspoken agreement between the families that ran the other cartels that they would not interfere with plazas belonging to others and this was aggressively enforced. The main concern for everyone involved was how to breach the U.S. border, as this was much more fortified.

"Francisco, Armando's solid. If he were playing both sides, we'd have seen signs before now. He's been one of our best earners."

"Something has obviously changed. We're hemorrhaging money there now," Francisco snapped. He sank into his chair and crossed his arms over his broad chest. His fingers drummed against the polished wood. "I want you to go to Tijuana and talk to him and his people. I want names."

"I'll handle it," David said, his tone serious.

Francisco hung up without another word, staring out the window at the sprawling backyard below. He pictured Armando in his mind. He always seemed so calm and composed. Maybe he was just a good actor.

That night, Francisco lay beside Blanca in the dark and stared up at the Blessed Virgin. Blanca's breathing was soft and even, but his own mind refused to settle.

He thought of Armando's son, studying business at university. *He's ambitious, like his father. He wants to secure a legacy of his own.*

The black fist amulet sat on the nightstand, and Francisco reached for it, caressing its smooth surface.

"What if you've already betrayed me, Armando?" he whispered to himself.

David arrived in Tijuana at midday, the cars in his caravan kicking up a trail of dust as he approached Armando's offices. Armando greeted him at the gate, with dark circles under his eyes, the lines around his mouth deeper than David remembered.

They sat across from each other in Armando's opulent office. A Frida Kahlo self-portrait hung on the wall, the artist's unibrow staring down at them.

David leaned forward, blinking rapidly, his tone all business. "Francisco isn't happy, Armando. Two shipments in a row. What's going on?"

"I don't know yet." Armando's voice was steady, but his eyes betrayed the tension he tried to hide. "I've been combing through my team, looking for leaks. I'll find the rat."

David said nothing but eyed Armando. "What if you are the rat?"

The color drained from Armando's face, and for a moment, the room felt unbearably still. His shaky hand reached up to wipe sweat from his brow. Then, his voice came, hoarse and raw. "No. You can't believe that. I've been loyal to La Familia for years. You know that, David."

"You have been a good earner until now, but you have cost us a lot of *pesos* lately. You say that you are loyal, but loyalty has a price," David said coolly. "Sometimes, people are willing to pay more."

"David, I swear on the lives of my children," Armando insisted, his voice rising. "I've done absolutely nothing to betray Francisco."

David noted Armando's trembling hands. "Francisco's patience is wearing thin right now with all of the seizures lately. If you're lying, we're going to find out about it."

"I'm not!" Armando cut him off, desperation bleeding into his tone. "You've known me for years. You've seen the work I've done here, what I've built!"

David jumped up and walked toward the door. "Then you'd better find out who's behind this before Francisco finds someone else to run this plaza," he warned. "Someone who doesn't make him doubt."

Francisco's phone buzzed on his desk the next morning, pulling him from a restless trance. He saw a message from David.

"I met with Armando. He denies everything. He's either innocent or a good liar. Still digging."

Francisco paced, thinking. The clouds outside his window turned dark, mirroring his mood.

"Armando," he murmured to the empty room. "What are you hiding?"

13

A shley was busy writing up some offer documents when she saw **Mom** flash on her cell phone screen. *Not today, Satan.* She hit Decline.

She sighed and went back to her work on the offer she was drafting for the La Jolla Shores house. Her Hong Kong clients were a nightmare, especially the wife. Every house had to meet an impossible criteria checklist: near top-tier schools, modern design, ocean view, and no "4" in the address. She even insisted on testing every bathroom to ensure that the flush was acceptable. It was Crazy Town.

Ashley knew all she could do was smile and nod. After all, the customer was always right. She recalled how she'd strained to keep her customer service voice during the last walkthrough of the home. This time, though, the client swore she had "a good feeling" about the house. Ashley had no choice but to submit the offer at lightning speed.

Her phone vibrated again.

She swore under her breath when she saw it was her mom again and answered. "Mom, I'm swamped. Can this wait?"

"Hi, honey," Janice said, ignoring her daughter's rushed

tone. "I'm sorry to disturb you, but I'll be quick. I'm thinking of selling the Avalon condo."

That stopped Ashley cold. "Selling the condo? What brought this on?"

"I don't use it anymore, and I could use the cash for... unexpected expenses."

Within seconds, Zillow was up on Ashley's laptop screen. She calculated the condo's current market value and what one-third of the proceeds—after deducting her agent fee—might look like, and this made her heart beat a little faster.

"I've been telling you for years to sell or rent it out. Are you finally seeing the light?"

"Something like that," Janice said vaguely.

"What about Ruby? She's still living there, right? She's not going to like this."

"Well, she'll have to figure something out. It's not fair to you and your brother. It's time."

Ashley's lips curled into a tight smile. "Okay. I'll get started on the listing."

That evening, Ashley initiated a FaceTime call with Ruby and their brother, Jack. The screen lit up with Ruby's tired face, her blonde curls frizzy from the ocean breeze. Jack joined moments later from his living room couch, children screaming in the background.

Ruby immediately noticed that Ashley looked flawless, even at the end of a long day. *Does her lipstick even smudge?* she thought, both impressed and irritated.

Ashley didn't waste time with small talk. "Mom decided to sell the Avalon condo. I'm listing it."

There was a stunned silence.

"What?" Ruby finally said, her voice rising. "She didn't tell me that! Where am I supposed to live?"

Ashley shrugged. "Not my problem. When the condo sells, you'll get your share, eventually. Mom wants the proceeds in her estate."

"Ashley, are you sure this is what Mom wants?" Jack asked, frowning. "What's the rush? None of us is in dire straits."

Ruby's voice shook as she said. "Ashley, I have a chronic illness, and this condo was supposed to be my safe place. Mom agreed—"

"Temporarily," Ashley interjected sharply. "It was never supposed to be a permanent arrangement. Maybe it's time to stop hiding on the island and move back to the mainland. You're more than capable of getting a real job."

Ruby's face flushed red, her chest tight. "You don't understand anything about my situation."

"And you don't understand money," Ashley shot back. "Mom's covering for you, but this isn't sustainable."

Jack's angry voice cut through. "Ashley, where's your compassion? This isn't just about numbers."

"It's not about compassion," Ashley retorted. "It's about reality. Mom decided, and it's her property."

Jack glared at her. "It's funny. You're sounding more and more like her the older you get."

Ashley looked like he had physically struck her. "Screw you, Jack. You always side with Ruby." She turned her attention back to Ruby, her tone cold. "You'd better start packing."

With that, she ended the call, leaving Ruby staring in shock at her blank screen.

14

Caleb Jackson groaned when he heard his alarm clock beep that morning. He sat up in bed and pressed a hand to his aching knee. The first few steps were always the worst, sharp reminders of last year's ACL tear during the homecoming game. The pain after the surgery was intense, and the post-surgical rehab had been brutal, but as an athlete he was used to pushing through physical pain. Now, even with a brace and months of physical therapy, the joint still twinged with every move.

He limped across the room, the floor cold against his bare feet, and stopped at the dresser. He saw the small orange bottle that once held oxycodone, but it was empty now. His doctors had cut him off, telling him that he shouldn't need it anymore. But Tylenol did nothing for his pain. He opened his backpack and fished out a single yellow tablet that he had bought from his classmate. The surface felt chalky to the touch. He popped it into his mouth and swallowed it down with water. The discomfort in his knee would ease soon enough.

Caleb splashed cold water on his face. When he looked at his reflection in the bathroom mirror, he saw a face that looked older than his eighteen years. He brushed his teeth with one hand and checked his Snapchat account with the other. He heard his mom calling him from downstairs.

"Caleb! Breakfast's ready!"

He stuffed his school supplies into his backpack and made his way downstairs, masking the stiffness in his knee as best he could. His mom, dressed for work, stood by the stove frying eggs for him and his sister.

"Don't forget to talk to Mr. Jones about your UC application today," she said, sliding a plate onto the counter.

"I've got it handled, Mom," Caleb replied, grabbing a granola bar. His appetite wasn't what it used to be when he was working out hard every day.

"Have a great day!" she called as he headed out the door. "I'm so proud of you!"

He smiled as her words echoed in his mind as he climbed into his old Jeep.

By the time Caleb settled into his first-period AP U.S. History class, the tablet had begun to work its magic. The throbbing in his knee dulled, replaced by a soft haze that made everything feel distant, even the teacher's animated lecture about the Civil War. Caleb felt drowsy, and he had trouble concentrating.

At first, he thought he was tired, another late night of college essays, practice drills, and homework catching up to him. But then came the nausea. His stomach churned. He felt cold sweat prickling the back of his neck. His breath grew shallow, and the air in the classroom felt thick.

Something's wrong, he thought, his fingers gripping the edge of the desk.

"Caleb?" his teacher's voice broke through, sharp with concern.

Caleb heard her, but he couldn't answer. The room spun, his

vision faded, then darkness. His ample frame toppled out of the chair and hit the classroom floor with a sickening thud.

"Caleb!"

His classmates froze, their murmurs rising into a wave of panic as the teacher dropped to her knees beside him, directing a student to call 911.

Caleb's story ended there, but how it had come to this was a tale of tragic intricacy.

The oblong yellow pill imprinted with "10/325" he swallowed that morning wasn't the Percocet he thought it was. It had traveled a long way before landing in his palm: chemicals from China smuggled into Mexican naval ports, processed in a La Familia cartel lab, and pressed into innocent-looking pills with the same markings used by the true manufacturer of Percocet. These pills, laced with fentanyl, fifty times more potent than heroin, slipped across the U.S. border hidden in truck compartments and inside car engines or carried by human "mules". In fact, there was no end to the creativity and inventiveness the cartel used in smuggling drugs into the U.S. which included all manner of cars and trains and things that go such as submarines, aircraft, fishing boats, buses and container ships.

Once stateside, local distributors passed them along, hiding their transactions in encrypted apps such as Snapchat and WhatsApp. The cartel received the laundered cash proceeds back via cryptocurrency or the Chinese underground banking system created to circumvent the strict rules of the Chinese government to prevent exportation of dollars from China. Caleb's supplier, a junior trying to make quick cash, did not know how lethal the product truly was.

Caleb's collapse was met with confusion. "He's having a

seizure," someone whispered. Another suggested dehydration. Caleb was a good student, a talented athlete, a nice kid who was going places. No one considered the tiny pill that Caleb had swallowed earlier, a pill that had stolen his breath and silenced his heartbeat.

Had they known, had they suspected, they might have reached for the naloxone nasal spray in the nurse's office—a lifeline some school districts were brave enough to stock. Kids in other, more conservative districts weren't as fortunate, as their parents felt that keeping naloxone at school would just promote drug use in teens, and that besides *their* kids would *never* use drugs. But in the critical moments before the paramedics arrived, that spray remained untouched, its life-saving potential unrealized.

Mrs. Jackson stumbled into Caleb's hospital room, her face pale and her lower lip trembling. Caleb's body lay on the gurney, tubes sticking out from everywhere.

"Your son..." the doctor began, his voice tight, but his words felt distant to her. The entire scene before her felt unreal. She had just seen him that morning at breakfast.

Mrs. Jackson's legs gave out beneath her, her proud words to Caleb from that morning echoing in her mind.

15

uby looked out her rear sliding glass door towards the ocean below and dialed her brother's number.

"Hey, Ruby," Jack greeted her loudly, trying to make himself heard over the chaos of bedtime routines. "Hold on—Justin, put down the toothpaste! Sabrina, can you help him with the cap? Sorry. What's up?"

"I think one of my clients is laundering money."

There was a pause on the other end, followed by the sound of a door shutting as he entered his bedroom. When Jack spoke again, his tone was serious. "Okay. Start from the top."

Ruby walked back to her desk and sat down, looking at the laptop screen. "I was reviewing one of my client's bank statements. He's a surgeon who also owns an art gallery I do the books for as well. And there are these weird transfers. Payments from a charity called the Second Lives Foundation into the art gallery account, and then wires from the gallery to some clinic in Mexico. A place called New Me."

"Mexico?" his voice rising slightly. "That's a little concerning."

"Exactly. And each transaction is under ten grand but just barely. It's almost as if—"

"They're trying to avoid getting flagged," Jack finished for her. "You mean like ... what do they call it? Structuring?"

Ruby stood up again and started pacing. "Yeah. It's how people keep law enforcement from noticing large cash flows. You break up the money into smaller transactions to fly under the radar."

"You probably learned that from all those hours you spent watching *CSI* or something," Jack joked.

Ruby rolled her eyes. "No, Jack. This is my *job*. And for the record, banks don't report anything under ten thousand dollars, unless—"

"Unless it looks suspicious?"

"Exactly." She opened the bank statements again to double-check her first impressions. "And this definitely looks suspicious. Transfers from a nonprofit? To an art gallery? Then straight to a clinic in another country?"

Jack's wife, Sabrina, chimed in from the background. "Did you say Mexico? Maybe it's something drug-related?"

"Oh, hi, Sabrina," Ruby told her sister-in-law. "I didn't realize I was on speaker."

"Sorry, you know how nosy I am," Sabrina laughed. "But really, money going to Mexico like that makes you think."

Ruby bit her lip and felt her stomach tighten. "Dr. Carter's a successful surgeon. It's not like he needs the money. Why would he get mixed up in something illegal, if anything is in fact going on?"

"Maybe he's not," Sabrina offered, but she sounded skeptical. "But you're right; it doesn't add up. There could be a legitimate explanation though. Maybe he is making donations to a charity or something."

"I hope you're right," Ruby said, rubbing her temple. "I don't want to find out this has anything to do with drugs. It would just ... ugh, it's so wrong."

Jack's voice softened. "You're thinking about Aunt Frida, aren't you?"

"Yeah," Ruby admitted. Her throat tightened as the memory surfaced of Frida's haunted eyes, the way she held John's photo like it might bring him back.

Thinking of her cousin John and the photo that Frida always kept nearby, Ruby's mind jumped to the trip to Acapulco she had taken with her roommate. The two women had ventured out of the hotel one night for dinner. They sat on the outside patio of a restaurant that, although recommended by the hotel concierge, was a little too touristy for Ruby's taste. As they sat drinking margaritas in glasses with salted rims, a middle-aged woman, her Aztec-featured face lined by tragedy and exhaustion, approached their table. She handed them a flyer with the photo of a man in his early twenties and pointed at his face.

"*Mi hijo,*" she repeated. *My son.* The woman was soon chased away by the restaurant security guard, who scolded her for bothering the guests. Ruby watched her move down the crowded street, stopping frequently to distribute more flyers.

"What do you suppose that was about?" Ruby had asked her friend.

"No clue. Maybe he is a missing person?"

"Strange. Why wouldn't she just go to the police?"

"No idea."

Neither woman had given the encounter a second thought. *Until now.*

"Look," Jack said, his tone practical now, "if you think something's off, keep digging. But don't jump to conclusions yet."

"Yeah, I know," Ruby sighed. "Hopefully, I'm making a mountain out of a molehill. I need to figure out if anything is going on or if it's just a big misunderstanding."

16

"**G**ood morning, Coastal Surgical Associates. How may I direct your call?"

When the call transferred to Jacklyn, the familiar, gravelly voice of Ruby Simon came through the receiver.

"Hi Jacklyn, I'm sorry to bother you. I got the bank statements you sent over, but I need some clarification on a few items. Did you have a chance to discuss this with Dr. Carter?"

Ruby's tone was calm, but there was a sharpness to it that put Jacklyn on edge. They went over the statements in detail, Ruby asking pointed questions about certain transactions. Jacklyn answered the best she could but felt as though they were going in circles. By the end of the call, Ruby still wasn't satisfied with Jacklyn's explanations.

"I'll tell you what. Let me talk to Kevin again to get some clarification, and I'll get back to you," Jacklyn promised.

Ruby hung up with a tight feeling in her chest.

That evening after the kids were in bed, Jacklyn found Kevin sitting at the kitchen table with his feet up on a chair reading the JAMA Surgery journal. He was working on a bowl of pistachios, cracking them open one by one.

She stood in the doorway watching him and then took a deep breath. "Kevin, I need to ask you something."

He looked up at her with a tired smile. "What's on your mind?"

"I got a call from Ruby Simon today. She had a few questions about the gallery bank account. She said there were some confusing transactions, something about consulting fees going into that account. I tried to answer her the best I could but she still has more questions."

For a second, Kevin looked like a deer caught in the headlights but quickly recovered. He put the journal down on his lap, and the pitch of his voice rose when he answered.

"What? That doesn't make sense." He forced a laugh. "She must be misunderstanding something in the bank statements."

Jacklyn filled her mug with hot water to make tea. "She sounded pretty sure. Is there anything going on at Shipshape? Has anything changed?"

Kevin waved a hand dismissively, his smile tight. "It's nothing you need to worry about. Tell Ruby to ignore it. Her only job is to prepare the financial statements, like she usually does. It's all above board."

His voice was casual, but he didn't meet her eyes.

Jacklyn observed her husband for a moment, a sudden wave of nausea hitting her. She knew him too well, better than he realized. He sounded calm, but his eyes betrayed his nerves.

"Okay," she said finally, her voice even. She didn't feel like fighting tonight. She was too tired, and the thought of her book and robe waiting upstairs was too tempting.

Kevin let out a huge breath as Jacklyn turned and headed upstairs to shower.

When Kevin heard the sound of running water, he made his way into the garage. He slipped into the driver's seat of his silver Mercedes, the leather cold against his back. From the glove compartment, he retrieved a disposable prepaid phone that Marcelo had given him.

He pressed a button and lifted it to his ear.

"Yes?" A gruff voice answered on the second ring, skipping any pleasantries.

"It's me," Kevin said, glancing over his shoulder toward the house. "We might have a problem."

17

Marcelo López ended the call with Dr. Carter and exhaled in frustration. The doctor's fear that his accountant was asking questions played again in his mind.

The doctor sounded calm, even flippant, but Marcelo wasn't buying it. The accountant, Ruby Simon, wasn't just curious, she was digging for information. Marcelo paced the small office in his home. Too much was at stake now for careless mistakes, especially by a gringo who thought his charm and position could fix everything. These Americans were so naive.

Marcelo frowned. He didn't trust Dr. Carter's explanation about his wife Jacklyn "accepting" his story. People like her and the accountant didn't just drop things when something smelled wrong.

With more than a little concern, Marcelo dialed David's number, and he picked up the call on the first ring.

"Bueno?" The familiar voice on the other end sounded agitated.

"It's me. I just got off the phone with Dr. Carter," Marcelo said, his voice tight.

"Dr. Carter? Why is he calling? *Ese pendejo* knows to only call when it's serious."

Marcelo got straight to the point. "It concerns his accountant. She's apparently asking questions about his bank statements and has been talking to Dr. Carter's wife too and asking for clarification."

There was a pause, and then a sharp, frustrated exhale. "*Hí-jole*. That *pinche gringo*. I told you he wasn't careful enough. Who's this accountant?"

"Her name is Ruby Simon. She lives in Avalon on Catalina Island. It's a small place, so it shouldn't be too hard to find her if we need to."

The line went quiet again before David responded. "We've worked too hard on this venture to let some nosy *metiche* accountant ruin it. The fewer people who know about it, the better. I'm going to talk to Francisco."

Francisco listened as David explained the situation with Dr. Carter's accountant. Francisco didn't respond at first, but his breathing quickened. When David finished, Francisco reached for the black amulet around his neck, rubbing it in slow, deliberate motions—three times with his right hand, three with his left. It wasn't just a habit; it was a ritual to temper his fury.

"The accountant could be a loose thread," Francisco said finally. His tone was deadly serious. "I want you to go to the island and find her. Watch her and see who she's talking to and where she goes."

"And if she's more than just curious?" David asked.

"Then we tighten the noose. Have someone get inside her home, bug her phone, and install keystroke software on her computer. I don't care how you do it; find out if she's a problem. If she is..." He didn't finish the sentence. He didn't need to.

David nodded, already planning his next steps. "Understood. I'll take care of it."

The next call David made was to Rafael, a La Familia associate who ran a used car lot in Los Angeles. Rafael owed David a favor, the kind that wasn't negotiable.

"Rafael," David said when the man answered, "I need you to handle something for me."

"No problem, anything for you, boss."

"I need you to file a complaint with the California Board of Accountancy against a CPA named Ruby Simon. File it anonymously."

"Got it. What's the complaint?"

"Tell them she's skimming money from clients, that she's helping others evade taxes. Make it sound convincing. I want her under scrutiny, understand?"

Rafael snickered. "That sounds like fun. I'll take care of it tonight."

"Good. Let me know when it's done." David ended the call and leaned back in his chair, staring at the ceiling. The pieces were moving now, and soon, he'd know whether Ruby Simon was a minor inconvenience—or a real threat.

18

R uby studied the bank statements open on her laptop again, downloading the transactions and highlighting certain transactions that she found suspicious. Something wasn't right. She felt it in her gut, but intuition wasn't enough. She needed an expert, someone who could confirm or dispel her suspicions before she got herself into trouble letting her imagination run wild.

She thought about Doug Baker, an old colleague from the CPA firm where they had both worked. Doug was no longer a mere accountant auditing corporate financial statements now but rather trained as an FBI forensic accountant specializing in securities fraud. If anyone could give her perspective, it was Doug. Ruby found his profile on LinkedIn and sent him a quick message.

To her surprise, he called her back less than thirty minutes later.

"Ruby! Long time no talk," Doug's voice boomed through the speaker. "How's life on Catalina?"

Despite the serious reason for their call, Ruby smiled hearing his voice. "It's good. I left the CPA firm and set up my own practice. My commute is a five-second walk to the desk, and I have ocean views all day. I can't complain. How's the FBI treating you?"

"Not bad! I'm working out of the Los Angeles field office. I've gotten a few high-profile cases under my belt, one a Medicare fraud case and another a large corporate embezzlement. But enough about me. I'm sure you didn't reach out to me just to chat, did you? Is there something I can help you with?"

Ruby hesitated, glancing at the statements again. She cleared her throat and stammered. "I need your advice, Doug. Hypothetically, if someone wanted to figure out if money laundering was happening, what would they look for?"

The line went quiet for a moment, then Doug's tone shifted and became serious. "That's not exactly light water-cooler talk. Is this tied to a particular client?"

"I don't know," she blurted, her fingers tightening around the phone. "It's just a hunch. But I'd like to understand what to watch for."

"All right," he said, his voice thoughtful now. "I'll give you a quick rundown. Money laundering usually involves 'cleaning' money so that illegal proceeds become legitimate income. First thing you'd look for is structuring, small deposits just under the reporting thresholds. Criminals don't want to smuggle cash out; it's risky, so they trickle the money in and wire it out later."

Ruby took notes on a legal pad, her thoughts racing. "Okay, that makes sense. Is there anything else I should pay special attention to?"

"Yes, you would also need to look at whether transactions make sense for that particular business. For example, if it's a dental office but they're wiring money internationally or buying expensive equipment they don't use for dentistry, that would be a red flag. You might look more closely at any discrepancies in cash flow or sudden changes in business practices."

Ruby's breathing sped up as Doug spoke. The patterns on the Carter's bank statements suddenly felt more like clues to a puzzle. *Maybe I* do *have something here.*

"Listen, Ruby," Doug warned. "If you're seeing things that raise alarms, you need to involve the authorities. These things are bigger than one person, and they can get dangerous sometimes. Don't play detective on your own, okay?"

"Understood. Thanks, Doug. I might circle back to you if I need more advice."

"I'm always happy to help. Thanks for reaching out," he said warmly. "And Ruby? Be careful."

As the call ended, Ruby looked at her notes, Doug's warning still reverberating in her ears. She thought about the Carter transactions again, the frequent, small deposits that didn't quite add up. The details wouldn't leave her alone, as if begging for answers.

But then the doubts crept back in. *Why stick your neck out?* she thought. She was in a good place, a quiet, low-stress life that kept her MS stable. She didn't need any trouble. If Dr. Carter was laundering money, was it even her business?

Her gaze fell on the stack of statements again, and her mind tugged in two directions. *Let it go,* one side whispered. But the other side, the side that had always needed to understand, to dig, pushed back.

Her fingers trembled as she reached for the statements again. *I'll just take one more look,* she told herself.

19

David picked up the phone and called his contact at the DEA, Miriam Rojas. When she answered, he told her "There will be a truck carrying avocados that will come through the border crossing around 2 p.m. tomorrow. Inside the aftermarket hidden compartments, you will find something special in both the tractor and the trailer."

"Okay, thanks. I appreciate the tip. Is this a competitor's load?"

"It sure is, and they have no business being there."

"Got it!" Miriam hung up the phone. Before calling in the tip to the border patrol, she thought about the meaning of the call. Miriam alerted La Familia when she thought it was too dangerous for a truck to cross the border or when she knew they might be searched on the U.S. side. Was this "I'll scratch your back if you scratch mine?" she wondered. It didn't really matter to her. She would get paid either way. Let these cartel pieces of crap kill each other for all she cared. The drugs would flow north in the hands of someone. The only difference was who would get the proceeds from the sale, and that was none of her concern.

The next day, David received a phone call from his crew that there had been another seizure at the border, this one worth eleven million dollars. He knew that Francisco would be apoplectic when he found out. Then he called Francisco to tell him the bad news.

"Someone is fucking with me. Nobody fucks with me! I want you to bring Armando to me right now." Francisco felt disoriented and spent most of that night unable to sleep, staring up at the ceiling of his bedroom, taking slow, deep breaths to calm himself.

The next day, Armando's stomach clenched on the way to see Francisco, and he thought he might shit himself. Once they were face to face, Francisco told Armando, "I have known you for a long time. You have done good work over the years but these seizures can't be random. We must have a rat. Have you been working with someone else who wants to take over our business in the plaza?"

"No, Francisco, I swear on my family's life that I know nothing about that." Armando started to tear up.

"Tell me," Francisco cooed. "It will be better for you if you are honest with me."

"No! I swear on the Virgin Mary that it's not me! You have to believe me!"

Francisco knew it was Armando. *Who else would have the power there to know where the trucks would be and when? No, it must be Armando. He is trying to destroy me and deserves to die,* Francisco thought. *I'll just replace him and see if the seizures stop. Then I will be sure that it was him. In any case, I need to make an example of him so everyone will know what happens when you double-cross me.*

Armando was weeping by now. "It's okay," Francisco told him gently. "Calm down. I will be right back."

As soon as Francisco exited the room, two of La Familia's enforcers entered. "Come with us," they told Armando as they each led him by one arm. "We don't want to make a mess in Francisco's office."

20

obin's hands gripped the wheel as she navigated the early morning traffic. The dull gray road stretched ahead like the past two years of their journey to parenthood. She glanced at Ken, his jaw clenched, eyes fixed on the road. They'd been through it all in the past two years of trying to conceive: endless tests, hormone injections, the bitter disappointment of each failed attempt.

The car was quiet, each of them in their own heads, but Robin felt the anxiety pulsing between them. She took deep breaths and tried not to focus on the grueling hormone shots she'd endured over the past month. But today was different. Today was supposed to be the day they would finally get what they'd longed for. Today, they would harvest her eggs. They had made it this far. But the fear and the ever-present doubt wouldn't let go.

In the passenger seat, Ken fidgeted, rubbing his forehead as if he could will away the stress. He reached across and squeezed her hand reassuringly, a reassurance that he didn't really feel, and they both knew it. "It's going to work this time," he said, though the uncertainty in his voice betrayed the confidence his words tried to project.

Robin nodded and smiled slightly for his benefit. She wanted to believe him, but after all this time, the scars of every disappointment left her skeptical. "Let's just get it over with."

Across town, Monica sat at the kitchen table, her phone pressed against her ear, listening to her soon-to-be ex-husband's voice on the other end. He was furious at her, his words cutting and cruel. She barely registered them, her mind more focused on the pain in her lower back, the cramping in her stomach and the cold sweat she was experiencing. The constant stress had become her companion, her only consistent one.

Monica's hand shook as she set the phone down. She reached for the pill bottle that she had gone down to Tijuana to get once her doctors had cut her off. Her hands shook as she twisted the cap. *Just a few more,* she thought, even as a sliver of guilt pricked her. She'd told herself she could stop at any time, but she knew that was a lie. She swallowed a pill and felt immediate relief washing over her like a soft blanket. For a moment, she allowed herself to close her eyes, letting the edges of the world blur into something softer and more manageable. The anxiety she was feeling abated.

When she got to the fertility clinic, Monica checked the time on her phone. She'd been up since the crack of dawn, dealing with the fallout from the custody fight, and now she was at work dealing with patients. The day had already spun out of control. The first batch of pills she'd popped had helped, but now she felt just as bad as when she'd woken up. The small vials of fentanyl stored for patient use called to her the same way that the sirens of Greek mythology lured sailors to the rocks with their irresistible song.

Her footsteps slowed as she entered the storage room of the clinic, her mind clouded with the need for something, anything, to take the edge off. When she saw the fentanyl vial meant for Robin, neatly tucked in its usual place, a cold shiver passed over her. She hesitated. *This isn't you,* she reminded herself, *you're a nurse who takes the duty of care of your patients seriously.* But the truth felt farther away now than it ever had.

Without another thought, she removed the fentanyl from the vial and replaced it with saline, as she had done so many times before. The quick rush of guilt almost made her stop, but then she imagined the relief, the momentary bliss, and she couldn't resist. She didn't know how to resist anymore.

During the egg extraction procedure, Robin's eyes blinked open. She realized that she was not asleep and feeling no pain like they told her she would be. Her whole body felt exposed, and she experienced the strange sensation of something cold and sharp inside her.

Nurse Monica was standing by Robin's side, her voice distant as she reassured her patient disingenuously. "It's a little discomfort, dear. You're doing great."

Robin took deep breaths to calm herself, but the sharp pain of the needle moving in and out of her engorged ovaries sliced through her like a knife. It was like nothing she'd ever experienced. In fact, thanks to Monica's addiction, what Robin had received for sedation was pure saline. She gasped, unable to take the pain. "That hurts so bad! Please, I can't do this!" Her voice broke, desperate, and she heard the nurse's soft laugh brushing her off.

"It's normal to feel some discomfort, Robin," Monica assured her, gaslighting her. "You're fine, breathe through it."

Breathe through it? Robin felt a sob rising in her throat, and her body tensed with each thrust of the needle. This was not what she had expected. This wasn't the sedation they promised. Her focus was entirely consumed by the excruciating pain.

She couldn't hold back her tears any longer, and she started shaking from the pain. The more she begged for relief from the pain, the more dismissive the clinicians seemed. One of them gave her a "there there little girl"-pat, telling her, "You're doing great. Man up! You'll be fine. You'll have a baby in your arms soon."

Robin's head spun, the pain continuing to shoot through her like jagged needles, but it wasn't only the physical pain that unsettled her. It was the sense of betrayal at not being taken seriously. She was exhausted by the intense pain and finally realized that something wasn't right. One thought kept echoing in her mind: *I can't trust them.*

Ruby sat curled up on the couch, the soft weight of Abacus's head resting on her lap. The rhythmic sound of the dog's breathing did little to calm the storm inside her. She absentmindedly twisted a curl of her hair around her finger, a nervous habit she hadn't outgrown since childhood. Her mind kept returning to her conversation with Jacklyn Carter. She turned the pages of the book on her lap, but nothing was sinking in. She flipped back to the beginning of the chapter. *Wait—what did the Chief of Police want with Harry Bosch again? And what had Harry done to piss him off?* Ruby exhaled and closed the book. She'd read the same sentence five times.

She thought about Andy. Normally, when he was away on the mainland or out on the ship, their communication was minimal—just the daily "Good morning, beautiful" text from him, followed by her "Have a great day" response. But today, her mind wasn't quiet. She remembered Nick, how he'd wanted to know where she was every second, always questioning her and criticizing every decision. Nick's presence had been suffocating, and she still felt the residue of it. But Andy was different. She felt like she could *breathe* when she was with him.

Being able to live her life without constant criticism felt gratifying. She wanted to hear Andy's voice tonight but didn't know if she should call him. She wasn't used to reaching out during the work week unless she had a good reason.

On the third ring, Andy picked up sounding rushed. His familiar voice sounded comforting.

"Hi, my love. I'm happy you called. I just got back from Masters Swimming practice and was about to jump in the shower."

"I hope I'm not bothering you..." Her words trailed off, hesitation tightening her chest. She didn't want to seem needy, but she needed this connection, needed to hear him.

"No way, I love hearing your voice. I'll sleep better tonight."

Her shoulders relaxed. She was no longer sure why she'd hesitated before calling him. It felt good just to talk. Their connection, once tentative, was slowly becoming something more solid.

There was a slight pause, and Ruby couldn't shake the feeling that Andy wanted more from their relationship than she was ready to give. He didn't pressure her, didn't push her, but she felt it in the way he listened to her. It made her want to both stay and run away.

She bit her lower lip. *What made me hold back? What is wrong with me?*

She eyed the front door, half expecting someone to walk through it.

"Actually..." she began, her voice tentative, "I wanted to run something work-related by you."

She recounted the conversation with the Carters, the strange transactions she'd noticed, the nagging feeling that something wasn't right. The words conveying her suspicions tumbled out faster than she intended.

When she finished, there was silence on the line. Her stomach tightened. "So, what do you think? Am I being a drama queen?"

When he spoke, his voice was serious, catching her off guard.

"You know, I know nothing about accounting," he said, his tone warm but laced with caution, "but what I do know is that you do. And you're the most practical person I know. If something's off, you need to handle it carefully. Don't share this with anyone yet. I wouldn't even mention it to people you trust, at least not until you know more."

Ruby felt her heart beat faster. She hadn't expected Andy to take her suspicions seriously, but she noted the quiet alarm in his voice.

"And Ruby?" His voice was lower and more serious now. "Go lock your front door."

A chill crawled up her spine. She was used to living alone, but for the first time she felt truly vulnerable.

"Now who's the drama queen?" she forced herself to joke, acting unbothered.

But Andy wasn't laughing. "I'm serious. They don't mess around."

Ruby's throat tightened. She knew he was right. She had no reason to be afraid—not yet. But the gravity in his voice, the low rumble of warning, made her wonder. She looked at the front door again, suddenly aware of the silence in the house.

"It's white-collar crime, not armed bank robbery," she said, brushing it off, but the words felt hollow as they left her mouth.

"Yeah, but people do strange things when money's involved. Tread lightly, and watch your six."

Ruby looked around the condo with fresh eyes, feeling exposed. She felt the weight of Andy's words, even after the call ended. She slowly walked toward the front door, the echoes of the conversation ringing in her head. *Tread lightly, watch your six.*

With a slow, deliberate motion, she turned the lock.

22

uby heard Jaime and Robert talking next door, the sound of their voices muffled through the wall that separated their condos. They sounded so casual and relaxed in contrast to her own worried state. She kept glancing back at the financial documents on her laptop screen, switching back and forth between the medical practice and the art gallery. *Am I overthinking this?* she wondered.

She had already reviewed the transactions three times, but they still made little sense. Her stomach tightened. There had to be an explanation for the money flowing between the Second Lives Foundation, the art gallery, and that clinic in Tijuana. She felt a pang of self-doubt. It was a mix-up, something innocent. But if it wasn't...

She pushed the thought away. *No, I'm being paranoid.* But the unease wouldn't go away. She had gotten to know Robert and Jaime well over the past year. Robert was an FBI agent. He was smart and not easily rattled. If anyone could make sense of the mess in front of her, it was Robert. *Should I ask him?* She wasn't even sure how to bring it up.

With a sigh, she shut the laptop, put her hair up into a ponytail and stood. She hesitated at Jaime's door for a moment, biting her lip, then knocked on the front door. She felt the sudden weight of the unknown pressing in as she waited for them to answer.

Robert's warm, easy smile welcomed her as the door opened. "Hi Ruby, to what do we owe this pleasure? Come on in! Can I get you a drink?"

His relaxed demeanor calmed her, but the bad feeling lingered. She stepped inside, forcing a smile as she made herself comfortable on their couch. "I wouldn't say no to a little red wine. How are you guys doing?"

"You know," Robert said, waving a hand towards the ocean outside, "it's paradise, so how bad could it be?"

Jaime appeared in the doorway, his usual bright smile in place. "What's up, Ruby?"

Robert Jones grew up in the church, where Sunday wasn't just another day of the week; it was an event. From sunup until sundown, he sat in the wooden pews of a packed Memphis sanctuary. His father's voice boomed from the pulpit, his preaching rising and falling like the gospel choir behind him. His mother, an educated woman with a soft touch, sat primly in the front row, nodding along, always with a book tucked into her bag.

"Education is the key, baby," she would tell him as she read to him each night. "No one can take knowledge away from you."

The church aunties adored him. They constantly straightened his tie and pinched his cheeks. The aunties did the same with his sisters, but their attention lingered a little longer on him, as if they saw something in him they didn't want to. "I been prayin' for you, baby," they would tell him. "I know the Lord's got big things for you."

He knew who he was from a young age, but in a world built on scripture and tradition, that knowledge felt heavy. He smiled, nodded, and fulfilled his obligations. He experienced stolen moments and "on the down-low" encounters in his teens, but secrecy and guilt always burdened him.

Then he met Jaime.

Loving Jaime was never a choice. It was like stepping into sunlight after years in the shade, like finally exhaling after holding his breath for too long. And for the first time, the fear of what his parents might say wasn't enough to make him hide. He couldn't hide his truth anymore. He wanted more.

After college, FBI Special Agent Robert Jones put his sharp mind and desire to help people to work on the Memphis police force. The job fit, but something in him pushed for more. He wanted to be where the cases were bigger, where his instincts could stretch further. Detective work suited him, but the FBI had always been his long-term career goal.

Years later, when he finally stepped into the Long Beach field office, badge clipped to his belt, he carried everything with him—the preacher's son, the teacher's boy, the teenager in the pews who once wondered if he'd ever be able to live in the open. Now, there was no more hiding.

He knew exactly who he was, and where he was meant to be.

Ruby returned the smile, but her mind wasn't on casual conversation. She picked up her wineglass, swirled it slowly, and thought about how to bring up her concerns without sounding crazy.

"What are you working on these days?" she asked, pushing her concerns down.

"I'm actually part of a task force that's preventing fentanyl smuggling through the southern border," Robert said, his expression growing more serious. "The government is finally getting smart, getting everyone—federal, state, local, tribal—on the same page. But to be honest, it's like spitting into the wind. Supply and demand are both massive. Over 100,000 Americans OD'd last year. These kids have no clue of the risks they're taking with even one pill." He shook his head. "One guy they call the 'Skittles Man' was making rainbow-colored fentanyl pills that looked like candy to target kids. It's disgusting."

Ruby's stomach lurched. She'd heard the statistics, but hearing them from Robert made it hit home harder. "That really *is* disgusting. I'm sure it feels like a losing battle. But you're doing the Lord's work, Robert."

Jaime chimed in, his voice full of pride. "Yeah, you are. That's my man."

If Robert's skin weren't so dark, they both would have noticed the subtle flush creeping up his neck. He cleared his throat. "Aww, thanks, but you guys are embarrassing me."

Ruby took a deep breath, slowing her pulse. She needed to steer the conversation to something less personal, more pressing. "But what about the famous 'War on Drugs'?" she asked, hoping to sound casual. "Haven't we spent a fortune on that? Are we making any progress?"

Robert leaned back on the couch, his hands folding together. "Oh, yeah. A trillion dollars—*with a T*—and it's barely made a dent. These cartels are well-funded and ruthless. The drugs keep coming."

Feeling her anxiety ramp up again, Ruby took some deep breaths. "What about the Border Patrol? Don't they catch some of this stuff before it gets through?" she asked.

"They try," Robert said, frustration lining his voice, "but the border is like a sieve. For every bust they make, there are dozens more getting through into the U.S. These bastards are clever, and they've got money and technology on their side."

Ruby sipped her wine, the liquid doing little to calm the tension in her throat. "But what about the Mexican government? Doesn't the U.S. support them in stopping this at the source?"

"Yeah, I mean, it's in our best interest, right?" Jaime asked.

Robert sighed. "Mexico's been at war with the cartels since 2006. Billions of U.S. dollars have gone into modernizing their security forces, reforming the judicial system, and creating job opportunities so that young people have options besides getting involved in the drug trade … but with that much money comes a lot of corruption. And human rights violations. Mexicans and Central Americans are coming across the U.S. border in large numbers to escape the violence. The situation is complex."

Ruby nodded, staying engaged despite the growing sense that the world Robert described was much darker than she had imagined. *And the cartels don't care who they hurt.*

"Jobs are important," she agreed. "But as long as the violence continues, people will risk everything for safety." She paused, looking at Robert and Jaime, then cleared her throat. "But anyway, we're not solving the world's problems tonight. I came over for a different reason. I wanted to get your thoughts on something, Robert."

He raised an eyebrow, his interest piqued. "Sure, what's up?"

Ruby set her wine down, her fingers feeling clammy, and pulled her laptop out of her bag and opened it. "I think you know I do the books for different clients, right? One of them's a doctor in Orange County, and his wife handles the back-office stuff. I haven't been able to understand the bank statements she sent this month, no matter how hard I try."

Robert sat up straighter, his attention focused. "Go on."

Ruby laid out the details of the transactions she was concerned about, her voice quiet but resolute. "I'm probably overreacting, but there's a pattern that doesn't sit right with me. Do you think you could ask around about this clinic in Tijuana and the 'Second Lives Foundation'? I just ... I need to know if I'm missing something."

Robert nodded and then promised her, "I'll see what I can dig up. My team might be able to help."

Ruby felt somewhat relieved, but her chest still felt tight. "I really appreciate it, Robert. Thank you." She chugged the dregs of her wine, feeling the warmth spread through her body, though it did little to soothe her mind.

"No problem, Ruby," Robert said, grinning again. "That's what friends are for."

As Ruby stood up to leave and head back to her condo next door, she couldn't shake the feeling that she was just one step away from something bigger and potentially dangerous.

23

usana Gutierrez's shoulders ached as she wheeled the stroller up the cracked sidewalk toward her apartment in Wilmington, north of Long Beach. After a day of caring for the baby, grocery shopping, and picking up her older son from school, she was exhausted. She glanced up at the entryway to her building and saw that the lights that should have lit up the walkway were still burnt out. The management had been promising to fix it for weeks. The thick cloud cover obscured the moonlight, and the pathway was unnervingly dark.

She handed her keys to Sebastián, her ten-year-old son. "Open the door for me, *mijo*," she whispered, careful not to wake the baby. Sebastián struggled to unlock the door without light but finally pushed it open. Susana cradled the baby while Sebastián grabbed the grocery bags from the basket under the stroller, locked the door behind them and turned the deadbolt, like his mom had taught him.

She set the sleeping baby down in the crib in her bedroom and then went straight to the kitchen. Susana had eaten nothing since breakfast, and now she was too tired to cook. She opened the fridge, grabbed the ham and cheese, and made some quick sandwiches for herself and Sebastián. They ate together in silence, the only sounds being the occasional police siren from the street outside.

After dinner, Sebastián, already in his pajamas, grabbed his bedding and lay down on the couch where he slept every night.

"Good night, *mijo*," Susana said, planting a kiss on his forehead.

"It's a school night, so no TV," she reminded him. Sebastián didn't need any convincing as he was already nodding off, too tired to want to watch TV.

Susana sat in the quiet of the living room for a moment, playing on her phone. She always felt on edge in this neighborhood once night fell. She reached for the TV remote and turned it on low so as not to wake the sleeping baby. In this neighborhood, the threat of violence was never far, just beyond her locked front door.

She heard a sudden crack of gunfire over the sound of her TV.

Susana froze, her heart skipping a beat. It wasn't the first time she'd heard gunshots tearing through the night air. The tension between the MS-13 and Florencia 13 gangs had been heating up, the competition over the "last mile" of drug routes that started deep in Mexico making the streets feel like a war zone. But this time, the sound was too close. She barely had time to react before another wave of gunshots followed, and then another. Sebastián's soft gasp from the couch broke her out of her trance.

Before she could shout for him to get down, she saw the red splatter on the floor, his blood, hot and sticky, splashing across the worn carpet.

"Sebastián!" she screamed, her heart leaping into her throat. She ran to him, but the sickening sound of his gasping for air made her feel faint. He was holding his side, his face terrified, looking up at her for help.

"*Mamá,* it hurts so bad," Sebastián sobbed, his voice shaking as he pressed his hand to his side. Susana's whole body shook as she held his small head in her lap, but her mind spun, unable to comprehend the dark reality of what was unfolding.

The screech of tires outside told her the gangbangers had already made their getaway, disappearing into the night like they were never there. She didn't even have time to register who had done this. Her sweet, innocent Sebastián lay there suffering. And for what?

A flood of sirens pierced the air as police and paramedics arrived and burst through the front door. Susana barely registered the first responders, unable to look away from Sebastián, his face contorted in pain and his breath shallow and ragged.

At the hospital, the news was even worse than Susana could have imagined: L1 spinal cord injury. Sebastián, her beautiful boy, would never walk again. The words echoed in her ears. She wanted to scream and to fight against the unfairness, but she felt only numb. The trajectory of her innocent son's life had changed forever with the trajectory of a bullet carelessly fired by someone fighting over the right to sell drugs in the neighborhood. A victim of a world that didn't care who it hurt.

The police came asking the usual questions, the same ones they always asked in these cases. Did anyone see the shooting? The car? But no one had seen anything. The fear ran too deep in this neighborhood. No one would dare cross the line, even for justice. *The malandros,* the thugs, *hold this place hostage,* Susana thought bitterly. *We're all just prisoners here.*

The media swarmed the next day—cameras, microphones, and reporters asking questions Susana couldn't answer. The mayor stood at the podium, his eyes misty with fake sympathy as he promised justice. But nothing would change. Not for Sebastián, traumatized and maimed, the latest victim of the ongoing quest for gold by competing Mexican cartels feeding Americans' unquenchable thirst for drugs as the drug traffickers' silent partners. Not for the rest of them.

When the dumbass gang member who had shot Sebastián took to Snapchat, flashing his AK-47 and bragging about his "accomplishments," it was too easy for the authorities to track him down. Justice, when it came, felt hollow. The criminal would be charged, yes, but it was too late. In a flash of gunfire, someone had already stolen Sebastián's future and shattered his life. The mayor's tears and the FBI's efforts couldn't erase the truth: *Kids like Sebastián are nothing more than collateral damage in a war they didn't start.*

Susana sat in her son's hospital room, the weight of the disaster pressing down on her, suffocating her. The mayor would say his words, the city officials would offer their condolences, but nothing would ever bring her son back whole.

And on the streets outside, the local gangs would keep fighting for a piece of the action that started in Mexico, innocent bystanders be damned. And they would keep winning.

24

R uby heard the waves lapping the shoreline below as she curled up on the couch, the sound of Abacus's snoring a comforting rhythm. The book she was reading lay open in her lap, but she couldn't concentrate, her mind on something else.

The ringing of her phone startled her. When she saw Robert's name flash on the screen, her heart skipped a beat. She felt curious as she answered.

"Hi, Robert. I didn't expect to hear back from you so soon."

"Ruby, I hope you're sitting down! You won't believe the news I have!"

Ruby's stomach tightened, and she sat up straight to hear better. "Well, spill it!"

"I asked some people on the task force if they'd ever heard of the Second Lives Foundation," Robert said, his voice low and urgent. "It turns out that the Foundation is *already* under investigation by the FBI for financial crimes, including money laundering."

Ruby's breath caught, the words sending a sharp jolt through her. *No way.* She sat up straight, taking deep breaths. Abacus, sensing her sudden shift in mood, lifted his head and stared up at her. "Are you shitting me?" Ruby blurted out, her voice barely above a whisper.

"And it gets worse. Do you know about Suspicious Activity Reports or SARs?"

She blinked, her throat going dry. "Yes, I have heard of them. That's the system they use to track terrorism, right?" she said, her voice shaky. "But what do they have to do with this?"

"Okay, I'm fixin' to tell you," Robert said, his tone laced with excitement. "SARs are not just for suspicion of terrorism. It's anything that smells wrong. You know SARs are reports filed by banks when they spot transactions that seem unusual. Banks send them to the Treasury, specifically, the Financial Crimes Enforcement Network, or FinCEN. It's how they track money laundering and fraud. And this is exactly what happened with the Second Lives Foundation. There's a Suspicious Activity Report that was filed against them."

Ruby's mind raced and her pulse quickened as she considered the implications. *Money laundering through a charity?* "What does the Second Lives Foundation's SAR say?"

Robert's voice dropped lower, almost conspiratorial. "I can't send you the full report since it's an active investigation, but I can read you an excerpt."

Ruby stood up and calmed her breath. "I'm all ears."

"Alright, listen to this. The SAR says..." Robert cleared his throat, and Ruby's stomach twisted.

"This Suspicious Activity Report is being filed to summarize suspicious inbound and outbound wire transfer activities conducted by the Second Lives Foundation, Account #965402102 at Commonwealth Bank in Fresno, California. Wire transfers into the Foundation's account by one individual are followed almost immediately by wire transfers out to a company called Ship-shape, Inc., in Laguna Beach, California, Account #898404332 at Mission Bank and Trust in Marin, California. An internet search identified a website for Shipshape Gallery, which claims to specialize in nautical art. Suspicious activity follows a pattern—dates and amounts too close together—February 1st, $9,780; February 4th, $9,950; February 6th, $9,890; February 8th, $9,960; February 12th, $9,880, and finally, $540 on February 14th, for a total of $50,000. The Foundation's wire transfers to Shipshape mirror this pattern."

Ruby's heart skipped. *Fifty grand ... routed through the art gallery?*

"There's more," Robert continued. "The report says it looks like they might have structured these transactions to avoid triggering the Bank Secrecy Act. The amounts are just under $10,000, which is a common tactic to avoid detection, which you already know. But what really stands out in the SAR revolves around the question of why money is flowing from an organ donation foundation to an art gallery."

Ruby's mind spun; the puzzle pieces she'd been grappling with felt like they were falling into place. "Jesus," she breathed shakily. "So, what will they do with this information?"

"Right now, they're tracking the money, building a case. But the link to Shipshape and the New Me Clinic in Tijuana has raised eyebrows," Robert said. "The task force wasn't aware of that clinic before this. It could be a key part of something much bigger. We're getting the Mexicans involved in this. This could be a game-changer for us."

Ruby sucked in her breath. *Tijuana. The New Me Clinic. Shit was about to get real.*

"So, what happens now? Which Mexican agency's getting involved?" she asked, her mind moving too fast.

"I'm not sure yet," Robert replied. "Most likely the *Federales* and local law enforcement from Baja California. But the important thing, and the reason I called you so late, is that the FBI wants to meet with you as soon as possible. And they need you to send me the bank statements you've got. They're gonna bring in their financial forensics team to look them over."

Ruby felt a shiver of dread. She hadn't realized how much was at stake until now. "I really don't have much information, only a few documents, but maybe it's enough to get you started. I'll email them over to you once we hang up. I can catch the ferry over tomorrow afternoon and be there by about two. Will that work?"

"Perfect. I'll let them know," Robert said. "And Ruby, this is important. The investigation is still under wraps. No one can know about this yet."

Ruby nodded, feeling nauseous. "Understood."

She ended the call, her hands shaking. Abacus whined, sensing her unease, and she reached down to scratch his ears absentmindedly. *How deep does this go?*

Ruby walked out onto her balcony, feeling the ocean breeze on her face. The outside world felt more dangerous. The pieces of the puzzle were fitting together, but she wasn't sure if she was getting closer to the truth or digging herself deeper into something she couldn't escape.

25

r. Feinerman's night in the ER had already been eternal. After ten years as a Level 1 trauma center emergency medicine doctor, not much fazed him. The usual frequent flyers were there — the old man with chest pain; the young man who complained of back pain and needed opioids because "nothing else worked"; the unhoused diabetic woman who drank her dinner, slipped into a diabetic coma, and was brought to the ER by ambulance; the combative meth addict yelling about how it was "Crooked Joe's fault" that he was there. That was background noise to Dr. Feinerman.

In one hour, he told himself, I can go home, take a shower to wash the bodily fluids off of me, and get in bed. Suddenly, a middle-aged man with a beer belly and a hirsute torso and buttocks ran buck naked through the waiting room doors as the nursing assistant was pushing a wheelchair with a pregnant woman through. His gray hair glistened from the coconut oil that covered his entire naked frame, and he shouted, "Mother made me do it!" at the top of his lungs, eyes wild and looking around in all directions for the obvious danger that was pursuing him.

Dr. Feinerman groaned in frustration. "Can we get security in here stat?" he shouted to the nursing station. A little blonde nurse, a newbie based on the shocked look on her face, ran out to the waiting room for help. The more battle-worn ER nurses' expressions said, "nothing to see here, folks." The security guards ran back and subdued the noncompliant psych patient quickly, but it was like a mud-wrestling contest as they attempted to gain purchase of the man's greasy arms so they could handcuff him.

Once the patient had finally been vanquished, Dr. Feinerman slid open the cloth curtain to what he hoped and prayed would be his last patient of the night, Mrs. Rogers. After greeting her and her husband, who stood anxiously by her side, Dr. Feinerman perused her chart and lab results. He looked at the woman and saw that she was quite ill. She mumbled to him, "I saw a grizzly bear walk by." *Altered mental state.*

"She's confused," her husband told Dr. Feinerman. *No shit.* "She's been throwing up and complaining that it's hard for her to swallow. And slobbering. And she's also having trouble breathing. Could this be connected to her kidney transplant from three weeks ago?" *Bury the lede much?*

Dr. Feinerman looked up, startled. This question got his full attention. "When was this exactly? Was it done at this hospital?"

The husband looked away. "No, not here."

"Where then?"

"A few hours away," he said noncommittally, staring at the wall behind the nurses' station.

"Your wife is clearly sick. We are going to have to do a full workup, including imaging, a lumbar puncture, and more labs. Something is clearly affecting her neurologically. However, I've been here all night, and I'm going home soon. I'll get you started, and then Dr. Lew will take care of her, but I'll check back tomorrow. Please give him the information for her transplant surgeon so we can follow up with him as well."

"I don't really have that information. My wife knows, but she's in no condition to remember."

"Okay, well we'll know more after we run more tests."

When Dr. Feinerman woke up, his first thought was of Mrs. Rogers. After he showered and ate, he called Dr. Lew who was still on shift.

"She's getting worse. Her imaging shows significant encephalitis. She's immunocompromised from the transplant, but we haven't identified any specific bacteria, virus, or parasite. We gave her IV antibiotics and antivirals, but we had to intubate her. According to the husband, she's had symptoms for days but refused to go to the hospital."

"Don't you find it strange that she didn't follow up at the transplant center? Did you get the name of the transplant surgeon from Mr. Rogers?"

"No, he was being kind of cagey about it. Things don't look good for Mrs. Rogers. We're admitting her to the ICU."

26

F rancisco began. "As you know, heroin, cocaine, and fentanyl are our bread and butter, and we have made a fortune selling them to the *gringos* and will continue to do so. However, I have high hopes for our medical venture in Tijuana, which has proven to be profitable lately. Not only does it provide a diversified revenue stream, but it also helps us to move product into the U.S. in places that the DEA isn't looking. Nobody wants to delay an ambulance carrying a critically ill patient seeking medical treatment from reaching a hospital. So far, we haven't had a single ambulance stopped even once!"

"Yes, Paco. It was an imaginative tactic."

Francisco went on. "I've learned that we can make money by selling not only organs but also other body tissues, such as shoulders and corneas. I have been pushing the team there to use all of the meat from the 'cow' and avoid any waste, like they do in China."

They nodded their agreement.

"The problem now is that we have a supply chain issue. We rely on American doctors to refer paying customers to us. It seems that the demand is definitely there. Desperation and wealth can take you far. Our problem is on the supply side. We need more product to sell."

"So, what are you thinking?" one lieutenant asked. Do you want us to keep spreading the word among the *falcones* that we will pay volunteers cash? Or increase referral fees? I'm sure people in financial need will come forward."

"Actually, I am thinking of a more proactive approach. Let's spread the word that we will pay a bounty for each young, healthy patient that is brought to us. Rather than shooting someone who won't be missed or was disloyal and throwing them into a ditch or a shallow grave, let's be smart about it. They can be cash cows for us."

One lieutenant looked doubtful. "Are you talking about abducting someone off the street and bringing them to the clinic?"

"Yes, that's exactly what I'm saying. So many people disappear every year that a few more won't raise any eyebrows. The last I heard, over 120,000 people in this country are already 'missing.' That's perfect for us. I'm hoping that we can continue to expand this same business model at a medical facility across the Texas border in Ciudad Juárez, Matamoros or even Reynosa," Francisco fantasized.

Even if any of the lieutenants objected to Francisco's plan, they would never dare to express any reservations to him.

A short time later, Francisco washed his hands and joined Blanca and the girls at the dinner table, planting a kiss on top of each one's head.

"And how was your day, *amor?*" Blanca asked Francisco.

"It was productive," he told her and smiled gently. "No complaints."

27

uan had been the man of the house for six years, ever since the day when the tractor had rolled over his father and crushed his skull. His father's blood had stained the earth, dark like the soil he'd worked, and left Juan filling his large shoes. A mere ten years old at the time of the accident, Juan had felt the weight of his mother's gaze as she looked to him, her tired eyes asking him to be the man she needed.

Every day after that, Juan had worked, pulling at the land and scraping together whatever money he could. His hands, calloused from farming, always moved as he worked to provide for his mother and younger siblings.

But money was tighter than ever now. This evening, the small house smelled of beans and fresh tortillas as his mother, Amparo, stood by the stove, dark circles under her eyes as she stirred the pot. As she spoke to Juan, she stirred more aggressively and then cleared her throat. "Juan, if we don't bring in more money, José and Chuy will have to drop out of school too. They'll have to work."

Juan felt his throat constrict at the thought of his brothers walking the same path he had all those years ago. He had sacrificed his future for them so that they would have a chance at a better life. "No, *mamá*. I'll figure something out. I won't let them drop out."

But even as the words left his mouth, his mind raced. *How?* The thought gnawed at him. In the cantina, he had asked around, but the few remaining men in town were barely scraping by. Those who departed went to the North, to *El Norte,* to find work as gardeners or in meat processing plants, and sent money home to their families. That was the way it was here. *El Norte or nothing.*

On his way out the door the next morning, his neighbor, Martín, waved him down. His gruff voice was low, urgent. "Juan, I hear you need to make some quick money."

"You heard right," Juan said, his eyebrows drawing together. "My brothers need to stay in school."

"I understand," Martín said, his voice low as if afraid someone might overhear. "Do you remember when my daughter needed that surgery for her foot?" Juan nodded. "My daughter had been in pain for weeks before I was able to raise the money. I never told you how I got it. Just between you and me, I went up to Tijuana and donated a kidney. They paid me $1,500 cash."

Juan blinked, staring at his neighbor in disbelief. "*How* much?" he asked, his voice barely a whisper.

"$1,500. Cash." Martín's eyes shone with a strange mixture of pride and secrecy. "Not bad money for a couple of hours of work, right?" he laughed.

Juan's chest tightened. *$1,500.* He could already imagine what that money could provide, like his brothers staying in school, and his family's problems being relieved. But the idea of selling an organ scared him.

Martín must have seen it on his face, because he leaned in, pressing a scrap of paper into Juan's hand. "Here's Jorge's number. He's the one who hooked me up. It might be worth a call at least."

Juan stared at the paper for a long moment. The choice was simple, but the consequences weren't. *It's illegal,* he reminded himself. *And dangerous.* But the thought of his little brothers stiffened his resolve to at least investigate the possibility. *I can't let them drop out.*

The next day, after a sleepless night, Juan dialed the number that Martín had given him. "You're looking to make some money?" Jorge asked Juan.

Juan hesitated for a second. "Yes. How can I get involved in the 'medical research'?"

Jorge's laughter came through the phone, but then he said conspiratorially. "I'll buy your bus ticket. We'll meet and talk about it. I'll front you a little cash for your trouble."

The bus ride up to Tijuana felt like an eternity to Juan. By the time he arrived, his stomach churned with a mixture of anticipation and dread. *In a few days I'll have the money,* he reassured himself. He passed the physical exam with no issues. He was young and strong after so many years of working the land. In his short life, he'd rarely seen a doctor, and felt intimidated.

On the day of the surgery, he had expected some pain and discomfort afterwards, maybe a small permanent scar. But what he hadn't expected was an overwhelming feeling of unease.

The operating room was too bright. They strapped him down before he could protest, and the anesthetic clouded his mind. When he started to come to, everything felt wrong. He felt as if someone had carved out the core of his body, leaving it hollow.

His side ached with a deep pain, and his head was spinning. The realization hit him slowly, then all at once: *They took more than they were supposed to take.*

The smell of the sterile operating room was still in his nostrils as Juan's body betrayed him, slipping into unconsciousness once again. This time, there was no more hope of returning home.

Juan was gone. His family would never know what happened, not really. The authorities wouldn't be able to help; he was already in the shadow of the 120,000 who had vanished, slipping into the same darkness as so many others before him.

28

FBI Special Agent Robert Jones strode inside of the Long Beach field office, rolling his shoulders to shake off the stiffness from the drive, Aretha Franklin's "R-E-S-P-E-C-T" still echoing in his ears. The building was alive with movement, phones ringing, fingers tapping against keyboards, and agents engaged in intense conversations.

Now, in the conference room, he absentmindedly clicked the top of his pen, the rhythmic click-click-click filling the silence of the conference room as he waited for the meeting to start. He made sure his tie was meticulously knotted, and his shirt was without a single crease. In fact, he never let himself look sloppy, a lesson drilled into him early. "If you want respect, you dress like you deserve it," his father used to tell him.

The door opened, and agents began filtering in, taking their seats. "Good afternoon," Robert greeted his colleagues, setting down his bag. His accent in the professional setting no longer carried the traces of his Memphis roots.

Robert stood up as Ruby entered the conference room and greeted her as she took a seat. Six agents surrounded the table, their faces all business, their seriousness filling the room.

She wiped her sweaty palms on her pants as she steadied her breath. She had prepared for this moment, but the reality of it felt different. This wasn't an office or a quiet meeting with clients. This was the FBI, and Ruby was a civilian.

She took a deep breath and reminded herself: *You're a professional. Put on your big-girl panties.* Her hands gripped the strap of her computer bag as she sat straighter in her chair, nerves jangled. Robert's face appeared like a small lifeline. His reassuring smile, though faint, was the only thing keeping her from running out of the room.

"Ruby," Robert's voice cut through the tension, confident. "Let me introduce everyone on the task force."

"Task force?" Ruby asked uncertainly.

"The FBI collaborates with other federal agencies to coordinate responses and utilize resources to combat transnational organized crime, encompassing money laundering and drug trafficking. Fighting these organizations is a challenge for the U.S. government because they are so well funded and organized, and the government also needs to be well funded and organized in response.

"This is Jerri Simpson from the economic crimes division," Robert began, gesturing toward a sharp-eyed woman dressed in a navy power suit. "Diego Fontánez from the transnational drug squad," Robert continued, nodding toward a man with a thick mustache and dark, intelligent eyes.

Ruby nodded politely, ignoring the sudden heat that spread across her neck. *I'm just here to help,* she repeated to herself.

"We also invited our partners from the other agencies on the front lines with us," Robert said, his voice steady. "This is Agent Miriam Rojas from the DEA, and this is Agent Danny Ortega from the ATF."

Ruby's heart rate picked up speed at the mention of the DEA. *This is the big leagues.*

After a few more introductions, the agents passed their business cards over to Ruby, and she felt herself being scrutinized by each. "It's nice to meet you," she said, her voice coming out more tentative than she intended.

Jerri's cool and sharp gaze didn't help.

Robert cleared his throat, sensing Ruby's discomfort. "Let's get started. Ruby, can you please tell us a little about yourself and how you became suspicious about the transactions?"

Ruby swallowed hard. As she reached into her bag and pulled out her organized binder, her hands shook slightly. She glanced around the table, the weight of their eyes on her making her throat tighten.

"Good afternoon, everyone. I'm a CPA, and I handle business and personal taxes for private clients. One of my clients, Dr. Kevin Carter, is a surgeon in Newport Beach. I've been doing his financials for years now." She paused, her voice catching. She knew she had to keep it together, but she felt uncomfortable being in the hot seat.

Her voice cracked like a middle-school boy. "This month, the transactions on their bank statements didn't add up. Payments came in from a nonprofit to the doctor's art gallery and then were sent out from the gallery to the New Me Clinic in Tijuana. It felt to me like something wasn't right."

She had their full attention now. Robert nodded encouragingly, but there was none of the usual warmth behind his gaze. He was dead serious now. "Can you explain further?"

Ruby flipped through her binder, pulling out the bank statements that she had printed for the meeting. The papers rustled in the tense silence as she laid the documents down in front of them. "Here, this one, for example. This isn't a standard payment. It's too frequent, and there's no legitimate reason an art gallery would be wiring funds to a plastic surgery clinic, especially in another country."

Jerri's brow wrinkled as she looked through the pages. Diego's expression remained unreadable, but Ruby felt that he was focused on her every word. "And the Shipshape Art Gallery and the New Me Clinic?" Miriam asked, her voice a sharp cut through the quiet. "What do you know about them?"

Ruby nodded, feeling the weight of the moment. "I know the Second Lives Foundation has been on the FBI's radar before, right? But I think the connection to New Me Clinic is new. This could be tied to something bigger."

There was a pause as the agents exchanged looks and whispered to each other. Miriam Rojas looked like she was about to speak, but she caught herself, looking back at Ruby.

Robert looked around at his teammates, rubbing his jaw thoughtfully. "We really appreciate you bringing this to our attention. This is valuable information, Ruby. We'll follow up on this. But..." He hesitated for a moment, weighing his words. "We'll need more. Keep digging as much as you can, and we will keep working on our end. We'll get back to you soon."

As the meeting concluded, Ruby felt the tension in the air. She stood, and her knees felt a little shaky. DEA Agent Miriam Rojas was the first to exit the building. The door clicked shut behind her, but Ruby didn't notice.

Outside, Miriam pulled out her burner phone, looking around as she dialed.

"David, you should know," Miriam's voice was low and businesslike. "The FBI task force is onto the New Me Clinic. We met with an accountant today, Ruby something, and she's been tracking funds between the Second Lives Foundation, Shipshape, and the clinic."

Miriam no longer had any qualms about making a call like this. It was all just a game of cat and mouse. There was no way that the flow of drugs would ever stop because the appetite for drugs in America was insatiable. At first it was just a few dollars here and there that she had accepted when she was a rookie, but as she rose through the ranks to more and more important positions in the DEA, her value to the cartel grew and so did her compensation. She knew better than to spend any of the money ostentatiously on a BMW or a Rolex watch, but it gave her a little wiggle room, and she was padding her nest for retirement. She justified to herself that if it weren't her, it would be someone else.

David's voice came through the line, strained but calm. "What's her name? Where can I find her?" His voice carried an edge of something sharp, dangerous. Miriam could hear the tension in it, the low growl of concern that was just beneath the surface.

As Miriam walked back towards her car, she felt the heat from the conversation seep into her bones. She didn't care about the accountant, but she knew this game was bigger than her and bigger than the task force. This was about keeping the wheels turning. Keeping the game in motion.

Miriam tucked the phone back into her pocket, keeping her face impassive and looking around to make sure she was still beyond earshot. She felt the chill of her decisions settling over her like a second skin.

29

"Hi, Ruby, I'm surprised to hear from you again so soon. Did anything develop with that money-laundering client we talked about?"

"Hi, Doug. Sorry to bother you again. I wanted to update you and pick your brain a little more."

"Sure. Shoot. What's going on?"

Ruby took a deep breath, wrapping a piece of hair around her index finger. "I met with the FBI. They've got a task force in Long Beach that's been investigating money laundering and drug trafficking."

"Wait, hold on. The FBI? What are you doing with the FBI?"

As the pitch of Doug's voice rose, Ruby could almost hear his eyebrows rise as well, his voice tinged with disbelief. She felt her pulse quicken as she spoke. "They're investigating the Second Lives Foundation. You remember I mentioned to you the one with the strange transactions? And it turns out there's a plastic surgery clinic in Tijuana that's been getting money from one of my clients, an American doctor."

Doug's tone slipped into something more serious. "You're saying these funds are being moved from the U.S. to Mexico?"

"Yeah. Lots of money is being moved in and out, but it's not clear exactly what is happening. The FBI was already looking into the nonprofit foundation, but they didn't know about the funds being sent down to a clinic in Mexico until now. They're trying to figure out where the money is going, and why. But I need to ask your advice about something."

There was a brief silence on the other end, then Doug's voice came back, slower, more deliberate. "Okay, I'm listening."

Ruby's throat tightened as she went over the details again and how the money flowed. She could almost hear the gears in Doug's mind turning, connecting the dots. When he spoke, his voice was laced with suspicion.

"Ruby, the most obvious answer is still the one you first considered. If it looks like money laundering is going on, it probably is. But there could well be something else here, right?" He paused, choosing his next words. "These transactions are all linked to a foundation focused on organ donations and a clinic that could be involved in organ transplants, right?"

Ruby's breath caught in her throat. *Organ transplants?* The words conjured an image in her mind that she couldn't shake.

"Do you really think this could be something like that?" Her voice shook despite her best efforts to stay calm.

Doug's voice softened, and he spoke to her more gently. "Have you thought about the possibility that this might be tied to organ trafficking? I don't know, Ruby. I've never seen it firsthand, and I don't want to scare you, but it's a possibility. Have you thought about it?"

Ruby felt a chill race down her spine. Her thoughts scattered, but she forced herself to focus on the conversation. "What would I even look for if that were a possibility?"

Doug hesitated. She could almost hear him sifting through

his experience, sorting out the words he didn't want to say. "Transactions that don't match up with normal business activities, unusual payments, especially large ones, going to medical centers, especially in places like Mexico. Look for a pattern of transfers between nonprofit organizations and medical tourism sites, or any sign of things that just don't make sense."

Ruby's mouth felt dry. "And what if I see something like that? Then what?"

"Ruby, if you even *suspect* that something like this could be happening, you need to let the FBI handle it. This could be bigger than money laundering."

Her stomach churned. She had been afraid of this. But now, the possibility loomed over her like a shadow. "I don't know, Doug. It just feels so unlikely."

Doug's tone softened again, but there was no comfort in it. "I wish I could agree with you, but I can't. These things are happening right now. They're out there. And if this is what it looks like, we're talking about people's lives."

Ruby fell silent, her thoughts racing. She couldn't shake the images Doug's words had conjured, the reality of what he was suggesting. Her chest felt tight, and she had trouble taking a full breath. "I don't know, Doug. Maybe I'm overthinking this, letting my imagination run away with me."

"I hope that's the case," he mumbled. "But if you're right, Ruby, you need to let someone know. You can't just let this slide." There was a finality in his voice, as though the gravity of the situation was finally sinking in.

Ruby closed her eyes, her head spinning with the weight of what she might have uncovered. *What if this is real? What if it's worse than I imagined?* She let out a shaky breath. "Okay, I'll keep digging. If I find something solid, I'll bring it to the FBI."

"Keep me posted, Ruby. If you need anything, anything at all, you know where to reach me."

The call ended, and Ruby found herself alone in the silence, with Doug's words still hanging in the air. She stood up, her legs unsteady beneath her. She glanced at the stack of papers on her desk with her research, but now it felt so much darker, that she was getting closer to something dangerous.

But was she ready to uncover it?

30

Jack was sitting at his desk grading homework when Ruby called. He noticed the worried look on her face when the FaceTime call started.

Finally, he broke the silence. "So, I'm dying to know. How was your meeting with the FBI?"

Ruby exhaled sharply, thinking back to the experience. "It was stressful," she said, almost whispering. "They asked a lot of questions, and I told them everything I knew."

Jack lifted his eyebrows expectantly. "And?"

"They think there could be something there with the money laundering. They're still investigating, putting a case together."

They were both silent, and then Ruby offered, "It may be bigger than I thought, Jack. I can't walk away from this."

Jack looked back at her, arms crossed. "You're taking on a huge risk, Ruby. You know that, right? Are you sure it's worth it?"

She looked up at him and nodded. "What if it's for something more than money laundering? What if it's drugs or something worse?" Her voice quavered. "If I don't speak up, who will? What if someone gets hurt because I kept quiet? My God, Jack, what if someone dies?"

Jack started to speak but stopped himself.

"What if it were cousin John's life? Or someone like him? Isn't that worth the risk?" She didn't know if she was trying to convince her brother or herself.

Jack rubbed his temples, letting out a slow sigh. "You sound like Dad," he said finally. "Do you remember that story he used to tell us all the time about a little girl who was rescuing starfish that had washed up onto the sand after a big storm by throwing them back into the ocean one by one? About how a man asked her why she was bothering when there were thousands of starfish on the sand and her minor efforts couldn't possibly make any difference?"

Ruby smiled faintly, though it didn't reach her eyes. "Yes, I remember. She told the man, 'It made a difference to *that* one!' as she threw another starfish back into the water. I think about that a lot. How sometimes it feels like we're just drops in the ocean, but every drop makes a ripple and changes the tide, even if we can't see it right away."

"Right." Jack shook his head. "You've always been a cautious person, Ruby. You live on a hilltop, in your little house on your little island. You don't make waves, don't take risks."

"You're right," she admitted, her voice breaking. "But maybe that needs to change. It's time to stop being so cautious. If it could make a difference and save someone, wouldn't it be worth it?"

Jack's gaze softened, but his shoulders were still tense. "I'm all for courage, but this is different. You could be going up against powerful people, dangerous people."

Ruby looked him in the eyes and then said, "I'm scared, Jack. I won't pretend I'm not. But if I don't do this..." She trailed off, shaking her head. "Then what kind of person am I?"

Jack stared at her for a long moment, his jaw working as he chewed on her words. Finally, he exhaled a deep breath. "I'm worried about you, Ruby. I don't want you to get hurt."

"I won't," she said, her voice firm. "I'm being careful."

But as she said it, she looked back toward her locked front door.

31

avid, Pepe, and Ramón slipped through the border into the U.S. under the cover of night. The boat ride from San Diego to Catalina Island that followed felt like a blur of saltwater spray and seasickness. The associate from La Familia who piloted the boat spoke little, but his eyes kept searching the horizon for other boats as he navigated the choppy waters toward the island. By the time they docked in Avalon Harbor, Pepe and Ramón looked like ghosts, their sweat-streaked faces gray with nausea.

Once inside Miguel's apartment, Ramón, tall and lean, splashed water over his face in the cramped kitchen sink, trying to cool down, while Pepe, thick-set like a wrestler, paced the living room floor. He paused every few steps to chug some Coke to settle his stomach from the turbulent sea.

David eyed them both, a smirk on his face. "Are there any decent tacos on this island?" he asked Miguel mockingly.

Miguel glanced over, unfazed, as he pulled a beer from the fridge. "Tacos? Sure. A lot of *paisanos* live here. Do you want me to grab some fish tacos?"

The mere mention of food made Ramón gag. He gave a low

groan, pressing his palm to his forehead. Pepe just shook his head, taking another sip of Coke.

David chuckled, eyes narrowing. "You babies. I feel fine. We've got work to do. You need to grow a pair."

David turned back to Miguel. "*Sí, güey.* Go get some tacos with salsa, guacamole, the works." He ignored the looks Ramón and Pepe exchanged.

While Miguel set out for food, the rest of the men gathered around the kitchen table to start with the preparations. Joaquin, their tech expert, was already in the middle of setting up the gear. He laid out a phone recording adapter, a USB stick with hacking software, and a handful of other small devices on the kitchen table.

"This," Joaquin said, tapping a black adapter with his finger, "we'll install on her phone line. And this,"—he pointed to the USB—"goes in her laptop. The rest"—he held up the devices like a magician showing his tricks—"we'll plant around the house in smoke detectors, Wi-Fi routers, and lighting fixtures. We'll have to figure out the best spots once we're inside."

David's gaze hardened as he processed the plan. This was bigger than he'd initially thought. Every piece of technology and every move they made had to be precise. Anything less could expose them.

After they ate, at least those who could stomach the food, Miguel disappeared into the bedroom, leaving the others to their planning. The hours stretched long as they prepared for the next phase.

The next morning, Joaquin, Ramón, and Pepe, disguised as hikers, baseball caps pulled down low over their faces, set out on foot until they reached the condo development where Ruby lived. The men took up their positions with the casual ease of professionals, yet there was an undercurrent of tension, an awareness that they could be spotted at any moment. David stayed in the apartment and was in contact with them through his phone, receiving text messages updating him on the surveillance.

Multiple hours passed with little action. Ruby did not leave the house for the entire day. Still, the men remained vigilant, taking turns eating and relieving themselves. They waited silently, their eyes never leaving the condo.

Finally, late in the afternoon, the moment arrived. Ruby, along with her dog, left the condo and headed toward town. Joaquin's message flashed on David's phone. "Go time."

Joaquin wasted no time. He crept into the condo, moving through the rooms like the professional that he was. David watched the screen of his phone, eyes narrowing as Joaquin's updates came in, one by one. First, he tapped the phone line, then compromised the laptop, and finally he hid listening devices in the walls, the ceiling, and the furniture.

David held his breath until he received the final text. *"HECHO."* All done, Joaquin's message flashed.

The men reconvened at the apartment, settling in for a long night. Joaquin set up a small command center to track Ruby's every move, studying her interactions, her online activity. For the next few days, they followed her like predators, noting every search, every click, and every detail.

It didn't take long before they saw it. Ruby was researching the Second Lives Foundation and the New Me Clinic on her laptop. The significance of the searches wasn't lost on David. *This was not a good sign,* he thought, the tension in his chest tightening.

He had enough data now. It was time to inform Francisco.

32

John Fernández pulled his rusted brown pickup truck into the parking lot of the gas station, the old engine complaining as it sputtered to a stop. He had been unemployed since the latest round of layoffs at the plant, and the days had become a blur of empty hours and nagging phone calls from his ex-wife, Marina. She wanted the child support that he owed her, but what little he managed to give her was never enough. "You can't squeeze water from a rock," he had told her more times than he could count, but it didn't make the calls any easier.

He yanked the door to the gas station convenience store open, and the bell above it jingled as he stepped in. He didn't expect to see Jesse, a coworker of his from the plant that he never cared for, standing in front of the refrigerator picking out an energy drink.

"Hey, man, how've you been?" Jesse's voice was low.

"I've been okay," John muttered, avoiding Jesse's gaze. "Money has been tight, and Marina's been on my case about the payments. You know how it is." He glanced at the floor, embarrassed, shoving his hands into his jacket pockets.

Jesse shrugged, a sympathetic look passing over his face.

"Yeah, I feel you, man. I'm in the same boat. The unemployment check is better than nothing, but it ain't much." Jesse paused and then said, "If you're looking for some extra cash, I might have something interesting."

John's eyes narrowed, feeling suspicious. "Freelancing, huh? What's the gig?" His gut tensed, but he was too far in debt to care all that much.

Jesse glanced around, lowering his voice. "I have something small for you if you want it. It pays well, all in cash, and no questions asked."

John hesitated. It sounded too good to be true, but he wasn't really in a position to be choosy. Desperation made him lean in closer and ask, "What do I gotta do?"

Jesse smiled, the kind of smile that didn't reach his eyes. "It's simple, man. You're a patriot like me, right? A real Second Amendment guy? I need you to pick up some firearms, that's it. It would only take a couple of hours of your time. You won't even break a sweat."

John stiffened and stepped back, a chill crawling up his spine. "What kind of firearms?" he asked skeptically.

"A few hunting rifles," Jesse said, glancing over his shoulder. "Nothing to worry about. They're for my buddy, okay? He can't buy them himself."

John looked at Jesse, his stomach tight. "That sounds a little fishy. Why can't the buyer get them himself?"

"Don't worry about it, man." Jesse waved it off, his voice lowered to a near-whisper. "You would be helping out a friend. It's no different than buying a case of beer for a guy without ID."

John's pulse quickened, but the thought of cash sitting heavy in his pocket soothed him. It would buy him some time, take care of Marina for a little while, maybe even pay down some of his past-due rent. He exhaled slowly and then nodded. "Alright. I'm in."

Jesse clapped him on the back. "Great. I'll give you the details Monday night. Just make sure you're ready."

Two days later, John pulled up to the sporting goods shop with the thick envelope of cash burning a hole in his back pocket. John barely noticed the store's massive sign looming over him. His mind was on the cash and the endless bills he couldn't seem to outrun. Every glance in the rearview mirror made him feel like someone was following him. He parked in the rear parking lot, trying to look inconspicuous.

He saw the gun counter towards the back and felt his hands sweat as he walked toward it. He spotted a pale teenager with pockmarked skin behind the counter. The kid, whose name tag read "Blake", looked half-asleep. His head was down, clearly counting the minutes until his shift ended.

"Hey, man. How's it going?" John greeted him, his throat tight.

Blake mumbled, barely looking up from his cell phone screen. "I'm a little hungover, to be honest, just waiting for my shift to end."

"I feel you," John replied, trying to sound casual. He forced his voice to stay steady, but his hands shook at the riskiness of what he was doing. "I'm just here to pick up some hunting rifles."

Blake barely looked up at him. "We got plenty," Blake said, sounding bored. Do you want something that feels good in your hands?" He stood unenthusiastically and led John to the racks.

John nodded, the words feeling like they came from someone else. "Yeah, show me some of the popular ones."

Blake guided him through the display, pointing to rifles without much enthusiasm. "This one's the WASR-10, real reliable. Then there's the Anderson AM-15. The Barrett's pretty impressive though." He gave a slight smile. "It can penetrate iron plate from over a mile away."

John felt a slight shiver crawl up his spine at the mention of the Barrett, but he kept his face neutral. "I'll take ten of those." He tried to sound as casual as possible, but the words came out sharper than he intended.

Blake paused, his eyes looking at the rifles and then back to John. For a split second, John thought the kid might question him, but Blake just nodded, unperturbed. "They're for my own personal use for hunting," John added, hoping Blake would suspend disbelief that his customer would use these for deer hunting, which is also what John indicated on the firearms transaction forms. John's right hand shook as he filled out the form but took a deep breath, remembering what Jesse had told him: There are no specific laws against gunrunning. The worst he could get if he got caught for lying on the form was probation and probably nothing at all.

"Okay. Anything else?"

"No, just the Barretts and ammo," John said quickly, pulling the envelope from his pocket and handing it over. His hand shook enough for him to notice, but Blake didn't seem to care. Transaction complete, John walked out with two carts full of weapons and ammo, not looking around, a "nothing to see here" vibe.

That night, John met the buyer at a nearby truck stop. The gravel crunched as his truck pulled up and stopped next to the buyer's truck. Wordlessly, John transferred the weapons into the back of the man's vehicle, his heartbeat pounding in his ears. The rifles would join others as part of the "iron river" of weapons flowing south to Mexico and beyond. There was no verbal acknowledgment between the two men and no handshake, just the quick anonymous exchange.

John's mind raced as he walked back to his truck. He knew the guns could end up anywhere, maybe in the hands of the cartel gunning down a Mexican policeman who couldn't compete against the better armed criminals. Or worse, he thought, an American border patrol agent. His stomach twisted, but he shoved the thought further down.

The War on Drugs is bigger than me. It's not my business if America has a drug problem that makes cartels fight in Mexico about who will fill that need, he told himself. *I need to worry about my own problems, like making child support payments and paying for beer and rent, in that order. If it weren't me, it would just be some other guy trying to pay his bills.*

As he started his truck, the low rumble of the engine barely registered. His thoughts focused only on the cash in his pocket and the look on Marina's face when he would hand some of it to her. He had no choice, and he'd do it again if it meant surviving. When he thought about it, it was the easiest money he ever made.

33

Two days later, when Dr. Feinerman was back on shift, he looked at Mrs. Rogers's chart and saw that she was deceased. *Not surprising.* He called down to the hospital's pathology department, his scientific curiosity getting the better of him. His old medical school classmate was working there now.

"Dr. Cooper, it's Jeff Feinerman."

"Hey man, how's life in the ER?"

"It's a battle zone, but it's *my* battle zone."

Dr. Cooper chuckled. "What can I do for you?"

Dr. Feinerman explained Mrs. Rogers's symptoms and her quick demise. "Can you please call me when you determine the cause of the encephalitis?"

"Will do. It may take a few days though if the cause is not obvious."

"Understood, thanks, man."

Dr. Feinerman was playing whack-a-mole in the ER a few days later when he saw a call come in from Dr. Cooper.

"You're not going to believe this. Take a guess?"

"HSV? West Nile? TB?"

"No, not even close. It's rabies!"

"Oh, come on. You can't be serious!"

"Serious as a heart attack. You'd better call the Department of Health and Human Services to interview the husband. Maybe she got bitten by a bat or something."

"Maybe," he responded, but he sounded skeptical.

34

The black Nissan pickup truck rumbled into the parking lot near the *zócalo* of the small Mexican town, the tires grinding on the cracked pavement of the main square, which was La Familia territory. The air was dusty and warm, but the men inside the truck were stone cold. They wore tight black balaclavas, their eyes dark slits of focus as they checked their weapons, rifles at the ready.

Pedro ran his fingers against the "Barrett" logo hand-stamped into the receiver of the rifle, and then tightened his grip, his breath shallow, finger on the trigger. The instructions from David had been simple: *Kill as many as you can, make it quick, and then get out.* The money was good, too good to pass up, but the stakes were higher than ever. They couldn't afford to get caught. If they got caught, David would kill them, if the cops or rivals didn't do it first.

His men sat next to him without speaking, their faces set in grim determination. Pedro nodded to them. It was time.

"On the count of three, let'er rip," Pedro muttered under his breath.

The world around them paused for a second. Then, at Pedro's signal, the truck's doors flew open and chaos erupted.

The deafening sound of gunfire tore through the air. The men squeezed off rounds, moving their guns in a murderous arc around the square. They heard the bullets slamming into flesh mixing with the panic-stricken screams of the innocent victims.

The young mother pushing a stroller collapsed in a spray of blood, the baby's screams muffled by the chaos. Two ten-year-old boys walking in their school uniforms turned towards the noise in confusion just as the bullets found them, their *paletas* dropping to the ground uneaten. An old janitor, bent over his broom, didn't even see it coming. His body fell backward as the force of the gunshots knocked him off his feet.

The pickup truck's tires screeched as the assailants sped off, their laughter echoing as they sped down the narrow streets, the adrenaline already wearing off. It was just another day at the office for them. Minutes later, they ripped off their balaclavas, jumped out of the truck with their rifles and into a waiting white utility van, the engine roaring to life. The bloody pandemonium they had left behind on the square was like a nightmare, the distant wail of sirens rising in the background as law enforcement arrived en masse.

The white van carrying the men swerved through the town, blending in with the regular traffic, and soon they were out of sight as if nothing had ever happened.

Back at the *zócalo,* the Mexican public security forces flooded the scene, sirens blaring, their boots heavy on the ground. Uniformed officers scrambled to secure the area, tending to the stunned injured and moving the dead. The once-vibrant square was now a grisly tableau of blood and confusion, the smell of gunpowder hanging in the air.

The law enforcement officers' presence on the plaza, while reassuring for civilians, did nothing to ease the tension for La Familia. The rival group that had carried out the massacre, or at least what had been made to look like a rival group, had done more than kill innocent civilians. The attack had drawn law enforcement's attention right to the heart of the town in La Familia's plaza, leaving the cartel unable to conduct its normal operations. The rival cartel had *heated up* La Familia's plaza, a move that would allow their own men to operate unencumbered in another part of town where law enforcement was now scarce.

David paced in his office, wiping his hand across his sweaty forehead. He knew what would happen if Francisco ever found out about his betrayal of La Familia, and now he had to break the news of the attack to Francisco.

He dialed Francisco with shaky hands. When the call connected, he could almost feel his cousin's rage on the other side of the line before Francisco's voice erupted through the speaker.

"Who the fuck is doing this to me?" Francisco's voice roared, a guttural sound of pure fury. "I'll cut off their balls and stuff them down their throats! I'll—"

David pulled the phone away, wincing at the volume of Francisco's rage. When he put it back to his ear, the anger was still there.

"Someone is out to get me, David," Francisco seethed. "They're treating me like a limp dick, like I'm nothing. When I find out who they are, I will make them pay dearly for this."

David said nothing, just listened as Francisco's anger drowned out everything else. The man's fury was palpable, raw, and unrelenting.

But David knew that something more than rage simmered beneath the surface. Francisco's grip on power, and on sanity, was slipping, and he knew it. And that was more than okay with David. He was betting on it.

As he set the phone down, David's thoughts turned cold and calculating. La Familia had become more than a business. It was a war, and in a war, there were no friends and no cousins, only enemies.

35

The first light of morning slipped through the blinds. Jacklyn Carter blinked into the soft glow, her eyes adjusting to the daylight creeping in. She turned her head, the gentle rise and fall of Kevin's balding head on the pillow across from hers barely audible in the quiet of their bedroom. She noted that when he was still asleep, his face was soft and free of the sharp, controlling edge that often defined his presence when awake.

The sheets, tangled around her legs, felt cool against her skin. Jacklyn stayed still for a moment, feeling the weight of the separateness between them. *Gone are the mornings when we'd wake up tangled together,* she thought. The once-frequent mornings of hasty, passionate embraces had faded into something more routine, just like their days. She sighed, lifting the sheets up to her neck, savoring the comfort for a little longer. *Maybe I can stay in bed until the boys wake up, or at least until I have to get them ready for school.*

Kevin's habitual morning routine would begin soon enough: the sound of his sneakers hitting the floor, the rustling of his Vuori running gear as he pulled it on. He'd be out the door before long, his focus shifting to his cross-country runs, a habit that had persisted since high school. Jacklyn didn't mind. *Let him run,* she thought, sinking deeper into the pillow. *He will be a little calmer when he gets back.*

Her thoughts drifted to their early years together, how her parents had disapproved when she married a "người khoai tây" (a "white boy," as they put it), but how the disapproval had softened when Kevin's surgical career promised financial security. Growing up, Jacklyn spent many hours doing her schoolwork in her parents' cramped shop, dusty bolts of fabric and colorful spools of thread lining the walls. Her parents, as always, looked ahead. *We'll have you, our good daughter, taking care of us in our old age,* they had said. But Kevin never fully earned their respect. *No, he didn't even try,* Jacklyn thought bitterly. Jacklyn knew in her heart that Kevin had married her in the hope that, as an Asian wife, she would be more deferential to him. He liked to be in control. Maybe it was true that marital strife in Asian marriages was more subdued and harmony was valued over conflict, but at the end of the day Jacklyn was an American born and bred.

Despite his stature, his polished career, and their shared life, he had carried a dismissive air about those he deemed "beneath" him—her parents included. The nurses at the hospital had often whispered about his attitude, the way he treated people like his personal playthings. Jacklyn hadn't defended him; she couldn't.

As the years passed, Jacklyn had quietly stepped away from her own career as a beloved pediatric nurse practitioner, the kind of woman who could put a worried parent at ease with a smile and a few kind words. But motherhood and managing Kevin's practice, Coastal Surgical in Newport Beach, had replaced that. Now, she wasn't Jacklyn the nurse any longer, only Jacklyn the manager. She missed being appreciated and having her own money to spend. *I can't say I like this,* she thought, though there was no room to argue. Kevin's work took precedence, his image of success the one they both tried to live up to, even as it pulled them apart.

The Coastal Surgical office was like a shrine to Kevin's career. Sleek white marble furniture, mirrored walls, and artificial fuchsia orchids were carefully arranged in the waiting room. *He insisted on ultra-modern,* Jacklyn remembered with a half-hearted smile. She would have preferred something more comfortable and welcoming for their home, but it, much like the clinic, had become a monument to Kevin's ideals, and Jacklyn had long since stopped protesting. There was no use in fighting it. She had learned, as she always did, that some battles weren't worth waging. She wasn't going to use up her "marriage capital" on home decor decisions.

The soft slap of slippers against the floor snapped her out of her reverie. Kevin sat up, stretching as he tied his robe around his waist. "Babe, are you up?" His voice was groggy. "I have a scientific advisory board meeting after work. I won't be home for dinner."

Jacklyn grunted a reply, barely lifting her head. *Right. Another Foundation meeting.* A wave of resentment about her husband's involvement with the Foundation and the time it took away from her and the kids rolled through her, but she buried it quickly. She already did almost all the child-rearing and shuttling to extracurricular activities. Kevin's one job when the kids were little was to get them bathed and ready for bed, but they were too old for that now.

Jacklyn felt lonely with Kevin away so much, but she knew that there was no other woman. For all his faults and idiosyncrasies,

Kevin had been a faithful husband, and she did love him. Besides that, she felt reassured by the fact that he was a committed germaphobe; she couldn't imagine him risking a sexual encounter, even with a full-body condom.

When Jacklyn had confronted Kevin about her concerns about his time away from the family when he first told her about the offer to join the board, he dismissed her, saying "You don't seem to mind the extra cash which lets you live in a nice home in Laguna Beach, drive your Tesla, and send the kids to private school." She never wanted that Tesla anyway and felt it was too ostentatious, but Kevin had insisted. *The income from the surgical practice is more than enough for our family. He should spend that time at home.*

Jacklyn felt like she was treading water now and had been for some time. But her parents' voices echoed in her head. "Family is everything." She knew she would never put the American idea of self-actualization and personal happiness over the good of her own family.

She heard him moving around, shuffling, getting dressed, the rustle of fabric that punctuated the silence. Jacklyn closed her eyes for a second longer, tuning out the sounds of Kevin's morning routine. She had grown accustomed to them, just as she had grown accustomed to the slow erosion of their connection.

As he left, she felt the faintest pang in her chest—almost like regret. *I miss you.*

Jacklyn sat up in bed a little later, the house still and quiet.

She looked at the suitcases by the door, her sunhat resting optimistically on top—the ones they had packed for their anniversary trip. Kevin had promised her a special celebration. He could write off the trip as a business-related expense if he visited the art gallery that they owned in Avalon. *Maybe some time together, a cruise to Catalina and Ensenada could help us reconnect.*

36

gent Rosie Ramírez marched into the Long Beach field office, the weight of her badge clipped to her belt grounding her. She had been there for two years now, but the enormity of it still pressed against her shoulders, the kind of weight her father once carried.

She adjusted the strap of her laptop bag and exhaled, steadying herself before stepping into the conference room. A transnational organized crime task force meeting was nothing new, but today she'd be the task force's primary liaison with their Mexican law enforcement counterparts, making good use of her Spanish language skills. It was a moment that mattered, one she had spent years preparing for. Her fingers brushed the edge of her strap, and for a brief second, she wasn't in the FBI office anymore.

She was back in Indio, in California's Coachella Valley, in her family's backyard at the base of the picturesque San Jacinto and Santa Rosa Mountains, the desert heat melting into the coolness of evening. String lights stretched across the patio, casting a warm glow over the celebration of her high school graduation. The aromas of carne asada, tamales, and her grandmother's famous pozole bubbling away in a massive stockpot wafted through the air. Laughter burst from the women in the kitchen as they pressed masa into corn husks, their hands moving with generations of practice, mixed with the sound of clinking bottles and the shuffle of chairs on the concrete.

Her grandfather sat near the barbecue, holding a beer and watching his grandchildren play, marveling at their boundless energy. "When I was your age, we didn't have backyards like this," he had said, voice rough with time.

Rosie looked up at him questioningly. "Because you lived in Palm Springs, *abuelo?*"

He nodded. "Yes, we lived in Section 14, right near downtown." His eyes darkened. "We lived there until they burned it all down. They labeled it as a slum, that they needed the land for something better. Someone better." He took a slow sip of his beer. "They never gave us a chance."

She remembered how her father Lou had sat beside her grandfather, his own expression unreadable, the weight of their family's history resting between them. Lou had been one of the first Latino police officers in Palm Springs, carrying the burden of proving himself every day.

"When you wear this," he had told her years later, polishing his badge at the kitchen table, "people will make assumptions about you. Every minute of every day, you need to prove them wrong. You show them what a Ramírez can be."

She had clung to those words the day she graduated from the police academy, the same one her father had attended. She had carried his words through years of undercover work in Vice, through moments of doubt, through nights when physical and mental exhaustion made her question everything.

Now, standing in the doorway of the FBI conference room,

she stood up straighter. The past was always with her, but it did not define her.

She stepped inside the conference room, her badge at her hip, her mind sharp.

It was time to get to work.

37

Robert's knuckles cracked against the conference table, silencing the muted conversations going on around him. He surveyed the room, his sharp eyes meeting those of each agent, ensuring their attention.

"Okay, people. We've got a lot on our plate, so listen up." His voice was controlled, but there was an edge to it. "Jerri, I need you to dig into the Second Lives Foundation and the Shipshape art gallery. Get the subpoena for the Carter's personal and Coastal Surgical financial records, and don't stop there. Connect with the special agent who's been on the SARs from earlier and squeeze him for everything he's got. If it takes bringing in others from the financial crimes squad, so be it."

"No problem, I'll get started today," Jerri replied, her fingers already tapping away at her tablet, focused.

"Luis, I want you out there now. Go talk to the employees, the ones who've been at Coastal Surgical, the Second Lives Foundation, Shipshape, anyone who's had access to Dr. Carter or his wife. Dig up any dirt before we pull him in for questioning."

Luis nodded, determined. "Got it, boss."

"Rosie," Robert continued, his gaze turning toward her. "I need you to reach out to our Mexican counterparts. Have them get eyes on the New Me Clinic. We need surveillance, and we need to know if they're laundering money, too. There's more going on here than plastic surgery. You need to get inside. If you can, get yourself in as a patient."

Rosie didn't flinch at the suggestion. He knew she had years of working undercover under her belt and was fluent in Spanish. "I'll do it myself, but I'll need backup. I'll coordinate with the Mexicans on that."

"Good. Let's move fast on this one," Robert said, already moving to the next person.

"Miriam," he said, looking in her direction. "See if the DEA can get anything from its confidential informant network in Tijuana. We need to know what's really happening across the border. And I don't want anyone missing anything."

"Understood," Miriam replied, her voice no-nonsense, her mind already on the phone with the DEA and other people who would be very interested in knowing this information.

"Luis," Robert added, his voice low, "stick close to Dr. Carter. I want eyes on him at all times."

"I've got it covered," Luis replied, already stepping toward the door.

Miriam, once out of the meeting, didn't hesitate. She grabbed her burner phone and dialed David's number, the weight of the news settling like a stone in her gut. Finally, David picked up, his voice thick with curiosity.

"David, I thought you'd be interested to know that the task force is digging into Dr. Carter and his businesses, looking into the clinic and interviewing people, but there's something else. Rosie Ramírez, an FBI agent, is planning to go undercover at

New Me. She's going to pose as a patient to get inside," Miriam said, her voice calm but urgent.

David didn't answer immediately. She heard the quiet in his breath before he spoke. "Well," he said, the word heavy with meaning. "That's unexpected. I'll let the management know. Send me her photo."

"I'm sending it over now," Miriam replied, already pulling up the picture on her phone.

38

Jacklyn tossed and turned all night, thinking about what shenanigans Kevin could be up to. He had definitely been acting cagey ever since she had asked him about the bank statements. She lay with her head on the pillow, cataloguing the possibilities in her mind. *Tax evasion?* He had been complaining for years about how much tax they had to pay. She always told him that paying taxes was a good thing because it meant that you had income to pay taxes on, but he was still salty about it. No, Kevin knew better than to mess with the IRS. He was always conservative when it came to their taxes. Was he trying to shore up the art gallery? Sales hadn't been too great lately. But then why put the money in and take it right back out again? That made no sense. But then again, she wasn't all that savvy when it came to finances. *They didn't teach that in nursing school.* Finally, she landed on cheating. *Maybe he had a woman on the side? A Mexican woman?* That made some sense, but she didn't think he was like that. The thought tortured her. Finally, at about 4am, she could take it no longer, and she nudged him awake.

"We need to talk," she told him, words that strike fear in the hearts of all men.

"For the love of all that is holy! What time is it? Can't this wait until morning?"

"No, it can't wait!" she sobbed.

"What's wrong? Is it one of the boys? Are you okay?" Now he was wide awake and sat up. With his back against the headboard, he reached for the lamp. He saw her tear-streaked face and the hurt in her eyes. "Tell me."

She choked out the question: "Is there someone else?"

He was confused for a moment. "You mean another woman? What are you talking about? Why would you think that?"

"The money! Where is the money going?"

Relief flooded his face as the realization dawned on him that she was continuing the conversation they had had previously. "No, love, never. I swear on our children's lives that I have never been unfaithful to you."

"But then where is the money going? I don't understand?!" she asked, her voice shaking.

"Come here," he said as he wrapped his arms around her. "That's not what this is."

"Then what is it?"

"I can't talk about it. It's better if you don't know."

"That's not good enough!" she sobbed.

Kevin was silent for a few moments before making a decision. "Okay, take a few deep breaths and calm down," as if telling someone to calm down ever made a person more calm. "I will tell you, but you can't tell a soul. Can you promise me?"

"I promise," she sniffled.

"Okay," he started. "There's a clinic in Mexico that is helping desperate people procure the organs that they need. All I do is perform physical exams to make sure that the recipients are healthy enough that the transplants have a high probability of success. If it weren't me doing the physical exams, it would just be someone else."

She stared at him. "But, isn't that illegal?"

"Yes, that's why they are paying me so much. But if someone is willing to sell an organ, and another person is ready to buy, what's the harm in that? We are helping people who could die if they wait for an organ through legal channels."

"So the donors are in Mexico? Are they at least getting paid well?"

"I'm not involved on that side, but I would assume so. I only do the screening exams, that's it."

Jacklyn felt sick to her stomach. It didn't really matter how Kevin positioned it. She knew in her heart of hearts that it was wrong. And she couldn't believe that Kevin could be involved in something so nefarious. She felt like she didn't know her husband at all. She would almost have preferred another woman. How could she possibly keep this colossal secret inside her? But she had to. She didn't want to destroy her family or take her boys' father away from them. *He could go to prison for this,* she thought. Lose his license. No, she would convince him to stop doing it. The people running the operation, though, would they let him stop? Or would he become a "loose end" that needed to be tied up? She shuddered at the thought.

39

Gordon Miller slammed the receiver down onto the charger with a little more force than necessary, the click of the phone against the base reverberating in the quiet kitchen. His fingers lingered on the edges of the device as if he could still feel the remnants of the conversation seeping into his bones. *Alimony payments, division of property, recriminations,* the words ran through his head, drumming in time with the thudding pulse behind his eyes. He rubbed his face, shaking off the sting of it.

There were no kids to fight over, thank God. At least there was that. He could avoid the whole mess of child support or custody fights. No, it was just him and the aftermath of yet another failed marriage. He exhaled, staring out the window at the rising sun. *How did I fuck up another marriage?* He wasn't really surprised, just weary of the cycle.

He reached for the half-empty bottle of Jack Daniels from the counter, his hand instinctively going to it like a man seeking refuge, but he stopped himself. Instead, he sat back in his chair, shoulders slumping as he stared at the glass of amber liquid, the last remnants of his most recent bottle catching the light in a dull, almost mocking way.

They don't know how good they had it, he thought bitterly. He didn't even know why he bothered with marriage anymore. The last one had been the same, just a different set of issues. Toward the end, when she had given him that ultimatum in counseling—her or the booze—he didn't even hesitate. He had always known what he was choosing, even if she hadn't. And deep down, he knew he couldn't quit drinking even if he wanted to. He'd been doing it since he was twelve years old, first stealing vodka from Tommy's parents' stash after school, then graduating to keggers, frat parties, liquid lunches and boozy golf.

His mind wandered to how it had started. *Sixth grade. A goddamn sixth grader.* He and Tommy had carefully filled the bottle back up with water, titrating it just right, making sure Tommy's parents never noticed. The rush had been electric, and after that, the idea of life without alcohol had never seemed possible. Drinking dulled the sharp edges of life, made everything feel smoother. The world wasn't so rough when you were a little buzzed.

The memory soured as it took root. Over the years, the hangovers had gotten worse, the binge drinking more frequent. And there were those moments, those girls he could barely remember, the ones who had whispered "no" when he kissed them. *But they were both drunk, weren't they?* He'd convinced himself it was all fine. *They wanted it, didn't they?* After a certain supreme court nominee's hearings brought the aspiring judge's sexual assault accusations from his ancient past back to life, Gordon's golf buddies from school took to playfully calling him "Brett", somehow seeing parallels between Gordon and another preppy, rapey, self-righteous attorney with multiple false accusations in his past.

Who cares? Gordon thought, wiping a hand over his face. The girls didn't matter. They probably regretted it later. *Those sluts.* He smirked bitterly to himself, the thought stinging more than it should. That was the problem with being a man like him. He saw the world as it should've been, people doing what they were supposed to do, keeping their roles in line.

As he stood up and walked to the bathroom, Gordon caught sight of his reflection in the mirror. He had always been a handsome man in a WASPy sort of way, but his looks had taken a hit, a combination of years of heavy drinking and advanced age. Years of drinking had also made his nose red and bumpy, and his cheeks were flushed with rosacea. The bloated belly stuck out like he was well into his second trimester, and his skin had a sickly yellowish tint to it now. The mirror didn't lie, but it didn't care either. It didn't care that Gordon had been drinking since he was twelve, that it had always been a part of his life. The kidney damage had been gradual, insidious, but here he was. Sixty-five years old and struggling just to stay afloat. He wasn't ready to pack up his toys and go home.

The swelling in his ankles had gotten worse, too. He grunted as he unbuttoned his shirt, stepping onto the scale to see how much water he was retaining. When the doctor had seen him last, he had suggested stopping drinking, but Gordon didn't think it was so simple. *What does the doctor know?* His parents had drunk until the day they died. His father made it to eighty-three, his mother to eighty-five. Drinking didn't kill them.

But now Gordon's kidneys were failing, and nothing could fix that. The only thing keeping him going was dialysis, which did the work of filtering his blood that his kidneys could no longer do, but dialysis was a joke. He knew he didn't belong in dialysis with those poor, fat diabetics. As a *real* American, he *deserved* a new kidney, especially more than all those illegal aliens and minorities. He hated every moment of it, the sterile smell of the clinic, the hollow feeling after every session. *Four hours, three times a week. It was a part-time job, for Chrissake.*

He'd been on the transplant list for so long he couldn't even remember when he'd been placed on it. His number hadn't been called yet, and with each passing day, it seemed less likely. He signed an agreement to abstain from alcohol and knew he could be randomly tested and kicked off the list if he tested positive, but the most he could do was cut back.

When he arrived at his nephrologist's office the following week, Gordon sat across from him, tapping his fingers against the cold metal of the chair's armrest. He felt the pressure of the dialysis sessions weighing him down, and the thought of waiting for a transplant that might never come gnawed at him.

"I'm just so tired of this," Gordon complained, rubbing his temple, "the dialysis, the waiting. I don't have the time for this. I'm too young for this."

The doctor paused mid-sentence, his eyes looking up to meet his patient's. He squirmed in his chair and considered his next words.

"Gordon," he said slowly, "there may be options for you. But discretion is key."

Gordon's ears perked up. *Discretion. What was he talking about?*

The doctor leaned toward Gordon, lowering his voice to a near whisper. "You didn't hear this from me, but if you're willing to make a sizable charitable donation to the Second Lives Foundation, say fifty-thousand dollars, there's a chance you could expedite things. You could go across the border and bypass some of the red tape. But, like I said, it would all need to be strictly confidential."

Gordon leaned back, staring at the doctor in disbelief. *A donation?* The wheels in his head turned. *Fifty thousand for a new kidney?*

The week following the conversation with the nephrologist, and after a pre-surgical physical with Dr. Carter, Gordon stood in front of *New Me Clinéca Médica* in Tijuana, a modern building in an upscale area of the city. As an American who never bothered to get to know the world around him beyond work, home, and the golf course, he hadn't even known that there *were* upscale areas in Tijuana or all of Mexico for that matter and it came as a surprise. His palms were sweaty as he entered the modern and posh clinic.

He sat in a well-appointed waiting room, flipping through a magazine on the table. Of course, he had the money. He could wire the fifty thousand to the Foundation from his brokerage account right now, no questions asked. *And my donation would even be tax deductible!*

Could it really be this easy? he thought, his pulse quickening. The clinic looked as pristine as any hospital in the States, but something felt off. He glanced around, his eyes landing on the pamphlets selling youth and beauty. It seemed almost too good to be true.

But Gordon had made up his mind. He needed that kidney, and if this was how he was going to get it, so be it.

40

Marcelo sat in his office reading through the latest donor files. One was a young woman, barely out of her teens. The cold, clinical details in the file seemed almost absurdly out of place given her youth. As his fingers scanned her file, the gears in his mind started to grind, and he was hit by a sudden flash of inspiration.

What if there's more?

He ran his fingers through his hair, staring at the picture of the girl in the file. What if he could push the boundaries just a little further to maximize revenues? Francisco's voice echoed in his head: *"Don't let anything go to waste."* Marcelo clenched his jaw. Could he apply this mantra in this situation?

The more he thought about it, the more the idea, which had started out amorphous, sharpened in his mind. We could get a "two-fer," he whispered to himself. The idea seemed promising, but he didn't know if it was feasible.

By the time Marcelo sat at his desk to call David, he was excited about his idea. He stood up and dialed David's number, pacing the length of his office.

"Bueno?" David's voice was gruff and hurried.

"David, I've been thinking. I have a business expansion idea that might increase our revenues significantly," Marcelo said, his tone carefully neutral, but he couldn't quite mask the excitement beginning to stir beneath his words.

In another universe, Marcelo's creativity could have made him a successful marketing strategist for a Fortune 500 company, but in this universe he ran the New Me Clinic in Tijuana.

David's pause was brief, just enough to make Marcelo wonder if he was hesitating, or thinking. "Okay, I'm listening, but make it quick."

Marcelo took a deep breath. *Don't overthink it.* "So, we're making money from plastic surgery procedures and, of course, the organ harvests. But what if we could squeeze more out of the young female patients before we take them down to the operating table for the organ harvesting?"

He heard David shift on the other end. "I'm intrigued," he said, voice steady. "What did you have in mind?"

Marcelo's words tumbled out faster now, fueled by a thrilling sense of possibility. "I've been talking to a reproductive endocrinologist. Typically, a woman releases one egg per month, but hormones could boost production of multiple eggs simultaneously. Selling the eggs is an option, as is fertilizing them to sell as embryos."

Marcelo paused, not wanting to oversell the idea and turn David off. He could almost hear the wheels turning in David's mind.

David's voice came back, lower this time. "What's the catch? How much would it cost?"

Marcelo was ready with an answer to this question. He didn't want to reveal everything yet, not until David showed he was on the same page. "We'd need another location just for this process. The organ harvests are obviously faster, but the hormone treatments would take a few weeks. But if we succeed in doing both, it would be very profitable."

David's calculating voice cut through the air. "Aren't you missing something, Marcelo?"

Marcelo frowned, his pulse quickening, but said nothing. *Was David going to shut his idea down already?*

David's next words made his stomach drop. "You're thinking too small. What if we didn't stop at embryos? What if we implanted the fertilized embryos back into the egg donors? In nine months, we could sell the babies, maybe produce twins or triplets to maximize throughput. The price for babies would far outweigh what we'd make on eggs or embryos."

Marcelo's mouth went dry. The idea felt so dark, but it did hold a certain sickening appeal. *Nine months would be a huge investment,* he thought, but he couldn't deny the numbers dancing in front of him.

"Yeah," Marcelo agreed. "But it would be a big risk. Nine months is a lot of time and money to invest."

"I know," David replied. "But with enough volume, this could be huge. There are always people desperate for babies. There would definitely be a market in America, Canada, and Europe."

Marcelo's mind raced, weighing the pros and cons of the idea. The pieces of the plan were falling into place faster than he could process them. It felt like the beginning of something monumental.

"I'll run the numbers," Marcelo said. "I'll do a cost analysis and see what we would need. But in the meantime, you should talk to Francisco and see if he's on board."

David didn't say anything right away. The thought of pitching this idea to Francisco felt like standing on the edge of a cliff. He had no idea how Francisco would react, but if anyone could see the monetary potential, it was him.

"Yeah," David said. "I'll talk to him."

41

lejandro's hands gripped the steering wheel as he coasted along the highway, singing along to the car radio in the silence of the early evening. He smiled at the thought of his mom's chicken enchiladas, the tender chicken wrapped in soft tortillas and drowned in her homemade salsa. He was looking forward to a rare weekend trip home. His phone vibrated, and he looked down to see Noemi's name flashing on the screen.

"Hey, *querida*," he greeted her, his voice light, "I'm almost there. I can't wait to see you later. Are you coming over for dinner?"

Noemi's voice came through full of affection as Alejandro pulled off the highway and into the gas station on the outskirts of Zamora. The gas station was quiet with only a few cars stopped at the pumps and in the market. He sat in the driver's seat while the gas pumped, exchanging casual words with her.

"Is everything good?" she asked, a flirtatious note in her voice.

"Yeah, I'm getting some gas. I should be there in an hour or so."

But then, out of the corner of his eye, he noticed a group of men walking toward him. At first, he thought maybe they were passing through. But something about the way they moved, the way their eyes locked on him, made Alejandro uneasy.

In an instant, everything changed.

Before he could react, the men grabbed him, pulling him roughly from the car. His phone slipped from his grasp and fell to the pavement with a crack. Before he could register what was happening, they placed a cloth hood over his head, and the world turned dark. He tried to struggle, but his arms were pinned to his sides by one of the men.

He gasped for air, his body tensing as he took a beating from all directions. He couldn't think or move. A sharp pain shot through his ribs, but the punches and kicks kept coming.

"Please!" he begged, his voice weak. "Take my car, my wallet, anything, just don't hurt me!"

They responded to his pleas with only more violence. He felt dizzy, and his vision blurred, the darkness closing in.

Then, just as suddenly as it had started, the beating stopped. The gas station was silent once again. His breath came in ragged gasps, but he heard no more sound, no shouting, and no footsteps. Only the fading roar of a truck's engine as it sped away with him inside of it. His chest tightened, his heart hammered in his ears, but then, nothing.

Noemi? His mind screamed, but his throat was too dry to form the words. His body went limp, too weak to even keep fighting for consciousness. He felt himself slipping away.

Meanwhile, Noemi's heart pounded as she listened to the terrifying silence on the other end of the line. The only sounds she heard were the faint static of the phone and her heartbeat in her chest. Her fingers trembled as she held the phone to her ear; the words stuck in her throat.

"Alejandro? Alejandro!" she cried into the phone, but there

was no response. A cold sweat prickled her skin as the seconds dragged on, each one longer than the last. Then, faintly, she heard an engine roaring to life, tires screeching as the vehicle tore away. Her chest constricted in panic. They had taken Alejandro and his screams with them.

No, no, no!

Her mind raced, the horrible realization sank in. *Something's happened to him.*

She grabbed the phone, hands shaking, and called Alejandro's mother. "Something happened to Alejandro. They took him!!"

Back in Zamora, fear paralyzed Alejandro's family, and uncertainty gnawed at their insides. They gathered around the kitchen table in grief as Noemi relayed every painful detail of the call.

But in their hearts, they knew something that felt worse than any fear. Someone had taken him away.

Since the line between law and crime was blurred beyond recognition in their town, they couldn't go to the authorities. Retaliation wasn't a possibility; it was a certainty.

They held their breath, each moment stretching into the next, praying for a ransom call, a voice, anything, but nothing came.

Hours stretched into days. Alejandro's sister and mother clung to the hope that they'd hear from him. But the posters they printed, each one bearing his smiling face and the words, *"Age 24, last seen January 20th wearing blue jeans and a green sweater,"* soon became part of the landscape of missing persons notices scattered throughout town. It felt like a cruel irony. Alejandro, once so full of potential, working his first job after earning a degree in civil engineering, was now another face in the crowd of the posters of the disappeared. The posters lined the streets, stuck to poles, plastered on bus stops, their faces fading in the sun. But Alejandro was gone. His fate was sealed, far beyond their reach.

Elsewhere, in the New Me Clinic's basement, Alejandro's dead body sprawled on an operating table. The clinicians worked efficiently to strip him of his organs. Anything of value would be harvested for profit.

But they weren't done with him. Once they'd finished, they didn't dispose of his corpse as they had done with the others. Since Alejandro was a larger man, they stuffed his body cavity with plastic bags of fentanyl pills, then sewed him back up to look like a sick patient traveling north for surgery.

The ambulance ride to the U.S. was routine, and the border crossing went quickly. They disguised Alejandro's body to look like a normal, living patient. Border patrol drug-sniffing dogs missed the hidden fentanyl because of the antiseptic smell.

Once in San Diego, they opened Alejandro up again, this time for a different harvest. They retrieved the bags of fentanyl and discarded his body like trash.

His loved ones would never know what happened to him.

42

Marcelo paced in his office, cellphone in hand, as he listened to David's report.

"Francisco likes the embryo idea but not the surrogacy idea, which would take too long," David said. "Embryos would have faster turnover and quicker profits."

Marcelo smiled in satisfaction and sat down in his desk chair. "I thought he might. Embryos are less complicated. Here's how it would work." He wrote his notes out on a legal pad, his mind already racing ahead, laying out his plan. "Once the girl's in the clinic, she stays sedated. Hormones will do the rest to stimulate her ovaries."

David said dryly. "And we don't care about the factory after production."

"Exactly," Marcelo replied. "The usual risks of overstimulation don't matter. By the time her eggs are harvested, her 'usefulness' is over."

"And fertilization?" David prompted.

Marcelo's lips twisted into a grin. "That's where we get creative. We could use a doctor's sample, something clean and convenient. Once we are up and running, we could use semen from the future buyer. Imagine the appeal: a child with the father's DNA but without the mother's 'advanced maternal age' dragging down success rates."

David whistled. "Custom embryos. High-end fertility with no messy and expensive procedures for the couple. All they'd need would be to prep the wife at home and then come down here for the transfer. Hell, the same bed we use for the donors could work. I like the efficiency."

Marcelo nodded. "Exactly. Minimal hassle and maximum profit. I would need to hire a reproductive endocrinologist, a lab tech, set up a referral network, purchase equipment, and medications. If we move fast, we could be operational in a matter of weeks and start marketing."

"Make it happen, Marcelo," David said. "Time is money."

Marcelo hung up and called Ricardo. "I need a location that is private but close to New Me, something discreet enough for sensitive operations."

Ricardo grunted in understanding. "I'll find something."

Marcelo didn't wait for the results to start recruiting. The endocrinologist he'd been courting months ago was eager, especially when Marcelo doubled the pay. The lab tech came with sterling credentials and had no qualms about maintaining confidentiality. Soon after, the team recruited nurses, attracting them with promises of high pay and vague job descriptions.

A week later, Marcelo stood in the newly outfitted clinic, a gleaming facility with state-of-the-art equipment. He surveyed the setup with a critical eye as Ricardo entered with their first subject, a girl in a pink miniskirt that was at New Me. Livia's steps were unsteady.

"Is she clean?" Marcelo asked, crossing his arms.

"I checked for everything," Ricardo assured him. "But we administered antibiotics and antivirals, just in case."

"Good." Marcelo glanced at the lab tech, who stood nearby. "Let's start her on the hormone protocol. I want a dozen mature eggs minimum."

The tech nodded, his expression unreadable as he wheeled over a tray of syringes. Livia whimpered as they placed the medication in her IV line, but Marcelo ignored her and turned his attention to the embryologist.

"What's our fertilization plan for this batch?" the embryologist asked.

Marcelo's grin widened. "Why not use me for this proof of concept? Besides..." He leaned closer, opening his eyelids wide to show his bright green eyes. "Maybe we'll get lucky and pass these on."

The embryologist hesitated but then nodded, jotting notes in the donor's file. Marcelo felt satisfied with how every detail was falling into place.

Days passed in a blur of activity. Marcelo kept tabs on Livia's hormone levels and ultrasound images of her ripening egg follicles. He met with his team daily, strutting through the halls like a peacock, feeling proud of his ingenuity.

Finally, the embryologist pulled him aside and said excitedly, "Her follicles are ready. We will administer the trigger shot tonight and schedule the retrieval for tomorrow morning."

Marcelo clapped him on the shoulder. "Strong work, doctor."

The next morning, Marcelo watched from the observation room as the girl lay unconscious, her arms strapped to the sides of the operating table as the doctor maneuvered the needle to extract the eggs from her ovaries. Marcelo's phone vibrated with a text from David.

"How's the beta test going?"

Marcelo typed back: "It's looking promising. The proof of concept is underway."

The embryologist appeared at the door, holding a tray of small glass test tubes. "We have ten mature eggs," he reported, smiling.

Marcelo grinned. "Great! Let's fertilize them. I'll supply the sample."

43

Janice's stomach flip-flopped as she sat in the modern office of the Liver Specialists of Orange County. She sat waiting as the hepatologist glanced at her chart and reviewed her latest test results.

"Your liver is hanging on by a thread," he said finally, his tone grave. "The only silver lining is that your condition will move you higher on the UNOS waiting list."

Janice let out a bitter laugh. "That's great, if I get to the top before my liver gives up the ghost. It feels like I have a ticking time bomb in the upper-right quadrant of my abdomen."

The doctor hesitated, his professional mask slipping for a fraction of a second. "I understand how you feel, Mrs. Simon. But there's still hope."

"You can't have it both ways," she interrupted angrily. "You told me my liver is barely functioning. So what's the plan here? Do we sit with our fingers crossed and wait for a miracle? Is that the plan?"

"Well," his voice dropped, and he said, "There is another option to consider. But it's 'unconventional.'"

Janice leaned forward to hear what he had to say. "Unconventional sounds better than dead. Can you tell me what it is?"

The doctor glanced toward the door, as though checking for eavesdroppers, stood up to close it behind him, and then opened a desk drawer. He slid a brochure emblazoned with the logo of the New Me Clinic across the desk towards Janice, complete with photos of smiling women and beauty transformations.

Janice frowned. "Plastic surgery? I think I missed the part where breast enhancement saves failing livers."

The doctor smiled grimly. "They don't advertise their *other* services. There's a facility downstairs that is separate from the plastic surgery clinic. They handle cases like yours, but it's hush-hush, and it's not cheap."

Janice studied his face, searching for any sign of hesitation. "And is this legal?"

He straightened in his chair, his expression neutral. "Let's just say it's an option. It's best not to ask too many questions."

Her pulse quickened as she reviewed the brochure. On the back, she saw a handwritten name and number that caught her eye. *Marcelo López.*

The next day, Janice sat at her kitchen table staring at her phone. The New Me brochure lay open in front of her, the images of beautiful smiling women taunting her own yellow and swollen face. Finally, she dialed the number.

A man answered after the second ring. "New Me Clinic, Marcelo López speaking."

"Mr. López," Janice began, her voice shaking slightly, "Dr. Patel referred me to you. I'm interested in learning more about the services that you offer."

There was a pause on the other end, just long enough to make her consider hanging up. Then Marcelo spoke, his tone professional and polite. "I see. Please send over your medical records, and I'll have our team review them. If you qualify, we'll arrange for a consultation."

By the end of the call, Janice's hands trembled. She hung up and began scanning her medical records, feeling hopeful about her future for the first time in ages.

A week later, Doris drove Janice to her appointment with Dr. Kevin Carter. The lavish office at Coastal Surgical Associates didn't hint at the secrets it may have held. Janice froze in the examination room, her heart pounding as Dr. Carter walked in, file in hand.

"And how are you today, Mrs. Simon?" he asked, his genial tone not quite masking the clinical detachment in his eyes.

"Well, I'd be better if my skin weren't the same color as a banana," Janice replied dryly.

Dr. Carter smiled faintly and began his examination, asking pointed questions as he went. He noted his observations, occasionally scribbling notes in the file.

When he was done, he removed his gloves and threw them into the biohazard trash can. "Mrs. Simon, your EKG and blood-work look good, apart from the liver-related abnormalities we expected. I can clear you for surgery."

Janice exhaled slowly, relief mingling with apprehension.

"There's just one thing," Dr. Carter added, his tone serious. "You'll need to be ready to leave at a moment's notice once they find a match. You can't tell anyone where you're going, not even family, and not the friend who brought you here today."

Janice raised an eyebrow. "Why not?"

He hesitated. "This kind of procedure requires discretion. Tell people you're going on a yoga retreat or something."

Janice knew that what she was considering would not sit well with her goody-two-shoes daughter Ruby and decided she wouldn't tell her. Ashley would be okay with it, but she didn't want to take the chance of Ashley letting it slip to Ruby or Jack. If it all worked out, which was a big "if" at this point, she would tell Ruby after the fact.

That night, Janice sat on the sofa, her own face visible on their nightly FaceTime call. Ruby's face appeared on the screen, smiling when she saw her mother.

"Hi, Mom! How are you feeling? How was your day?"

Janice forced a smile. "Oh, you know, the usual. Actually, I've been thinking about taking a little trip."

Ruby frowned. "A trip to where?"

Janice shrugged, feigning nonchalance. "I was thinking about going on a women's retreat, just to get away for a couple of weeks."

Ruby laughed, but sounded skeptical. "To get away from what? You're already relaxing at home with no responsibilities to get away from. And since when have you wanted to spend time with other women?"

Janice sounded defensive. "I'm considering it, that's all. Stop micromanaging me, Ruby."

Ruby's smile faded. "I've never tried to manage you, Mom, let alone micromanage you. I'm just asking because it doesn't sound like something you would normally want to do. Ever."

Janice waved her hand dismissively, ending the call soon after. As the screen went dark, she let out a deep breath. She hadn't lied to her daughter exactly, but she hadn't been truthful either.

She looked again at the New Me Clinic brochure on the table next to the couch. It seemed like a promise of salvation and danger rolled into one.

44

Janice had just settled into her recliner to watch Doc Martin, with a mug of chamomile tea on the side table, when a sharp knock shattered the quiet. She glanced at the clock. 8:30 p.m. It was too late for visitors, and she certainly wasn't expecting anyone at this hour.

Her first thought was that teenagers were selling candy or Jehovah's Witnesses were selling salvation. *Not tonight.* She set down her tea with a sigh, her annoyance already bubbling up. Grabbing her phone, she walked to the front door of her bungalow, her slippers flapping across the wood floor.

Through the peephole, she saw two young men that she didn't know. One held a bouquet like the kind you would send to a hospital patient. The sight should've eased her nerves, but it didn't.

She tightened her grip on the phone, thinking she could call the police if needed. "Who's there?" she called, her voice louder than she intended.

"Ma'am," the man with the flowers said in accented English, flashing a practiced smile. "We're friends of your daughter Ruby. She asked us to deliver these flowers to you."

Janice frowned, looking through the peephole of the door.

Ruby had never mentioned sending flowers, or friends for that matter. "Let me see the card," she demanded.

The man nodded, taking the card out of the flower arrangement and holding it up in front of the peephole for her to see. Someone had scrawled her name across the envelope. Against her better judgment, she opened the door a crack, keeping the chain latched.

She took the card and read it aloud. "Dear Mom, I hope you're feeling better soon. Love, Ruby."

It *looked* genuine. She hesitated and finally said, "Alright, give me the flowers, please." She slipped off the chain and opened the door wider.

That was her mistake.

Before she could react, the larger man surged forward into her home, shoving the door open and sending her stumbling backward onto the floor. He pointed a gun at her chest.

"If you scream, you're dead. Do you understand?" His voice was cold, and his eyes were hard.

Janice's heart thudded in her chest as she nodded, unable to speak.

"What do you want?" she finally managed, her words tumbling out in a rush. "Take my purse. It's right there on the counter. I have cash, credit cards, take anything you want, just don't hurt me! I'm sick. I'm an old woman."

The smaller man rolled his eyes. "We're not here to rob you, lady. This isn't about you."

Her legs trembled like a newborn deer. "Then what is this about?"

The larger man leaned closer, his breath hot against her cheek. "Your daughter, Ruby. She's been sticking her nose in where it doesn't belong."

Janice blinked, her confusion mixing with terror. "Ruby? That sounds about right, but what does she have to do with anything? She's an accountant. She does bookkeeping for small businesses! I don't understand why that would upset anyone?"

The smaller man let out a humorless laugh. "She'll know exactly what we're talking about. We need her to know that we're serious." He grabbed Janice's chin, forcing her to look at him. "You'll help us send the message."

Before Janice could scream, he swung his fist, catching her cheekbone, but the punch was gentler than he would have punched a man. He had some standards. Pain exploded in her face as she fell back again. Warm blood trickled down her nose and into her mouth.

"That's enough," the larger man said, pulling out a knife. He gripped Janice's head with one hand, the other steadying the blade. "It's time to make our point."

"No! Please!" Janice's plea ended in a sharp cry as the knife bit into her ear. White-hot pain surged through her, and the room spun violently. Her knees buckled, and she crumpled to the floor. Darkness closed in as she lost consciousness.

When Ruby called her mom for their nightly 9 p.m. FaceTime check-in and got no answer, a prickle of unease spread through her. By the time her third call went unanswered, unease had turned to panic.

She dialed Doris next.

"Ruby? Do you know what time it is? This better be important. I was in REM." Doris groaned, her voice thick with sleep.

"Doris, something's wrong. Mom's not answering, and it's not like her. You didn't have to take her to the hospital again, did you? Can you please check on her? The ferries aren't running this late, or I would come myself."

Doris sighed but agreed. "I'll head over to her house right now."

Twenty minutes later, Doris stood outside Janice's bungalow, flashlight in hand. She banged on the door, calling Janice's name, but there was no answer. She made her way around to the back of the house and looked through a partially open blind, heart pounding.

A pair of slippered feet stuck out from the doorway.

"Oh, no," Doris whispered, fumbling for her phone.

The police broke down the door, anticipating a medical emergency, only to be confronted with a sickening sight. Janice lay motionless on the floor, her wrists and ankles bound with zip ties. Blood stained her matted hair and streaked her face.

"Ma'am," one officer said gently to rouse her, cutting her restraints. "Can you hear me?"

Janice stirred, her eyelids fluttering. Her voice was weak but steady. "They said they'd kill my daughter if I talked. This is my daughter Ruby's fault," she complained to the officers as she sipped the glass of water that they had offered her. "She doesn't care what happens to me. I'm sick, and she can't be bothered to take care of me. She lives far away in Avalon." Once the paramedics arrived, they loaded Janice into the ambulance for medical treatment, her head bandaged like a mummy, Doris riding along in the back to comfort her.

"Oh, Doris, I can't believe this happened to me. The two men who attacked me told me they were there to send a message. They warned me, 'If your daughter doesn't stop sticking her nose where it doesn't belong, we'll slice your throat next time, not just your ear! If you tell the cops about this, your daughter is dead.' What has that girl gotten me into? Why can't she be more like Ashley?"

"Are you sure you're feeling okay? You're talking crazy now. Maybe you got a concussion when you fell."

"No, Doris. I heard what I heard. That's exactly what they said."

"Okay, well let's get you to the hospital for treatment. We can sort it all out later."

Doris called Ruby to let her know what happened and that her mom was not seriously injured and was in the emergency room getting first aid. Doris passed the phone to Janice, who scolded a horrified Ruby.

"This is the thanks I get for being a good mom? If you cared about me at all, you would be more careful, and not just always be thinking about yourself. Your sister Ashley would never have put me through this!"

"Mom, how could I have known that this would happen? I'm working on an accounting project, helping people."

"Well, you should have known better. Now I'm maimed!"

She must be delirious, Ruby thought. *She's talking crazy now.* "I'm really sorry that they hurt you, Mom."

It was too late for Ruby to take the ferry back to the mainland as they were no longer running, but she booked a ticket for the first boat of the morning. Ruby then called Andy to tell him what had happened. When she finished, Andy warned her, "Be really careful. I'm afraid for you now. Maybe you should refuse to continue cooperating with the FBI. These people are obviously violent and dangerous, and who knows what they're capable of?"

Ruby knew Andy was right, and she felt frightened for herself too, but she still feared that people's lives might be at risk and that justice needed to be served. *If I can help in my own small way, then I should do it.* She then called Robert to discuss the night's events and ensure that the FBI was involved in her mother's

Long Beach Police Department assault case, so Janice could be temporarily relocated.

"Things are escalating now," Robert told Ruby. "We must be getting somewhere with our case because we have touched a nerve. Otherwise, they wouldn't bother sending a warning through your mom."

45

A gent Ramírez sat at her office desk scrutinizing the New Me Clinic website. She had done her homework, read through their services, and now she had to decide.

She clicked through the photos of young, radiant faces, smiling women draped in towel turbans and spa gowns, and some before and after photos showing their aesthetic transformations. Her prior knowledge of the clinic made its flawless image seem suspect. But she knew what was at stake. She had a job to do, and the clinic was a piece of the puzzle.

She perused the various options. "Boob job?" She rolled her eyes. Her C-cups had served her well for years. She was an FBI agent, not dancing on the pole. Her fingers hovered over the different options on the screen, hesitating.

Finally, her finger tapped the picture of a perfect, sculpted nose. She clicked.

The text on the screen suggested she could get a consulta tion for her nose, with the added bonus of addressing some sinus issues. Her mind raced. "It's plausible," she thought. "I could use this." Sinus problems were real, after all. This could be her way inside the New Me operation. She wasn't there for a makeover, but she could act the part. And maybe she'd get the answers she needed. If she succeeded, this undercover operation could advance her career.

She picked up the phone and dialed the 800 number on the brochure. As it rang, she felt her adrenaline spike.

A cheerful accented voice answered on the third ring, smooth, like someone who had answered this call a thousand times a day.

"Good morning! Thank you for calling the New Me Clinic. How may I help you today?"

Rosie almost forgot to respond for a second, the professionalism of the receptionist throwing her off. She cleared her throat and then said, "Hi, I'm interested in getting a consultation about my nose. I've been dealing with some sinus trouble, and I was also hoping to straighten it. I understand you offer free consultations, is that right?"

"Absolutely! We would be happy to help you with that. We can arrange a Zoom consultation to start the process. Would that be okay with you?"

Rosie thought for a moment. A Zoom consultation would be too impersonal. She needed to see the clinic up close, to get a read on the place herself. Rosie was wary of how the clinic presented itself online. She couldn't put her finger on it, but the whole thing felt a little too polished, just "off" somehow.

"Actually, I was hoping to come down in person. I would prefer to see the facility myself. You know, to get a feel for the place."

"Yes, we can definitely set that up. Have you already seen a doctor in California? Do you have any imaging or medical records you can share?" The receptionist's voice remained businesslike.

"No," Rosie said quickly, "not yet. It's all preliminary. So when could I come down to the clinic?"

"Well, we have an opening next week on Tuesday morning. Would that work for you?"

Rosie hesitated. She felt the weight of the decision. This wasn't a visit for a nose job. This was research. She needed to get in to see things up close for herself.

"Actually, I'd prefer the afternoon. I'll be driving down, and I want to make sure I have enough time to cross the border. You know, in case there's traffic or delays."

The receptionist said, "I understand completely. Can you do Tuesday at 2 p.m.? Will that work for you? I'll email you the details."

Rosie smiled with satisfaction, her mind already planning what she would do on Tuesday. She would be there inside the clinic. *With backup.* She couldn't help wondering if this whole clinic was just a front. What exactly were they hiding behind the smooth exterior? She was determined to find out.

"That's perfect, thanks." Her voice was calm, but she could feel the excitement and a little bit of fear, the same way she had for every undercover operation she had been involved in. But something about this investigation made her feel like this could be more than a routine undercover investigation.

46

After a long day in medical school, Kevin Carter adjusted the collar of his shirt as he stepped into Josh's cramped apartment, the smell of marinara sauce and garlic bread wafting toward him. Josh clapped him on the back, handing him a glass of wine. "She's here. You'll thank me later."

Kevin didn't have to ask who. His eyes had already landed on her. Jacklyn stood by the window, her long black hair swaying as she laughed at something the girl beside her said. Her laugh was full and unguarded, the kind of laugh he hadn't heard since he couldn't remember when.

Josh nudged him forward. "Go on, say something."

"I—uh," Kevin stammered, clearing his throat as he approached her, holding out his hand. "Hi, I'm Kevin."

"Jacklyn," she said, meeting his gaze with a directness that was disarming. "So, Kevin, what's your story?"

Her straightforwardness caught him off guard. She didn't sugarcoat anything, not even small talk. But in her case, it wasn't intimidating. It was refreshing. For the first time in years, Kevin didn't feel like he had to perform.

Even then, years after leaving home, Kevin could hear his father's voice as if he were standing in the room.

"You only got an A-?" His father's tone was sharp, slicing through the excitement that fifth grade Kevin had felt seconds earlier.

"I—uh—" Kevin clutched his report card, feeling a lump in his throat. "It's still an A."

His father shook his head, pacing the kitchen like a caged animal. "Why didn't you get an A? Do you even think about what you're doing? Or is this good enough for you?" Kevin stood frozen, his shoulders tight as his father loomed closer.

Years later, the phantom of that voice still snapped at his heels relentlessly. It's not as though Kevin didn't work hard. He had always been driven to succeed. He did well in school, got into a well-regarded medical school and then fought his way through a surgical residency. He should have felt on top of the world, but he always heard his father's voice whispering in his ear that whatever he did and whatever he earned was never enough.

Once he and Jacklyn were married, Kevin remembered coming home after his first failed surgery, his hands still trembling. "I lost her," he said as the door clicked shut behind him.

Jacklyn looked up from the meal she was cooking. She didn't ask questions or offer platitudes. Instead, she walked over and wrapped her arms around him, resting her chin on his shoulder.

"It happens sometimes despite your best efforts," she whispered. "You're not a machine."

Her words had a greater impact than any praise. She didn't just accept his imperfections; she normalized them.

Dr. Carter glanced across at the older gentleman in his exam room, who looked a little worse for wear.

"Mr. Miller, how are you feeling today?"

"Like crap. Like my kidneys aren't working anymore."

"That's understandable. Let me see if we can't do something about that."

"Yes, let's. I'm sick and tired of going to dialysis."

"It's not easy," Dr. Carter commiserated as he palpated the glands in his patient's neck. He finished his exam and handed Gordon a lab slip. "Mr. Miller, you're as well as can be expected. Please go get this blood work done ASAP."

He took the paper from the doctor and said, "Thanks, Doc," as he walked out the door, feeling more hopeful than he had in a long time.

Three years back, while attending the American College of Surgeons conference in San Francisco, Kevin was approached by a young Mexican man. The man was looking for partners for their growing plastic surgery clinic south of the border in Tijuana that catered to American and Canadian clientele.

"Look, Dr. Carter," Marcelo said, swirling the ice in his glass while they sat in the bustling hotel lobby near the convention center. "We're giving patients a chance they wouldn't have otherwise. Patients like cancer survivors or people priced out of care in the U.S. Everyone deserves options."

Kevin looked over the glossy brochure for the New Me Clinic that Marcelo had slid across the table towards him. The facility in the brochure looked modern, but something about it felt too perfect, too artificial.

"What's the catch?" Kevin asked noncommittally.

Marcelo smiled, his green eyes shining. "There's no catch, my friend. We're cutting out the middleman. You help patients, and we compensate you for the referrals. It's a win-win for everyone."

Kevin hesitated, the weight of his father's disapproval echoing in his mind. He'd worked too hard to risk his career, but then, who else was helping these patients?

In his sales pitch to Kevin, Marcelo explained that the New Me Clinic would pay cash for each referral to the clinic. American patients would gain from using a clinic in Mexico, with procedures costing 50% less, and referring doctors would also profit. Dr. Carter couldn't find any flaws in his logic but remained unconvinced.

A few months later, Dr. Carter paid the New Me Clinic a visit to verify that it was legitimate. A black SUV picked him up from his Laguna Beach home and drove him straight to the clinic in Tijuana. Marcelo and his team wined and dined Dr. Carter that night and then took him back home. The New Me Clinic's operation, modern equipment, sound hygiene protocols and trained bilingual staff impressed Dr. Carter, and he signed on.

His first referral to the New Me Clinic was a woman who wanted reconstructive surgery after her battle with breast cancer that her insurance company did not want to cover because they deemed it elective. The patient went to the New Me Clinic and returned satisfied with her experience. After that, Dr. Carter referred several more patients and received a five-thousand-dollar referral fee each time. After a few months, Marcelo asked him to reach out to colleagues to see if he could expand the network of referring doctors and that he would get an additional cash bonus for each doctor in his network who successfully referred a patient, like Amway. Subsequently, Dr. Carter was able to bring a few of his colleagues on board.

Several months later, Kevin sat with Marcelo at a rooftop cafe in Laguna Beach, the outline of Catalina Island in the distance sharp against the fading afternoon light. Kevin sipped his beer, enjoying the view. Across the table, Marcelo looked relaxed and confident.

"You've been a fantastic partner," Marcelo said, stroking Dr. Carter's ego. "The referrals you've sent us have been top-notch. Patients love us and are happy with their results. But I've got something that could take this to the next level."

Kevin arched an eyebrow but didn't speak. He had learned that silence was often the best way to draw out the truth.

Marcelo went directly into sales mode. "We're expanding into a new, innovative area, conducting clinical trials related to organ transplants."

Kevin's stomach clenched. "Organ transplants?" He forced his voice to stay neutral, but something about this whole topic of conversation made him feel uncomfortable. "That's a far cry from cosmetic surgery."

Marcelo nodded casually, as though they were discussing what they would have for dinner. "It's not as different as one might think. We're helping sick patients who've been waiting years on the transplant list, but the system in the U.S. is so broken that it fails most people who need it."

Kevin looked away, hoping that Marcelo couldn't see his pulse throbbing in his neck. "And what about the organ donors? Who are they? Are they being coerced in any way?"

Marcelo laughed as though Kevin had told a funny joke. "Don't worry, Dr. Carter, everything is kosher. The donors are well-compensated, and everyone signs consent forms."

Kevin nodded slowly, but Marcelo's words still didn't sit right with him. From the rooftop, he looked out at the vast Pacific and watched the massive container ships headed north to the Port of Long Beach.

"And what would my role be in this operation?" he asked, keeping his voice calm.

"The same as before. You would continue to do screening exams and send us referrals, and we would handle the rest. Except now, you would earn ten thousand dollars per referral instead of five."

Kevin's throat felt dry, and he reached for his beer. He took a sip to give himself time to think and then looked up at Marcelo. "That's a considerable increase."

Marcelo's smile widened. "Well, this is a bigger market than cosmetic surgery. And you would be helping people, Dr. Carter, people who've waited for years on the UNOS lists that they may never get to the top of. And since we're working with the Second Lives Foundation, we're helping the entire community too."

Marcelo's mention of the Second Lives Foundation seemed to legitimize the whole operation and to mitigate Dr. Carter's doubts.

"And, as a surgeon, the Foundation would like to offer you a seat on its scientific advisory board. They are willing to pay you two-hundred and fifty thousand dollars a year, which is pretty generous," he offered, sweetening the deal.

Kevin glanced at Marcelo, who watched him, knowing he had him on the hook now and was ready to reel him in.

But the echo of his father's voice nagged at Kevin, sharp and scornful. *Do you think this is good enough? Do you think you won't get caught?*

"I need to think about it," Kevin said firmly.

Marcelo's smile didn't falter. He leaned back in his chair, playing the part of the generous host. "Take your time, *amigo*. But I know you, Dr. Carter. When you see the bigger picture, you'll understand this is the right thing to do for everyone involved."

Kevin nodded, but as Marcelo waved the waiter over to settle the bill, he couldn't shake the feeling of unease.

Dr. Carter wasn't dumb. He had doubts about whether this could, in fact, be legal, but by now he was making significant additional income working with New Me. *On the other hand,* he thought, *if a person is willing to donate an organ, then who am I to stop them?* Maybe it was American puritanism at play that prohibited fee-based organ donation. He would be helping people who had been waiting a long time for a kidney or liver. *And anyway,* he rationalized to himself, *I'm only one person. How could my involvement make any difference? If it weren't me,* he reasoned, *it would just be some other doctor.*

47

The soothing background music in the tastefully decorated but sterile reception area of the New Me Clinic did little to calm Agent Rosie Ramírez's nerves. She glanced at the receptionist's polite smile, her long red nails wrapped around her phone. Rosie fidgeted with her hair, acutely aware of the absence of her service weapon.

Rosie's hand trembled as she took the clipboard from the receptionist. *You need to focus. This is just another assignment. You've been undercover dozens of times.* She signed her name "Rosemary Jones" with care, her mind racing through possible exit strategies which she hoped she wouldn't need. She couldn't shake the feeling that she was being watched, even if there was no evidence of this.

Behind the reception desk, a security camera was tracking Rosie's movements. Marcelo sat in a back office, his phone vibrating on the desk with a text from Ricardo: "She's here." He looked closer at the grainy footage of the exam room hallway. "Make sure you stay close to her," Marcelo instructed Ricardo as a nurse led her to an exam room. Once the nurse left her alone, Rosie peeked into the hallway and, finding it deserted, decided to explore the facility to get the lay of the land. She walked into the hallway and headed away from the clinic's entrance.

Ricardo watched from his hidden vantage point as Rosie entered the hallway. A slight smile tugged at Ricardo's lips as he typed out an update for Marcelo: "She's heading down the hallway," who responded, "Don't let her out of your sight. I'm coming." Marcelo didn't want to bring the scrutiny that a missing federal agent would certainly bring but felt he had no choice now that the agent was inside the belly of the beast.

Rosie continued walking until she saw a sign that read *"Quirófanos".* Operating Rooms. Rosie stepped inside and heard the door click softly behind her. The air in that area turned colder and the smell medicinal. She moved cautiously, her heels echoing faintly on the tile floor. Through a small window in one of the operating room doors, she glimpsed masked and gowned figures bending over a patient. Her heart raced, but she forced herself to continue, her face neutral and her movements purposeful.

The green-eyed man approached her with a warm smile, but something about it made Rosie's skin crawl. "Are you lost, *señorita?*" he asked, his voice smooth and saccharine.

She nodded, forcing a laugh. "Yes, I was looking for the ladies' room. I must have taken a wrong turn."

He tilted his head, studying her like a puzzle. "Let me help you. This elevator will take you back to the entrance. The receptionist can help you find your way back from there."

"But I came from an exam room on this floor," she protested.

"I know this building can be confusing, but you do need to take the elevator," he said as he guided her inside. A security guard stepped into the elevator with them.

As the elevator doors slid shut before Rosie could react, she glanced at the security guard's phone, catching a glimpse of a text: *"Asegúrala!"* She knew that meant "Secure her!" A rough hand clamped over her mouth, muffling her scream. She kicked blindly, her heels striking something solid, but her attacker didn't flinch. The sting of a needle pierced her arm, and she thrashed harder, her vision swimming. "No!" she shouted, her voice strangled and weak. Her legs buckled, and darkness was closing in fast.

Rosie's body crumpled to the floor as the drug took hold, her vision blurring into darkness. The security guard crouched beside her, his voice a low growl. "You really thought you could walk in here unnoticed?" The green-eyed man chuckled behind him.

"What do we do with her now?" the guard asked, standing up. Marcelo instructed him, "Take her downstairs. We will send her out on one of the outgoing ambulances after a drop-off. They will know what to do so that she's never found."

48

FBI Special Agent Singh was on the phone with an epidemiologist from the Department of Health and Human Services who had called in about a recent human rabies-related death.

"We are working to identify the vector. We interviewed the husband of the deceased, who denied any recent history of wild animal bite, but he did say that his wife had recently traveled to Mexico. He claimed not to know where but said that she had gotten a kidney transplant there in the last few weeks. He told us, 'I guess now that she's gone there's no reason to hide.'"

"Do you know of any other cases besides this one?" Agent Singh asked.

"No, but if we hear anything, we will let you know. We also plan to contact the CDC to ask about this nationally."

"Do you know if this could be related to the kidney transplant, or do you think this has to do with being immunosuppressed or traveling to Mexico? Or some animal bite that the husband was unaware of? Do they screen organ donors for rabies?"

"Rabies isn't normally part of any routine screening for

organ donors, but who knows what the procedures are outside of the U.S. anyway."

"Okay, please keep me posted, and I will do the same. I will also enter this into the FBI system. How concerned should we be with only one death?"

"Only one death *that we know of so far.*"

Agent Jones looked up at the alert in his email inbox. He had set up an alert for anything related to organ harvesting and Mexico. He immediately called Agent Singh to get more information.

"Agent Singh, I see that you are working on a case related to possible organ transplants being done illegally in Mexico. What's going on?"

"Yeah, we got a report from the health department that an American woman who recently got a kidney transplant in Mexico died of rabies. They want to find the organ donor as soon as possible because if a donor had rabies, they could have placed the donor's organs and other tissues in other recipients. But the husband couldn't tell them where the kidney had come from exactly. 'Somewhere in Mexico' was all they could get out of him. The whole thing is pretty disturbing. What do you have going on in your case?"

"We are surveilling a clinic in Mexico that we suspect may be doing organ transplants, but we haven't been able to confirm it yet. Americans who can pay may be going down there to jump the line. But if that's what's happening, they may be getting more than they bargained for."

"Yeah, as they say, 'If it seems too good to be true...'"

"...It probably is," Agent Jones finished his thought, his tone grim. "We need to shut this whole thing down ASAP. Please keep me posted if they discover any other cases."

"Will do."

As Agent Jones hung up the call, he clenched his teeth thinking about the sheer greed and disregard for human life of these operators. He took a deep breath and vowed, "Your days are numbered. You will *not* get away with this."

49

The message came through at 3:17 p.m. Robert read it twice, a sinking feeling spreading through his chest.

"Agent Ramírez is missing. She entered the New Me Clinic but didn't exit. Her car is gone. The CEO of the clinic claims she was seen by a doctor and then left."

The words blurred as Robert stared at the screen. *Missing.* Federal agents didn't just vanish, not without help and not without a plan.

He called his Mexican contact. "You were supposed to be watching her!"

"We were," came the clipped reply. "Our people were stationed outside the clinic. No one saw her leave. It's possible she used a different exit, maybe even slipped out unnoticed. Or..." The pause hung heavy. "They knew she was coming."

Robert's gut twisted. He gripped the phone tighter. "If they knew, someone tipped them off. Was it your team? Or mine?"

"I assure you, we are loyal," the man said, his voice hard. "But you know how deep the cartel's influence runs. They buy loyalty. Maybe it was someone close to you."

Robert hung up without a word, the accusation lingering like a shadow.

Later that evening over drinks, Robert vented to Jaime, who was visiting Torrance for a few days. The bar was dim, the low hum of conversation masking their words. "It feels like they're always one step ahead of us," Robert muttered, staring into his glass. "I've been careful, tightening the circle, keeping things on a need-to-know basis, but it's not enough. There's a leak somewhere, and it could be anyone. The Mexicans. My own team." He ran a hand through his hair. "How do I track a ghost?"

Jaime leaned back, swirling his almost empty beer bottle. "You need a canary trap."

Robert frowned. "A what?"

"Like in *Patriot Games.* You feed each suspect a slightly different version of a story and see what leaks."

"Sounds like spy movie nonsense."

"It's not. They use it in real life too—'shake the tree,' like in *Tinker Tailor Soldier Spy.*"

"Thanks, Roger Ebert. Speak English."

Jaime smirked. "Okay, here's the deal: you've got a list of suspects, right? Feed each one a tailored story. If the cartel reacts, you've got your mole. Didn't they teach you this at FBI school?"

"I'm FBI, not CIA," Robert said, shaking his head. "But yeah. I see where you're going. I can't imagine it's one of the Americans, but you're right, I need to rule them out first."

By morning, Robert had a plan.

He contacted several agents and deployed them to Tijuana with instructions to surveil the entrances of hotels near the New Me Clinic. No one knew the full scope of the operation except him. Each agent was to report activity without drawing attention to himself.

Once Robert had laid the groundwork, he started making calls.

First, to Agent Jerri Simpson. "We're going to set up an FBI and Mexican police command center at the Grand Hotel," he said. "We're setting up surveillance there. Keep this strictly confidential."

Next, Agent Luis Romano. "We're going to set up an FBI and Mexican police command center at the Palacio Hotel. Don't breathe a word of this to anyone."

Finally, he relayed the same message to Agent Rojas from the DEA about the Holiday Inn Hotel.

Robert took a deep breath, relaxing his clenched jaw. "Let's see who bites," he muttered.

For two days, Robert received steady reports from his surveillance teams. Two of the hotels remained quiet. But agents reported an unusual uptick in activity, men coming and going at odd hours, cars idling too long in the parking lot at the Holiday Inn. The Holiday Inn was being surveilled by someone. It wasn't definitive, but it was enough to make Robert's pulse quicken.

Rojas.

Still, he needed more before he knew for sure.

The next call to Agent Rojas was more subtle. "We've intercepted WhatsApp communications from La Familia," Robert said, injecting just the right amount of urgency into his tone. "They're discussing Tijuana operations, and we're listening closely. But please keep this to yourself."

Hours later, cartel communications on WhatsApp went dark.

By the following morning, their activity had migrated to a different encrypted platform.

Gotcha!

Robert didn't waste time. He called the Office of the Inspector General at the DEA, his tone sharp and unwavering. "I have reason to believe Agent Rojas is compromised. I'm requesting an investigation. This isn't just about one mole; it's about saving lives."

As he hung up, Robert's chest tightened. He'd exposed the leak, but the cost was high. Agent Ramírez was still missing, and the cartel was on high alert. He wasn't sure if he'd saved Agent Ramírez or painted a bigger target on her back.

50

Robert's fingers tapped a pen as he looked up at the screen. The Zoom call was live, and he saw the muted faces of his team staring back at him like a Hollywood Squares game, but this was no game. He took a slow breath and spoke, his voice steady but commanding. "Alright, folks, let's get to it. Jerri, what's the latest on the Second Lives Foundation? What did you uncover from the financials and the suspicious activity reports? Any luck with Shipshape?"

Jerri nodded, her expression serious, her hands clasped in front of her. "I've been following the paper trail carefully." Her eyes looked up at the rest of the team, searching for reactions. "I met with the agent looking into the Second Lives Foundation. It's as shady as we suspected. They found several high-dollar donors with interesting histories." She paused, as if letting the weight of the information sink in. "All these donors? They're waiting for organs. Either they're on the UNOS list, or they're already in dire need of a transplant. Could it be a coincidence? Maybe, but it gets stranger."

The room grew still, everyone hanging on every word.

Jerri continued, "One donor, for example, contributed $50,000 to the Foundation. Then, a day later, *bam,* $45,000 gets wired to the Shipshape Art Gallery. They call it a 'consulting fee.' Then $5,000 is sent out from the Shipshape account to other physicians across the state. And here's the kicker. The Shipshape account wired nearly $30,000 to the New Me Clinic."

Robert's pulse quickened. "So, it's a loop, a big circle of money moving in strange ways. And the Foundation is the hub?"

"Exactly. It's not just the Foundation, though. The money trails connect the gallery, the doctors, and—" Jerri's voice dropped. "There's a pattern related to the New Me Clinic here that we can't ignore."

"Did they explain why payments went through an art gallery?" Robert's question was sharp, but his mind was racing ahead, already piecing things together.

"They claimed Dr. Carter gave them those banking instructions. But something's off. We spoke to some of the donors, and there's a lot they're not telling us. I suspect they're hiding something bigger."

A tense silence filled the air. The rest of the team exchanged looks, their eyes narrowing.

Robert nodded, already turning to the next item on the agenda. "Alright, moving on. Miriam, what have you learned about the New Me Clinic? Are there any developments on the ground in Mexico?"

Agent Rojas shifted in her seat, rubbing her forehead. "We've been surveilling the clinic for a while. Unfortunately, we still haven't located Agent Ramírez. She's gone dark." She stopped, then added, "But we did speak to Ricardo Méndez, Marcelo López's assistant. He claims he doesn't know much, but we're not buying it. We've got him under surveillance too. Meanwhile, ambulances have been coming and going at the back entrance of the clinic. It's odd, considering the clinic doesn't offer emergency services."

Jerri snapped her head up, her mind already locked onto that bit of information. "Ambulances?"

Jones nodded. "Exactly. And a nurse mentioned that there's a basement level she can't access. She's never been down there, says it's off-limits, and the elevator requires a code."

"Hmm..." Robert asked, his expression sharp. "What else?"

"There is one other thing. A couple of weeks ago, there were visitors to the clinic reported to be cartel members," Agent Rojas said, her voice tight with uncertainty. "One of them *looked* like Francisco Obregón, the infamous one."

The room went still. The name Francisco Obregón hung in the air like a lead weight. The very thought of him sent a chill through the task force.

Robert's voice cut through the tension. "*The* Francisco Obregón? The one who runs La Familia cartel?" His tone was filled with disbelief.

Rojas nodded. "It's a possibility. It makes sense. They've got connections to everything in Tijuana."

"But why would Obregón go to that clinic?" Agent Romano interjected, his tone skeptical. "He's a wanted man. That would be a very risky move on his part."

The room quieted again, everyone's mind on the possibility of cartel involvement.

"We'll definitely look into that," Robert said after a long pause, regaining control of the meeting. "We will get everything we can from the clinic's financials and bank wires and look further into the ambulances."

Miriam added, "The DEA's not focusing on the clinic since it's not directly drug-related, but we'll keep our eyes and ears open. As for Obregón, if he's involved, it's bad news, and we would definitely need to get involved."

Robert gave a sharp nod. "Alright, great work, everyone. Let's keep this investigation moving. We're not going to take our foot off the gas pedal now."

As the meeting adjourned, the atmosphere was tense, but outside the conference room, the real work was just beginning.

Miriam left the meeting and immediately gave David a call. "David, the task force is moving forward with its investigation. New Me is being surveilled and investigated by the Mexican authorities. Someone may have recognized Francisco. If everyone can lie low for a while, it would probably be best," she advised.

"Thanks, Agent Rojas." Then he dialed Francisco's number.

"Paco, it's me. I heard from a little mouse that the clinic is being surveilled by the police."

"You mean a little rat, but at least she's *our* little rat."

"What do you want to do?" David asked.

"Nothing yet. Let's wait and see." Francisco's voice was calm, but his heart was pounding. Out of instinct, he reached for his black amulet, rubbing it three times with the right hand and three times with the left.

51

Janice's phone vibrated on the counter as she finished folding laundry. She snatched it up eagerly when she saw the New Me Clinic's number flash on the screen.

"You're lucky, *señora*," the smooth voice on the other end said in accented English. "We have a probable match for you. This is very fast."

Janice's heart leapt. She gripped the kitchen counter for support, her knees suddenly weak. "Oh, thank goodness," she said, breathless. "When do I leave?"

"We'll send a car to pick you up within two hours. Be ready."

"I'll be waiting," Janice said, her voice trembling with a mix of excitement and nerves.

She hung up and rushed to her bedroom, pulling the small overnight bag she'd packed weeks ago from under the bed. She couldn't stop her hands from shaking as she checked its contents for the fourth time: toothbrush, nightgown, and com fortable clothes.

As she zipped the bag shut, nagging doubts whispered in her ear. Was this the right thing to do? Was she putting too much trust in strangers? But the thought of the new life that awaited her, free from the constant fear of her failing health, silenced the questions.

Janice called Ruby's phone, holding her breath as it rang, but it went to voicemail. "Hi, honey, it's Mom," she began, forcing cheerfulness into her voice. "I'm heading to that exclusive two-week women's meditation retreat I told you about. We'll be taking a vow of silence, so I'll be hard to reach. But don't worry about me. I'll call when I'm back home."

She left the same message for Doris, though it took more effort to sound convincing. Doris knew her too well.

Hours later, Ruby listened to her mom's voicemail message, raising an eyebrow as she heard her mother's phony cheery tone.

"She's taking a vow of silence? Since when does Mom do anything remotely spiritual?" Ruby shook her head in disbelief and called Doris to confer.

"I got the weirdest message from Mom," Ruby began.

"Let me guess," Doris said, cutting her off. "She's going on a two-week retreat and will be taking a vow of silence? It's absurd! Your mother doesn't stop talking even in her sleep."

"Exactly," Ruby said. "It just doesn't make sense. And why so suddenly?"

"It sounds fishy, Ruby," Doris said, her voice worried. "If you hear anything from her, let me know, and I'll do the same."

Janice squirmed in the backseat of a black SUV as it drove toward the border. The driver, a stocky man with dark sunglasses and tattoos on his forearms, hadn't spoken since he'd loaded her suitcase into the trunk and started driving.

Her excitement turned to fear as she approached Mexico. The reality of what she was doing hit her like a wave. She wasn't just traveling to a clinic across the border; she was crossing a metaphysical line, an ethical line.

She held her purse tightly to her chest, calming herself. "Are we almost there?" she asked the driver, keeping her voice steady.

The man nodded, his face impassive. "Almost," he said in accented English.

When they arrived at the New Me Clinic, two nurses in scrubs who spoke in accented English escorted Janice through a basement entrance. The walls were white, and the air in the clinic was cold enough to make her pull her sweater tighter around her. Her footsteps echoed as the nurses led her to a small room with a gurney and some medical monitoring equipment.

"This is getting real," she murmured to herself.

"Please lie down, *señora*," the nurse said, motioning to the gurney. "We are going to do some testing before the procedure and then get your IV hooked up."

An hour later, the nurse checked her and told her colleague. "*Tiene fiebre.*" She then turned to Janice and said, "You have a fever, *señora*. Unfortunately, your surgery will need to be postponed."

"What are you saying?" Janice's heart sank. "I feel just fine!"

"We can't take the risk. Your immune system might reject the liver. The organ will need to go to someone else. You need to recover and come back when you are well."

"But you might not have another match for me!" Janice protested, but to no avail.

The car ride back to Long Beach felt longer than the journey there. Janice sat in disappointed silence, staring out the window as the sun set, glancing at the outline of Catalina Island on her left. She felt a deep sense of disappointment but also shame. She had lied to her daughter and to her best friend, and for no reason.

Once she got back home, she called Ruby.

"I had to postpone the retreat," she told Ruby. "I'm running a fever and may have a bladder infection."

"I'm sorry it didn't work out, Mom," Ruby said, her voice empathetic. "I'm sure you'll get another chance when you're feeling better."

"I hope you're right," Janice said, but she didn't know if she would get another chance. She knew Ruby didn't believe her retreat story, and neither did Doris. They both knew her too well. And deep down, she wasn't sure she believed that she would actually get a liver before it was too late, from New Me or anywhere else.

52

uby opened her post office box with her key and pulled out the mail. She saw some bills, business mail, and the usual junk mail. But then a white envelope with the California Board of Accountancy's logo caught her eye. *Did I forget to pay my licensing fees? Was it a renewal notice?* She ripped the envelope open and scanned the letter, her eyes catching on the words *complaint* and *fraudulent activities.*

She inhaled sharply as she read the letter a second time. She was required to submit her client list and to appear before the board in two weeks. Ruby's thoughts raced. *This must be a mistake. Who could've filed a complaint against me?*

She walked out to her golf cart and sat down, her mind reeling. Just then, her phone rang, jolting her back to the present.

"Ruby, did you pay my homeowners' association bill?" Janice asked. "I got a nastygram from them."

"Good morning to you, too. Yes, Mom, I'm on it. The association changed payment platforms, so I need to set you up again."

"Good. I hate dealing with those people."

After hanging up, Ruby headed home. Once at her desk, she collapsed into the chair and pulled out the Board of

Accountancy's letter to reread it. The letter felt like disorder in her normally meticulous world, and she didn't like it one bit. She took a deep breath, shoved the letter into a file folder, and resolved to deal with it later. She had work to do.

That night, Ruby crawled into bed exhausted but still unnerved. She was drifting off to sleep when she heard her phone vibrate with a notification. She glanced at the screen and saw it was from her mom's bank. Dismissing it as another routine alert, she flipped her phone over and tried to fall asleep. Sleep that night was illusory, however, her mind churning with thoughts about the Board of Accountancy investigation and her livelihood.

The next morning, as she checked her email, Ruby noticed the bank notification from the night before again. When she clicked on it, her stomach dropped:

"Citi Alert: Your wire transfer has been successful. Recipient: SECONDLIVES; Amount: $50,000.00."

Ruby's heart pounded as she reread the message. She couldn't believe what she was seeing. She grabbed her phone and dialed her mom's number, her hands shaking.

"Why are you calling in the morning? You woke me up." Janice's voice sounded annoyed.

"Mom, is there anything you want to tell me?" Ruby asked accusingly.

"What are you talking about?" Janice replied, sounding defensive, an almost automatic response when she was talking to her daughter.

"Like the $50,000 wire transfer to the Second Lives Foundation, for example?"

"Oh, that." Janice's voice softened. "It's a charitable donation. I can spend my money however I want, Ruby. I'm a grown woman."

Ruby held the phone tighter in her hand. "Mom, I know

what the Second Lives Foundation really is. And I know what this money is for."

There was silence on the line before Janice responded, the defensiveness returning with a vengeance. "You don't know anything! And anyway, it's none of your business!"

"Mom, I can't let you do this." Ruby's voice cracked.

"Just stay out of it, Ruby! This is life and death for me. Do you want me to die waiting for UNOS to call?"

Ruby's mind raced. "Mom, you're gambling with more than just your life. Don't you care about where this liver is coming from? What you're trying to do is illegal!"

"Oh, spare me the lecture, Ruby!" Janice snapped. "You think your perfect life gives you the right to judge me? This is my chance to survive!"

Ruby clenched her jaw, fighting back tears. "Mom, promise me you won't go through with this yet, please!"

Janice's voice softened. "I'll think about it. But you'd better keep your mouth shut. Do not talk to anyone about this."

That night, Ruby lay awake, staring at the ceiling. Her mind played out a dozen scenarios, none of them good. What if the liver came from someone coerced or killed? What if the FBI uncovered this? Would they trace it to her too? She felt conflicted, but she couldn't betray her own mother, could she?

The next morning, Ruby's body ached from tension. Her jaw ached from grinding her teeth all night. *This is wrong,* she thought, *but I don't know what I can do about it.*

53

Kevin and Jacklyn arrived at the cruise terminal in Long Beach two hours early in order to hit the VIP check-in and get to their suite before the crowds. It took only one hour of cruising to get to Avalon.

The cruise ship swayed as it anchored outside Avalon Harbor. Jacklyn gripped the railing, her hair frizzy from the salty breeze. Below, they lowered the tender boats into the water, waiting to shuttle passengers to shore for the day. The iconic, red-tiled roof of the Casino poked out through the marine layer.

She nudged Kevin, who was scrolling through emails on his phone. "Look at that," she said, nodding toward the Casino and the hillside dotted with pastel-colored houses. "This view never gets old."

Kevin glanced up, squinting against the glare. "It'd look better if the sun were out," he complained.

Jacklyn frowned but didn't respond. She turned back to the view, her hands gripping the cool metal rail. The harbor shimmered in patches where the clouds broke, but the overcast sky prevented the harbor from sparkling as it would have done on a sunny day. She turned her attention back to the rows of boats bobbing in the harbor, yachts near the front, smaller vessels tucked behind them in an intricate pattern. For a moment, at least to her, the weather didn't matter one bit.

Once ashore, Crescent Avenue, Avalon's main drag, brimmed with life. Noisy rented golf carts whizzed past carelessly, their mostly intoxicated drivers laughing loudly, while other cruise ship tourists came in and out of shops and bars. The scent of the ocean mingled with fried fish, and the occasional shout of someone beginning their four-day bender broke through the din.

At the pancake house, Kevin barely spoke, preoccupied with something on his phone. Jacklyn focused on her plate; her strawberry waffles did little to distract her from the undercurrent of tension.

After breakfast and a stroll down Crescent Avenue together, they parted ways, Kevin to his appointment with Ruby Simon at the Shipshape marine-themed art gallery that Kevin had invested in years ago for the tax benefit, and Jacklyn towards the botanical gardens. At one time, Kevin studied painting and could appreciate talent when he saw it. Being a cash business, the gallery gave him more flexibility from a tax perspective.

Kevin, the gallery manager Simon, and Ruby sat down around the desk in the art gallery. Ruby admired the colorful landscape oil painting of Avalon Harbor and another of a giant flying fish suspended over the water with its fins spread wide.

The front door of the gallery opened, and a customer walked in. Simon said, "I'm sorry to interrupt, but I'm not involved in the bookkeeping for the gallery. I only report the monthly sales, so I don't know how much I can help in this conversation."

"You're right, Simon. Ruby and I can handle this. Why don't you help the gentleman who just walked in?"

Kevin sat on the edge of the desk, arms crossed, as Ruby

squirmed in her chair and then opened her laptop and angled it toward him.

"So," Ruby began, her voice tactful, "I noticed a few transactions that don't make sense to me. These—" she said, pointing to a column—"look like transfers in from an entity called the Second Lives Foundation. And these are outgoing payments to a clinic in Mexico. Can you clarify what these are and what their purpose is? I'm not sure how to account for them in your financials."

Kevin's face turned red as he responded. "Those payments are for medical consulting work I did for the Foundation," he said flatly. "And I am also serving on the Foundation's scientific advisory board now."

Ruby looked puzzled and then asked, "But the consulting fees should be paid into your personal account, not the gallery's account, right? I want to make sure everything's accurate."

Kevin sat up straight, his voice louder now. "Ruby, I don't need you second-guessing my accounts. If you have any questions or concerns, bring them to me directly rather than asking my wife. I don't think I like what you are implying."

Ruby's pulse quickened, but she forced herself to nod. "I'm sorry. I'm not implying anything. I just want to ensure everything is correct."

Kevin's eyes narrowed, his volume lower but his tone still aggressive. "It is. Now I want you to drop it."

As Ruby packed up her laptop, her hands trembled. Kevin's reaction wasn't just defensive; it was a calculated attempt to prevent her from digging deeper. Ruby knew one thing for sure. If she didn't navigate this carefully, she could be dragged into something far messier than accounting classifications. The other thing she knew for sure was that she refused to be involved in anything illegal. She had her CPA license and her livelihood to think about. She gave Kevin a brief smile as she walked out of the art gallery.

Jacklyn, meanwhile, was hiking up to the Wrigley Memorial and Botanic Garden, her tennis shoes crunching against the gravel path as she snaked her way through Avalon Canyon. The street had been quiet except for the ocean breeze blowing through the canyon. Her phone vibrated in her pocket, but she ignored it, preferring to focus on her lovely surroundings.

She stopped occasionally to admire the cactus plants lining the trail. Here and there, bursts of yellow or orange cactus flowers grew at all angles out of the cacti. She took some photos with her phone, making a mental note to send them later to her mom, a serious anthophile.

Once she entered the botanical garden, the imposing Wrigley Memorial loomed ahead, a tribute to the man who had made his fortune selling chewing gum and then used it to transform Catalina Island. Its blue stone steps and red-tiled roof stood out against the gray structure. She climbed the tall staircase, feeling her legs burn with each step.

Once she reached the top, she caught her breath. She stood between the Memorial's towering columns, which framed the landscape below, and admired the glimmering harbor and the boats of all shapes and sizes moored in rows. She closed her eyes and breathed in the scent of the ocean air, happy to be far away from the hustle and bustle of Crescent Avenue. This was her escape, a sanctuary from Kevin's moodiness and the unease that had been gnawing at her all morning. Jacklyn let out a deep breath she hadn't realized she'd been holding. *This is what I came for,* she thought.

Just before she descended the steps to head back down towards town, she finally checked her phone and saw a message from Kevin on the screen: "I'm done here. Meet me at the ferry dock at 2 p.m."

Jacklyn frowned, his tone in such stark contrast to her own zen-like state. As she took one last look at the panorama below, she felt a strange sense of foreboding settling over her.

54

As Jacklyn walked the winding canyon road towards town, the air turned colder, and the wind picked up. She shivered and untied the purple windbreaker from her waist, slipping it on and zipping it all the way to her chin. She smelled the eucalyptus trees lining the path on her left.

As she strolled, Jacklyn felt relaxed and was surprised to hear car tires crunching on gravel right behind her, seemingly appearing from nowhere. She looked over her shoulder and saw a white van pull up next to her and saw the passenger-side window slide down to reveal a young man in a hoodie leaning out.

"Miss, do you need a ride?" he asked her in a voice with a slight Spanish accent. "It looks like it's going to rain soon."

Jacklyn hesitated. Her natural instinct to decline an offer from a strange man softened by the man's polite tone and innocuous appearance. After all, Catalina was a safe place where everyone knew everyone. She smiled and then told him, "Thanks, that's sweet of you to offer, but I'm enjoying the walk. It's so peaceful here."

The man smiled back and told her, "Enjoy your walk." The van then rolled forward a few feet before stopping again, and she heard the van door slide open. Jacklyn felt a jolt of fear, and her eyes scanned the empty golf course on her right.

The driver of the van lunged from the driver's side, his hands rough as they wrapped around Jacklyn's torso. She gasped and tried to scream, but the man's palm smothered her mouth before any sound escaped her throat.

She thrashed against the man, her legs kicking his as she jerked herself away from his grip. The scents of eucalyptus and salt water in the canyon vanished, replaced by the less pleasant scent of a towel soaked in chemicals pressed against her nose and mouth. Her knees buckled as dizziness overwhelmed her, and the world faded away.

"Stop struggling, bitch!" a voice growled at her, but the sound felt distant. Her limbs grew heavy, and she saw only blackness.

Down at the ferry dock, Kevin clutched his phone at the meeting spot, repeatedly willing it to ring. The cruise ship's horns signaled an all-aboard call, and the deckhands on the ferry dock announced that the last tender boat to the ship would be leaving shortly. He dialed Jacklyn's number again, his panic rising when Jacklyn still did not answer.

She's always on time, he thought. *She would never miss the last call unless something was seriously wrong.*

Kevin stared at the crowd of passengers lining up for the tender boats. "Jacklyn!" he called out, his voice loud and desperate enough for those around him to turn and look at him in concern.

Jacklyn's lack of response filled him with nausea. He spoke to the cruise ship crew loading the tender boats to tell them that his wife had not arrived yet, and they advised him to go back on the ship to check for her, to see if this was all just a miscommunication. Back in their suite, his sweaty fingers tried to open the safe. To his dismay, he saw their passports were still in the safe and her bag was still open and unpacked. She hadn't come back to the ship.

He slammed the safe shut, his breath coming fast and panicked. The nausea hit suddenly, and he ran to the bathroom to vomit. The acid burned his throat as he looked at himself in the mirror, seeing a pale and haggard face staring back out at him.

This can't be happening.

His mind raced, and he thought back to his conversation with Jacklyn when she was asking about the financial transactions. He remembered his phone call to Mexico. He had assured them she would drop the matter, promised them she wasn't a threat to them.

What have I done?

As Jacklyn regained consciousness, her head throbbed, and she felt the cold, hard ground beneath her. Jacklyn winced and turned her head, feeling her cheek scrape against the rough floor, but something covered her eyes, preventing her from seeing her location. She tasted salt in her mouth and realized it was blood.

The thin plastic zip ties bit into the skin of her wrists and ankles every time she moved, and her muscles were stiff from cold. Panic and confusion surged through her, and she felt like she couldn't get enough oxygen with the duct tape sealing her mouth.

She dragged her face along the ground until the blindfold slid down and uncovered her eyes. The room was still dark, but she could make out a dim light from underneath the door. Her heart pounded as she scanned her surroundings, trying to make sense of it all. It appeared to be some kind of storage shed, empty except for some boxes in the corner and what seemed to be some gardening tools on the wall.

Where am I, and what is happening to me?

Jacklyn started hyperventilating through her nose, the tape covering her mouth. She strained against the zip ties, cutting into her skin even more, and her muscles ached. She didn't care about the pain; she cared only about getting back to Kevin and their boys.

Her mind raced as she wondered if Kevin was already looking for her or if he even knew she was gone. She forced back the tears.

Don't cry, girl. You need to think!

She rolled onto her side and felt the floor scrape her skin. She heard a hurried discussion in Spanish outside and lay frozen, afraid to move. *Were they coming back for her now?*

55

r. Carter sat at his desk drinking coffee to make up for the sleep he hadn't gotten the night before. The house was quiet except for the sounds of Jacklyn's parents cleaning up from breakfast and the kids getting ready for school upstairs.

The caffeine didn't help his pounding heart. His wife was still missing. The investigation into his life was hanging over him, growing more serious by the hour. The police had questioned him three times already, each session lasting a little longer than the one before. They were polite and not confrontational, but their eyes were suspicious and their questions too personal.

He thought about the New Me Clinic and knew he was already in trouble. All he had done was offer routine physical exams. He wasn't involved in the surgeries. And if it weren't him, some other doctor would have done the same thing, wouldn't they?

He took a deep breath, his head throbbing, and felt shaky. *I don't think I actually broke the law.* He rubbed his temples with both hands, trying not to think about it. But the way the detectives questioned him, like they already knew more than they were saying, made him doubt his own answers.

"Kevin?" He heard his mother-in-law knocking on his office

door, her accented voice calling him. He turned to see her petite frame standing in the doorway, her face haggard. "The kids are asking for you. They're wondering when you're coming to help them pick out their school clothes, like their mom always does."

He stood up. "Tell them I'll be up in a minute."

She looked at him, searching his eyes for the truth. He could almost hear her suspicions that, up until now, remained unspoken. *Does she actually think I had something to do with Jacklyn's disappearance?*

Jacklyn's father moved into view behind his wife and stood stooped, his hands buried in his pockets. "Jacklyn told us that you were good under pressure, that as a surgeon you needed to be," he said, his voice almost inaudible. "I guess we'll see, won't we?"

Dr. Carter's throat tightened as he turned away from Jacklyn's worried parents, pretending to organize the files on his desk. He couldn't stand the way they looked at him now a moment longer.

After getting the kids ready for school, he tied his running shoes on and headed out the front door for his daily run. He really needed the dopamine boost today more than ever to keep his panic in check. The early morning air was cool against his skin as he set off on the neighborhood loop along the beach paths in Laguna, his steps pounding rhythmically against the sidewalk.

His morning run ritual was normally a time where he could think and plan his day, or at least try to. The overcast sky was almost as dark as his thoughts as he replayed the detectives' probing questions in his mind.

"How is your marriage?"

"Does your wife have life insurance? Are you the beneficiary?"

The detectives took notes and wrote down his responses. He wondered what they were writing and how damning it would be.

His heavy breathing and physical exhaustion felt good as he

reached his front door. But then he remembered. *What if they find out about the referrals to the clinic or about the money?*

Back inside the house, the atmosphere felt stifling, and he felt Jacklyn's absence more acutely. Her parents sat hunched together at the kitchen table, and the house was silent. Jacklyn's mother folded her tiny hands on her lap. She seemed to have aged ten years since her daughter had gone missing.

"Kevin," she started, breaking the silence. "When was the last time you heard from her? Is there something that you want to tell us? Were you arguing?"

He stared at his in-laws, keeping his face neutral. "I already told the police. The day we had breakfast on the island was the last time I saw her. After we ate, she went on a walk while I had a business meeting at the art gallery. We were supposed to meet at the ferry dock, but she didn't show up."

"And she didn't say anything strange, anything out of the ordinary? Were you having any marriage problems?"

"No, nothing like that," he said too quickly.

Her eyes narrowed as she studied Kevin's face, trying to decide whether she believed him or not. His father-in-law's face already looked like he thought Kevin was hiding something from them.

Kevin cleared his throat and headed for his office. "If you'll excuse me, I have to call in to work."

He closed the door of his office, not intending to slam it, but the noise jolted him. His hands shook as he checked his email. He saw that the Second Lives Foundation had sent another payment confirmation for his consulting fees, a reminder of how deep he was already in this. He thought that it was only a matter of time until the police had access to his email too.

He felt trapped as he sat at his desk staring at the screen.

He looked over at a photo of Jacklyn near his screen, her deep brown eyes radiating the warmth that had attracted him to her from the beginning.

Jacklyn, where are you?

For a moment, he imagined her out there scared and alone, or maybe worse. His stomach cramped, and he held his head in his hands, anguished. He couldn't shake the feeling that every single decision he had made in the past year had led to the current unraveling of his carefully curated life.

56

The agents' faces on the Zoom call lined up like a Tic-Tac-Toe grid. The room around Robert was quiet, and the tension surrounding the case felt palpable even before the meeting began.

Agent Luis Romano, after spending hours combing through Dr. Carter's background, had found something unexpected. "The Laguna Beach PD confirmed that Dr. Carter's record is spotless. But, interestingly enough, his wife went missing only a few days ago," he informed the team. "There's an active investigation. I don't know, but that seems way too big a coincidence for me."

Robert thought about Jacklyn Carter's disappearance. He didn't buy that it was a coincidence for a second. Robert's brow furrowed and turned to Luis. "Get in touch with the LA County Sheriffs and the Avalon Harbor Patrol. We need to get every detail on her missing persons case. I don't like this one bit."

Maybe this isn't just about money laundering anymore. There could be something more here.

Luis was already on it, his fingers looking through his phone for his Los Angeles Sheriff's Department contact and jotting it on a piece of paper.

"Luis," Robert asked, "what did you get from the people *around* Dr. Carter?" His tone was earnest.

"Nothing concrete. Mrs. Jacklyn Carter is missing, of course. But we spoke to a few nurses at his office. They're all convinced that Dr. Carter is just a routine surgeon, nothing outside the norm. But when we talked to the art gallery manager, *that* was interesting."

Robert's eyebrows arched, intrigued. "And?"

"He said he knows nothing about the finances, but what struck me was his hesitation when we asked about the gallery's connection to the clinic. It's almost like he was hiding something." Luis's voice lowered. "We're watching him, though. If he cracks, we'll have him."

"Good," Robert muttered. "Luis, have you been able to interview Dr. Carter himself?" He was already dreading the answer.

"We've had a few discussions at his home but no formal interrogation yet. But we are watching his every move. He's keeping a low profile, going to work, taking his kids to and from school since his wife isn't there to take them. Nothing spectacular. I think his in-laws are staying with him, so that could make anyone run for the hills!"

Everyone chuckled knowingly.

"Has Dr. Carter been talking to anyone out of the ordinary? Did you find anything we can work with?" Robert looked at Luis questioningly. It felt more urgent now that the team knew that Mrs. Carter was missing, and they could feel time slipping by and being no closer to answers.

"We haven't seen anything unusual yet, but we're all over him like flies on poop," Luis added. "We are just waiting for him to slip up."

"Agent Sufuentes," Robert's voice cut through the Zoom

chatter, "I understand you've made some progress down in Tijuana?"

"Yes, Agent Jones," Sufuentes replied in accented English, his tone flat but his eyes hard. "We had a lucky break. We tailed one of the clinic's doctors and caught him leaving through the basement exit of the clinic late at night." He paused, letting his words settle. "It took some convincing, but he talked."

Robert's eyes opened wider. "What kind of convincing?"

"Let's just say we used some unconventional methods. The kind that wouldn't make it into the FBI handbook. It's probably better if you don't know." A grim smile tugged at the corners of Sufuentes's mouth before it vanished. "But lives were on the line, so we did what we had to do."

Robert nodded. "And what did the doctor have to say?"

"At first, he stuck to his story that the clinic was doing routine plastic surgery, nothing out of the ordinary. But when we reminded him how much he stood to lose, his license, his family, his kids' future, he finally cracked. He said he'd cooperate if the Mexican Attorney General's office could guarantee amnesty and protection."

"And?"

"He told us something shocking. The clinic upstairs performs routine plastic surgeries. It's a separate operation entirely." Sufuentes took a deep breath. "But there's a reason that ambulances are coming and going through the basement. The downstairs clinic is dedicated to organ harvesting and transplants."

The words hung in the air like a hand grenade that had been rolled into a foxhole but hadn't exploded yet. Robert's stomach churned, but he forced himself to ask, "Organ harvesting? You mean wealthy people are buying them?"

"Exactly. The buyers are mostly Americans, jumping the UNOS waiting list line, buying new kidneys and livers, all of it."

The gasps of shock were almost simultaneous across the call. Agent Romano muttered something inaudible and pushed his chair back from his desk, his face pale.

"That's not even the worst of it," Sufuentes said grimly.

"What could be worse than that?" Robert asked, stunned, barely above a whisper.

Sufuentes's looked downward for a moment and then looked back up with his jaw set. "The donors aren't always willing participants."

The silence was deafening.

"You mean—" Robert's voice cracked, and he cleared his throat. "Are you saying that they're killing people for their organs?"

"That's exactly what I'm saying," Sufuentes confirmed. His face was stone, but his voice betrayed the disgust he couldn't suppress. "And there's more. La Familia cartel seems to be heavily involved. They fund the operation and supply the 'donors'."

Robert's hands shook as he crossed his arms over his chest, visibly upset. As a policeman and then an FBI agent, he thought he'd seen every depravity that man could inflict upon man, but this? This was beyond comprehension. The team had been battling the cartel's drug operations and had seen firsthand its willingness to use extreme violence for years. They knew that the cartel had diversified into other lucrative areas such as extortion, arms trafficking, and human smuggling and trafficking.

He thought about the innocent, unwilling donors, surgeons who would intentionally harm their patients, their fellow Americans who were so entitled that they would benefit from this scheme at the expense of the victims and all the other sick

Americans patiently waiting for organs. But this revelation, if it could be believed and proven, was beyond the pale.

"I can't believe this," Agent Simpson muttered, her voice barely audible. "How do we take this down? We need to eradicate this atrocity immediately."

Robert forced himself to look at his colleagues in the camera, his gaze hardening. "We start by bringing every resource we've got to bear on this. DEA, ATF, CBP, and anyone else willing to get their hands dirty. We coordinate with the Mexican Attorney General's office. This operation is no longer an ordinary investigation."

Sufuentes nodded, his expression grim. "The cartel's reach is deep, and they won't give this operation up easily. But we've got the doctor's testimony, so it's a start."

"We'll make it the priority," Robert said firmly, and every other agent nodded in agreement. "This is evil on a scale we've never seen, and we are going to stop it, whatever it takes."

The meeting ended, but Robert didn't move even after the Zoom meeting was over. He could only sit and stare at the blank screen. In the pit of his stomach, a new resolve to put a stop to this burned hotter than the horror he felt. *The cartel thinks it is untouchable, but we are about to prove it wrong. Dead wrong.*

57

"Good morning, Ruby," Jaime called, his voice carrying over the sound of the surf below. He sat on their shared balcony, a steaming mug of coffee in one hand and a fleece jacket pulled tight against the early chill. "Andy made it to the mainland just in time. If this storm is half as bad as they're forecasting, they'll shut down the ferry service to the mainland for sure."

Ruby nodded, looking out at the Pacific and toward the mainland. The dark clouds of the impending storm had multiplied overnight, spreading across the sky. The air was damp and humid, and rain was coming. She shivered and tugged the hood of her blue-and-gold Berkeley sweatshirt over her head, zipping it up to her chin.

Her phone vibrated in her pocket, and she dug it out. *Good morning, beautiful!* Andy's daily text lit up her screen and her mood. A small, involuntary smile tugged at her lips, and warmth fluttered through her chest despite the chill. Instead of replying, she put the phone back in her pocket. She didn't want to think about the storm or the twenty-six miles of ocean now separating them.

Ruby spent most of the day at her desk working on a client's books. The desk was cluttered, the faint aroma of her mint tea mingling with the fabric softener of her newly laundered bedding. Her optometrist client had been negligent; months of missing bank statements stacked into a pile to be sorted out. By mid-afternoon, her head throbbed, and she dropped her mechanical pencil onto the desk with a deep sigh. Abacus padded over and nudged her hand with his wet nose.

"All right, you win, boy," she said, scratching behind his ears. "How about we call it a day?"

The old Robin Cook paperback she'd been meaning to finish waited for her on the couch, and soon she was curled up beneath a throw blanket. Abacus sat on the cushion next to her, his head resting on her lap. Outside, the wind started picking up speed and was now howling through the cracks in the balcony door. A weather alert dinged on her phone: *Atmospheric river expected to hit Southern California. Significant rainfall and gusting winds possible.* Ruby glanced out the window. She could feel the storm's imminent arrival in her bones.

She made a mental note to pick up groceries in the morning. *Better safe than sorry.*

Ruby slid into her golf cart, Abacus leaping into the front seat next to her. The early morning breeze chilled her, and the sky was fully gray. As the cart wound down the narrow road toward town, a stiff wind whipped through her hair.

She parked outside the small grocery store, giving Abacus a

quick pat. "Stay here, buddy. I'll be back soon." She connected his leash to the bar, and he sat obediently but sadly in the cart.

The electronic door opened, and Ruby stepped inside. The air was warmer here, and the store was full of other shoppers getting ready for the storm. *"Buenos días, César,"* she greeted the gray-haired man behind the cash register. *"Cómo estás?"*

"Buenos días, señorita!" he replied, his voice friendly despite the worry etched in his face. "Are you stocking up before the storm? It seems like it's going to be a big one. Lupe's already got the kids clearing the rain gutters and charging all of the electronics just in case."

"That's a smart move. Please send her my best and stay safe, okay?"

César nodded, his smile tight. Ruby grabbed a shopping cart and began making her way through the aisles. She grabbed a package of chocolate chip cookies. *To fortify myself against the storm.* She tossed them into the cart along with batteries, water bottles, and canned soup. Outside, the wind rattled the grocery store windows, making her glance up uneasily.

By the time she returned to the golf cart, Abacus was up and bouncing with excitement, his tail wagging furiously in greeting. Ruby loaded the grocery bags into the back and told him, "All right, let's go home."

Back at the condo, Ruby methodically unpacked the bags and filled the kitchen cabinets and fridge with the newly purchased supplies. The unease that she had been feeling all morning still lingered. She stepped out onto the balcony to pull in the patio cushions so they wouldn't blow away. The wind had grown stronger and more aggressive. Below, the ocean roiled violently, whitecaps breaking against the rocks.

Her phone dinged again, and a notification glowed ominously:

SEVERE WEATHER ALERT: Residents and visitors of Catalina Island are advised to leave immediately due to the potential for prolonged utility outages and dangerous conditions.

Ruby stared at the message, her pulse quickening. Abacus padded over, rubbing himself against her legs. She bent down, wrapping her arms around his warm neck. "Guess it's just us, buddy," she murmured. "It's a good thing I bought cookies!" The storm wasn't coming; it was already here.

58

That night, Robert sat in front of his laptop, biting his fingernails down to the nub. Jaime hated this nervous habit of his, but Robert still did it unconsciously in times of stress. His mind was still spinning from the meeting, from the revelations that were already surfacing. His hand hovered over the phone, and finally, he dialed Ruby Simon.

The phone rang twice before she picked up. "Ruby, it's Robert. There's something I need to ask."

"Of course," Ruby said, her voice a little too soft, as if she was waiting for him to continue.

"Why didn't you mention that Jacklyn Carter was a missing person?" Robert's voice was steady, but there was a bite to it now.

Ruby hesitated. For a split second, there was a strange quiet on the other end of the line. "Oh, I completely forgot to mention it," she said finally. "I didn't think her disappearance was relevant, honestly. And I figured you'd already heard about it from Jaime. It's all over the news in Avalon."

Robert's eyes narrowed. *Her responses seem too casual. Is she hiding something?* "No, Ruby. We only just found out as part of our investigation. I want you to know that we're taking this seriously, all hands on deck. I'll keep you posted as much as I can, but if you uncover anything else, let me know."

He didn't wait for her response before he ended the call. *Something's not adding up here.*

59

Ruby settled onto the couch to FaceTime her mother, as she did every night at 9 p.m., Abacus at her feet. "Hey, Mom. I wanted to check in. We're expecting a big storm on the island soon. I spent the afternoon stocking up on groceries and bringing in the patio cushions."

Janice's voice crackled over the line, sharp and matter-of-fact. "Please make sure the place doesn't flood and unplug the appliances before it hits."

Ruby rolled her eyes, her lips tightening into a thin line. *Not even a "Be safe, Ruby" or "Take care of yourself," huh?* she thought, biting back a retort. "I will, Mom. The condo will be fine," she said instead, but her voice carried an edge.

A heavy silence lingered between them.

On the other end, Janice sighed audibly, the kind of sigh meant to be heard. She traced a finger along the rim of her coffee cup, the ceramic cool against her skin. Her gaze drifted toward the framed family photo on the mantel. It was a younger Janice, her arm slung around her two daughters and her son, all three of them grinning despite their sunburned cheeks.

Janice leaned back in her chair, staring into the stillness of her living room. She knew she had always put her children first after their dad had died, even if Ruby didn't agree. But the kids were young and resilient. His death hadn't hit them as hard as it had hit her. She knew that Ruby still resented the fact that she had dated and married after their father had died, but she had still been a young woman and deserved to find happiness again, and it had been selfish of her daughter to prevent that. Yes, her taste in men had been questionable, but she was afraid of being alone. She had never lived alone, having gone from her parents' home to her marital home at twenty. And here she was, living alone with her daughters too far away to help her much.

"You know, I gave up everything for you kids," she said, her tone wistful, though her words carried the familiar weight of guilt.

Ruby pressed her lips together, clenching the phone tighter. "I know, Mom," she said, her voice clipped. She scratched the dog's neck, a tension tightening in her chest.

"When are you coming to visit again?" Janice asked, her voice softening but only slightly.

"In a couple of weeks," Ruby replied. "I'll let you know."

Janice harrumphed, the sound full of unspoken frustration. She set her *#1 Mom* mug down harder than she intended, the ceramic clinking against the glass table. "Weeks?" she muttered under her breath, shaking her head. "She has no husband, no kids, no excuses. Why wouldn't she come more often? Especially now." When the condo sells, she thought, Ruby will probably need to move back to the mainland, and then she can help me more.

The words burned on her tongue, but she swallowed them. Ruby's temper had always been sharp, and she didn't want another argument about *boundaries.*

"Andy seems like a nice guy," Janice said instead, her voice shifting gears. "When will I get to meet him?"

Ruby closed her eyes, willing herself to stay calm. *When hell freezes over,* Ruby thought. The mantra came to her mind automatically, the only thing keeping her from snapping. *May you be happy. May you be peaceful. May you be free from suffering.*

"Hmm?" Janice pressed when Ruby didn't respond.

"I don't know, Mom," Ruby said finally, her voice carefully neutral. "We'll see."

"Ruby..." Janice began, her tone exasperated, but Ruby cut her off.

"Mom, I have to go. The storm is picking up, and I need to check on things," Ruby lied, her heart pounding.

"Fine," Janice replied, the word as cold as the onshore winds blowing outside.

As Ruby hung up, she stared at her phone for a moment before setting it aside. Abacus rested his head on her knee and looked up at her with concern. Ruby scratched his ears absentmindedly, replaying the conversation in her mind.

Outside, the wind rattled the windowpanes.

60

The long nights spent hunched over anatomy books, the endless shifts in the ER where exhaustion blurred into routine, and the adrenaline-fueled moments in surgery had all led Dr. Justin Ross here. Now, in the home stretch of his fellowship, he was mastering the shoulder and elbow, complex joints that demanded precision and skill.

Justin flexed his right shoulder instinctively, a phantom ache reminding him of the countless hours he'd spent in rehab after his rotator cuff repair. Tennis had been his escape until the injury stole it. That's why he was here now, perfecting shoulder surgery, to give others a second chance at the lifestyle they loved, even if he'd lost his own.

Justin stepped into the cadaver lab, his nose assaulted by the sharp tang of antiseptic. The bright lights reflected harshly off the stainless-steel workbenches, and the heavily cooled air bit through his scrubs. He heard the clanging of the other surgeons adjusting their tools on the metal benches.

The instructor, tall and broad-shouldered with the effortless confidence of a former athlete, strode to the center of the room. "I'm Dr. Alexander," he said, a grin tugging at the corners of his mouth. "And yes, I know some of you think you've got it all figured out. But today, we're diving into what really matters: best practices, cutting-edge research, and technology that will make your work *better*." His gaze swept the room, daring anyone to challenge him.

Justin pulled back the sheet, exposing the left shoulder of the cadaver beneath. His hands froze. Staring back at him from the pallid skin of the shoulder specimen was a vivid tattoo of an eagle perched on a cactus clutching a rattlesnake in its beak. He knew the iconic image was the national emblem of Mexico, the same one that was imprinted on its currency, from the Aztec legend that seeing this image would signal to them where to build their city.

He leaned closer, his breath catching, and his mind racing. *This shoulder belonged to a young Mexican man, someone who probably had a story worth knowing.* Justin shuddered, feeling like he could almost hear Juan's mother Amparo calling out for him. *How did it end up here, halfway across the continent, in this cold, clinical lab?*

The questions came to his mind fast and unbidden. *Who was this man? How had he lived and how had he died?* Justin glanced around the room, half expecting someone else to notice the tattoo, to share in the jolt of realization. But the other surgeons were absorbed in their own specimens, and their chatter blended into the background noise.

What path had brought this shoulder here? The unsettling thought lingered as Justin reached for his scalpel.

61

The embryologist wiped a bead of sweat from his temple as he organized the last piece of equipment in the new lab. Marcelo paced behind him, talking on the phone, barking instructions to someone on the other end of the line.

"Time is money, *amigo.* Let's get this show on the road," Marcelo snapped, though a satisfied smile tugged at his lips. "We're almost there."

The doctor emerged from the adjacent room, still pulling off his gloves, and reported, "The patient is sedated and responding well to the hormone protocol," he said, tossing the gloves into the trash can. "Her body is producing a good number of follicles, and everything looks promising so far."

"Promising isn't good enough, doctor. We need results."

The doctor hesitated, glancing toward the patient beyond the closed door. "Stimulating ovaries to produce this many eggs is more of an art than a science, and it isn't exactly risk-free. I'm keeping a close eye on the patient's hormone levels."

Marcelo waved a dismissive hand. "That's what we're paying you for. Make sure we get the numbers we need." The reproductive endocrinologist had explained to Marcelo that it was just a numbers game. If they were able to grow fifteen eggs, perhaps twelve of them would be sufficiently mature. Of those twelve eggs, maybe eight of them would successfully fertilize. And then maybe six of those eight would survive to the embryo stage. But the first step was stimulating the woman's ovaries to produce multiple eggs.

The faint sound of Livia's breathing monitor beeped steadily in the background. Marcelo walked past the doctor and peered into the room. Livia lay motionless, her pale face almost porcelain under the dim light.

"She seems like the perfect candidate," Marcelo muttered to himself.

In the lab, the embryologist was already preparing for the next step, the extraction. "We'll know by tomorrow how many eggs are mature and viable," he said, not looking up from his work, and then we can start the fertilization process.

"Good," Marcelo replied, all business. "Make sure you text me the moment we have fertilization results."

The embryologist chuckled nervously. "Will do, but it's not immediate. You better pick out your 'viewing material' for the collection process so that we can prepare the sample for fertilization."

Marcelo nodded but said nothing, his mind already moving three steps ahead.

Later that evening, Marcelo sat across from Marisol at dinner, his meal untouched. She raised an eyebrow at his animated expression.

"So," she asked, cutting into her chicken, "what's got you so excited today?"

He looked up into her questioning eyes. "We're branching out. New Me isn't just about cosmetic surgery anymore. We're moving into fertility treatments."

Marisol tilted her head, with a guarded expression on her face. "Fertility treatments? That's different."

"Not really. It's about giving people what they want at a price they can afford," Marcelo said smoothly. "Same principle, different product. Couples from the States can adopt embryos made with eggs donated by Mexican women, which were fertilized with the husband's sperm. We're handling everything for them, the retrieval, fertilization, and storage. It's a win-win."

"And the patients? How are you convincing them to donate their eggs?"

Marcelo's smile faltered for only a moment, so brief it was almost imperceptible. "Let's just say we have willing participants."

Marisol frowned, setting down her fork. "Are they willing participants or desperate ones?"

Marcelo's expression hardened. "Does it matter? They're compensated, and everyone benefits. You don't need to worry about the details, Marisol."

Her face reddened at his tone, but she nodded and looked down. "I trust you, Marcelo."

At the facility, Marcelo watched through the observation window as the doctor retrieved the eggs. The embryologist meticulously recorded the count, his movements precise and experienced.

"There are ten eggs to fertilize," the embryologist reported later, handing Marcelo a clipboard with the results. "We will know the quality of the embryos in a few days."

Marcelo scanned the page, his mind already spinning with possibilities. "Good. Now we can start marketing. We'll target the clinics in Orange County, Los Angeles, and San Diego first. They're our biggest markets. Couples willing to travel will save thousands, and we'll take a cut every step of the process."

The embryologist hesitated. "And the patient? Do you want to send her back now?"

Marcelo glanced toward the room where Livia was resting. "Not yet. Let's see how the embryos progress first. Once we're sure, we'll transfer her back to New Me."

The embryologist's brow furrowed. "She completed the egg retrieval. She needs to be medically monitored. Keeping her here longer could cause—"

"Just do what I tell you," Marcelo interrupted sharply. "We're officially open for business."

62

Carlos adjusted the straps of his small backpack as he stepped onto the rickety bus. It was all he had left, his meager belongings rattling inside like loose change. The barbershop he'd spent years building in El Salvador had become his prison, drained dry by gang extortions. On his right forearm was a tattoo of the flag of El Salvador, the two blue stripes representing the Pacific and Atlantic Oceans and the white stripe symbolizing peace, a pipe dream for many decades. The jagged stump where his pinkie used to be, a constant, throbbing reminder of their last "warning", deformed his right hand. He hadn't waited around to see what would happen if he refused again.

The bus lurched forward, the uneven road jolting Carlos from his thoughts. He kept his gaze on the horizon, the border a distant hope that flickered faintly in his mind. He had heard the stories about the abductions, the ransoms, and the beatings, but there was no other choice. Staying meant certain death. At least he wasn't a woman, he thought grimly. He didn't carry *that* particular risk.

The bus slowed, a hiss of brakes slicing through the hot,

stale air. Carlos's heart sank as two men with rifles, *malandros,* boarded the bus. Their weapons were menacing with "BARRETT" stamped in bold letters along the barrels. The other passengers stiffened in their seats, their eyes darting toward the floor. The men didn't speak right away, letting their boots clomp down the narrow aisle, the sound louder than the engine.

"You, *muchachos,*" one of them barked, gesturing with his rifle. "Get out of the bus now!"

Carlos felt his stomach twist. A half-dozen young men, himself included, shuffled off the bus under the cold stares of the gunmen. The midday sun beat down on them as the gunmen lined them up on the side of the desert road, and the dirt felt hot and dry under their feet.

"Kneel and put your hands behind your neck," one of the men ordered, his face passive as though they were performing a tired routine. Carlos obeyed, the dust rising as he sank to his knees. His breath came in shallow gasps.

When it was his turn, a rifle butt nudged his chin upward. Carlos flinched, but dared not resist. The man with the gun crouched in front of him, his smile cruel.

"Name?"

"Carlos."

"Where are you headed?"

Carlos hesitated, his voice a strained whisper. "The U.S. border."

The man's smile widened, his gold tooth glinting in the sun. "Ah, so you've got money for the journey. Hand it over. All of it."

Carlos fumbled in his pocket, his fingers trembling as he retrieved a few coins. They clinked pathetically as he dropped them into the man's outstretched hand.

"This is it?" the man asked, mockingly inspecting the coins.

"It's all I have," Carlos said, his voice cracking.

The man's smile hardened, and he leaned in close. "Do you have family in *El Norte?* Anyone who loves you enough to pay your ransom?"

Carlos shook his head. "No. I'm from a small village in El Salvador. Nobody has anything."

A slap cracked through the air, and Carlos's head snapped to the side. His cheek burned as the man rose to his feet, laughing. Carlos didn't look up. He stared at the ground, trying his best to "become one" with the dirt.

The gunman exchanged a glance with his partner, who leaned in and whispered something. Carlos couldn't make out the words, but he caught the phrase "healthy young ones" and felt his stomach drop.

The first man turned back to Carlos, his grin now gone. Without warning, he grabbed Carlos's arm and yanked him to his feet. Carlos stumbled, his knees weak, but the man dragged him forward.

"Let's go," the man said, shoving Carlos toward the back of a black pickup truck.

"No! Please!" Carlos begged, but the sound of the truck's engine roaring to life drowned out his voice.

His wrists were bound tightly behind him, the rough rope biting into his skin. They threw him into the truck bed like cargo, and the metal burned his bare arms. Before he was covered by the tarp, he saw the bus pulling away without him, and its passengers stared blankly ahead, pretending not to notice.

Carlos's chest heaved as the truck sped off, each jolt slamming him against the sides. Above the rumble of the engine, he heard the men talking and joking as if this was just an ordinary day.

"We'll see if he's worth anything," one of them said, laughing.

Carlos closed his eyes and slowed his breathing. He had known the journey would be dangerous, but he hadn't expected this.

63

Nick crouched behind the scraggly hedge outside the condo complex, his knees aching from hours of waiting in the damp, salty air. The wind had picked up, whipping against his face and carrying the briny tang of the ocean. Above him, dark clouds churned, threatening rain. He tightened the straps of his backpack and stared up at Ruby's unit.

It had been a lucky break earlier, catching sight of her in the golf cart with her corgi. Lucky, too, that she'd carelessly left the sliding glass door unlocked. *Island life makes people sloppy,* he thought, his lips curling into a tight smile. She didn't know it yet, but tonight, he'd make her understand.

He stayed crouched until the last light in her condo flickered off, the faint glow spilling onto the balcony fading to black. His heart thudded in his chest, a combination of anticipation and anger. She *owed* him a conversation, owed him a chance to explain.

When he climbed onto the balcony, the glass door slid open silently. The condo was dark, but moonlight filtered in through the windows, glinting off the knife block in the kitchen. Nick hesitated. He didn't want to hurt Ruby; he loved her. *But what if she screamed before he explained?* His hand hovered over the knife handles before settling on the biggest blade. He grabbed it, the weight reassuring in his hand.

The air inside smelled faintly of banana bread, like she used to bake for him. He saw her tennis shoes and flip-flops lined up by the door, a throw blanket tossed over the back of the couch, the vintage movie posters on the wall. He tightened his grip on the knife and made his way toward the bedroom.

Abacus was the first to sense him. A low growl rumbled from the dark as the dog stepped into the hall, its body low and rigid.

"Shhh," Nick hissed, his breath shallow.

The dog lunged at Nick, who stumbled backward, nearly dropping the knife. He grabbed the dog by the scruff, getting bitten on his hand in the process. "Quiet!" he spat, dragging the animal toward the bathroom and throwing it inside, slamming the door.

Ruby stirred in the bedroom, alarmed.

Nick stepped inside. She was sitting up now, her hair tousled, blinking against the dim light. For a moment, she didn't move. Then, her gaze locked onto the knife in his hand, and her breath hitched.

"Nick?" she whispered, her voice hoarse with sleep.

He stepped closer, the metal of the blade catching the faint light from the window. "Don't scream, Ruby," he said, his tone deceptively soft. "I just want to talk to you. Do you understand?"

Her hands clutched the sheets to her chest, her body trembling. She nodded quickly, her eyes wide.

Nick exhaled, lowering himself to sit on the edge of the bed. The mattress dipped beneath his weight, and the faint scent of her body lotion wafted toward him. His fingers grazed the pillow beside her, his thumb rubbing the fabric in slow circles.

"It wasn't nice what you did," he said, his voice tight with barely restrained anger. "Spraying me like that. Why would you do that to me?"

"Nick, please..." Ruby's voice cracked, her trembling growing more pronounced. "You're scaring me. Put the knife down and we can talk."

He didn't seem to hear her. His hand flattened against the pillow, caressing it gently. His breathing slowed, and a faint smile crossed his lips. "We were good together, Ruby. We belong together. I love you so much."

Ruby's breath hitched. She inched backward, her back pressing against the headboard. Her hands gripped the sheets tighter, knuckles white.

"I remember," she stammered, her voice barely above a whisper. "We had good times, Nick. But this isn't the way to talk. Please, just put the knife down and I'll listen. I promise."

Her words faltered as he looked up at her, the momentary gentleness gone. "You don't get it," he said, his voice rising. "I've been out there, sleeping on couches, running from the cops, all for you! Everything I've done, I've done for us. Don't you *see* that?"

Ruby nodded quickly, her heart pounding against her ribs. "I see it, Nick. I do. Just give me a chance to explain."

But Nick wasn't listening. His free hand grabbed the sheets, and his eyes glossed over as if in a trance. "Deep down, I know you still love me."

Ruby's eyes darted to the door, to the knife, to the closed bathroom where Abacus barked and whined. She needed a plan, some kind of distraction, an opening, anything.

64

he two men crouched in the shadows outside Ruby's condo, rain beginning to fall on the leaves above them. Ramón, tall and lean with a pockmarked face, shifted uncomfortably, pulling his hood up and his jacket tighter against the damp wind.

"Pepe, look at that." He pointed a finger towards Ruby's balcony. A wiry gringo had appeared, climbing over the railing like a stray cat.

Pepe squinted, his stocky frame hunched as he leaned forward to get a better look. "Who the hell is that idiot? David didn't say anything about anyone else being here."

"It doesn't matter," Ramón muttered. "The dog's barking like crazy. If he wakes her up, this is going to get messy. Let's move."

Pepe nodded, his face grim. They crept to the front door quietly. Ramón jimmied the lock with ease, the faint click swallowed by the sound of the wind and rain.

Inside, the condo was dark except for the faint glow of a lamp in the bedroom. The dog barked furiously, the sound partially muffled by the closed bathroom door. Ramón's eyes adjusted, sweeping the space quickly. Ramón glanced toward the dark kitchen with the knife block resting on the counter and then padded quietly toward the living room. He looked up to see a giant buffalo and a Jaws movie poster on the wall. At the bedroom doorway, he froze and signaled to Pepe.

The target was there, sitting upright against the headboard, her eyes wide with terror. And on the bed with her was the lanky man, a butcher knife gleaming in his hand as he pointed it at her. The man holding the knife whipped his head toward them. His face twisted in rage when he saw them, and he shot to his feet, pointing the knife at them. "Who the fuck are you?"

Before Ramón could respond, the lanky man lunged at Pepe with a wild yell. "You leave her alone! She's mine!"

Pepe barely had time to sidestep, the blade slicing the air where his chest had been seconds before. Ramón reacted faster, grabbing the man's wrist and twisting it sharply. The knife clattered to the floor, but Ramón wasn't done. In one fluid motion, he yanked the blade up and plunged it into the side of the man's neck.

The *gringo* staggered back, clutching at the wound, blood spilling through his fingers. His mouth opened, but only a wet choking sound came out before he crumpled to the floor motionless.

Pepe let out a low whistle, nudging the body with his boot. "Well, shit. Now we've got to deal with him too."

In the corner of the room, Ruby scrambled out of bed, her breath coming in sharp, panicked gasps. She pressed herself against the wall, her hands frantically searching for anything she could use as a weapon.

"What do you want? Money? Take whatever you want, just don't hurt me!" she pleaded, her voice trembling.

Ramón turned to her with a smirk. "Money? No, *preciosa*, we're not here for that."

She looked around the room and finally grabbed the closest object she saw, a computer keyboard, and swung it wildly as Ramón stepped toward her. The plastic cracked against his arm, but he barely flinched.

"A feisty one," he laughed. "I like that. If we had more time…"

Ruby screamed, the sound raw and desperate, but Ramón was faster. He pinned her arms to her sides with one hand, the other clamping over her mouth. Her bare feet thrashed against the floor as she kicked at his shins, but her strength was no match for his iron grip.

The dog's barking grew more frantic from behind the bathroom door. Ramón rolled his eyes, pulling a roll of duct tape from his jacket. "Hold her still," he instructed Pepe, tearing off a strip with his teeth.

Ruby thrashed harder, her muffled screams turning into sobs as Pepe wrapped the tape over her mouth. They bound her wrists and ankles with zip ties and swaddled her in the bedsheets like a cocoon.

"This one's got claws," Pepe muttered, lifting her feet as Ramón grabbed her shoulders. Together, they carried her out of the condo, the rain drenching them as they made their way to the golf cart.

Ruby's heart pounded as they dumped her onto the floor of the back seat, her tears mixing with the rain. She wanted to scream for help, but the tape choked every sound.

The men went back for the gringo's body, dragging it out and buckling it into the back seat.

"*Vámonos,*" Ramón said.

The cart's motor whined as they navigated the winding, rain-slicked road. Ruby felt the cart lurch and sway, her stomach churning with every turn, worried that it would slide off the road and careen down into the canyon below. Halfway down the hill, the cart came to a stop.

"Let's get rid of him," Pepe said, nodding to the body in the back seat.

Ruby's muffled protests turned to sobs as they hauled the lifeless man out, his head limp as they carried him to the edge of the road. She had wanted Nick far away from her, but not dead! Without hesitation, they heaved his body over the side. Ruby closed her eyes, but she couldn't block out the crunching sound of his body rolling down the steep slope, the wet foliage breaking his fall.

When they reached the shed at the campground, Ramón slid the door open, the metal creaking. They carried Ruby inside and dumped her onto the floor. The room was pitch black.

Ramón crouched down, a slow, cruel grin stretched across his face. "Don't go anywhere," he murmured, his voice low but sharp as broken glass. He gestured with his gun toward the dark corners of the shed. "We'll be waiting outside for you if you try to run."

Ruby lay frozen, the sheets tangled around her, her body trembling. She felt a presence behind her. Her breath hitched as something soft brushed against her arm. Hair.

Her pulse raced. *Someone else is here.*

"Ladies," Ramón added, the word dripping with sarcasm, "you be good now."

The door slammed shut, leaving Ruby alone with the unknown figure behind her.

Jaime awoke to Abacus's frantic barking. He sat up in bed, straining to hear. A scuffle? A door? His heart thudded. Ruby had confided in him recently about feeling on edge, and with what he knew about the people involved in the FBI case, his stomach sank.

He listened carefully, the sound of a golf cart's motor cutting through the rain. He grabbed his phone and called Ruby but got no answer.

Slipping on a jacket, he pocketed the spare key Ruby had given him for emergencies and crept to her condo. Inside, the air was eerily still. Abacus was cowering in the bathroom, his low body trembling. Jaime's gut twisted as he moved to the bedroom.

The sight made his blood run cold.

The sheets were gone, the chair overturned, and Ruby's computer and keyboard lay shattered on the floor. Dark smears of blood dotted the bare mattress and trailed onto the floor. Jaime swallowed hard and dialed 911, his hands shaking as he explained the situation.

65

Francisco sat alone in his darkened office hearing the sound of the coyotes prowling the hills below over the silence of the house. A single candle flickered on the desk, casting restless shadows across the walls. He leaned back in his chair, put his boots up on his desk, and clutched the amulet hanging from his neck. His fingers moved in a rhythmic pattern: once, twice, three times with his right hand, then once, twice, three times with his left. The cool stone pressed against his fingertips, soothing him with its familiar shape.

David's wrong, he thought, his jaw tightening. *This isn't just a bad spell.* He stared into the candle's flickering flame, his reflection in the glass windows barely visible, fractured and distorted.

Voices drifted from the other room, breaking through the quiet. He froze, tilting his head to catch the words.

"Francisco is losing it," Arturo muttered, his tone low and conspiratorial.

"I agree," Gabriel replied. "He's no longer fit to lead La Familia. We need to start thinking about a replacement."

A sharp stab of rage coursed through Francisco's chest.

Those bastards. They think I can't hear them, that I don't know what they're plotting.

He sat motionless, letting the voices flow. Every word hammered at his pride, each one a dagger in his back. But he waited, seething. He wanted to hear it all, wanted them to bare their teeth completely before he struck. *No one betrays La Familia and lives.*

Minutes passed, and the voices stopped.

Francisco stood, his movements slow and deliberate, and slipped into the hallway. The faint glow from the office followed him, casting his shadow long against the tile floor. His footsteps were silent, his breathing controlled, his mind rehearsing the fury he would unleash on those traitors.

He reached the doorway to the adjoining room and stopped, his pulse thundering in his ears. He stepped into the room, ready to confront the traitors—

But the room was empty.

He looked around. The chairs sat neatly pushed in at the table. The air was still. The only sound was the steady ticking of the wall clock.

"*¿Dónde están?*" he whispered hoarsely, feeling confused. *Where are those* cabrones?

He turned, scanning every corner, but there was no sign of Arturo, no trace of Gabriel. A cold prickle ran down his spine.

Were they really even here?

The voices had been loud, clear, and real. He *heard* them. He was sure of it. But now, doubt crept in, worming its way into his thoughts. His chest tightened, and the room seemed to tilt.

Am I imagining things?

He stumbled back into his office and poured a shot of tequila, the liquid splashing over the rim of the glass as his hands shook.

He downed it in one gulp, burning his throat on the way down, but it did little to calm him. Another shot followed, then a third.

For the first time in years, Francisco felt the gnawing edge of fear, not fear of his enemies, but fear of himself.

That night at dinner, Blanca immediately noticed something was wrong with her husband. Francisco sat at the head of the table, his face pale, dark shadows of exhaustion under his eyes. He moved stiffly, as if he carried the weight of the world on his hunched shoulders.

"*Mi amor,*" she whispered, reaching across the table to touch his hand. "What is it? Are you okay?"

"I'm fine," he replied shortly, pulling his hand away from hers. His smile was forced and didn't reach his eyes. "I'm just tired. There have been too many late nights lately, and I haven't been sleeping well."

"Maybe you should rest tomorrow, take the day off from work," Blanca suggested.

"There's no rest for the wicked," he joked darkly, forcing a wink. But his voice cracked, betraying the strain underneath.

The next morning, Francisco bolted upright in bed, remembering the night before, his chest heaving. His hand reached toward the bedside table seeking the smooth stone of his amulet.

It wasn't there.

His pulse quickened. He threw back the blankets and

jumped up, pulling at the sheets and pillows frantically. The amulet was gone.

"Blanca!" he barked, his voice sharp enough to wake her.

She blinked drowsily, sitting up and looking at him questioningly. "What's wrong?"

"My necklace! Where is it?" he asked in a panic.

"What? *Mi amor,* calm down. What necklace?"

"My *amulet!*" he shouted. His hands shook as he tore the sheets from the bed, throwing the pillows to the floor. "It's gone! Every night I put it here on my nightstand, but it's gone. Where is it?"

Blanca's expression shifted from confusion to concern. "I don't know, *querido.* Maybe it fell somewhere. Did you check under the bed or between the headboard and the mattress?" she suggested.

"I checked everywhere!" he raged, teetering on the edge of panic. "Who was in our bedroom? The maid? The kids?"

"Just us, *mi amor.* Nobody else comes into our room at night," Blanca said gently, reaching for his arm to soothe him.

"Don't touch me!" he snarled, jerking his arm away from her touch. His chest heaved, and his face twisted with desperation. "Someone is *messing with me!* They're trying to drive me insane!"

"Francisco, please," Blanca pleaded. "You don't need the necklace. It's just a thing. We can get you another one."

"No!" His scream tore through the room, raw and pained, like a wounded animal. He staggered backward, his hands gripping his head. "I *need* it. Don't you understand? Without it," he stopped, his eyes wild, "everything falls apart."

Blanca stood frozen, her breath shallow, watching as her husband crumbled before her eyes.

66

Ruby heard muffled whimpering from behind her, which only added to her sense of dread. She smelled dampness and the stench of urine. With her wrists and ankles tied with the zip ties, Ruby's breath hitched as she wriggled against the cocoon of bed linens, her muscles straining with each contorted movement. The fabric dug into her skin, its rough weave biting. She gritted her teeth, ignoring the damp, metallic tang of blood on her lip from where they had slapped her.

Ruby was determined to unwrap herself so she could better explore and hopefully escape from her new prison. She tried to bring her knees to a ninety-degree angle to loosen the blanket, but it was wrapped too tightly around her. The duct tape on the outside of the blanket needed to be removed somehow. She was able to log roll her body sideways across the cold floor until she reached the rear wall of the shed.

Her cheek brushed against something cold and sharp. She froze. The faint scent of rust wafted to her nose, mingling with the ammonia-like stink of urine. A saw blade? She pushed her forehead against it, feeling its jagged edge press lightly against her skin, and held her breath as she worked to dislodge it and it finally clanked to the floor.

Her toes fumbled with the saw handle, the blade scraping against the aluminum floor with a metallic screech that made her heart hammer. *Too loud?* She froze, straining to hear if anyone outside stirred, but heard nothing. With trembling legs, she pushed the jagged edge against the zip tie, sawing in uneven jerks. Sweat stung her eyes, blurring her vision. The plastic held fast. "Come *on*," she hissed through gritted teeth, her desperation mounting with each failed attempt. Finally, she felt it snap. She kept working painstakingly with the saw blade until she freed herself from her swaddling.

"Who's there?" she whispered. "Where are we?"

In response, she heard only moans from what sounded like a woman. Ruby carefully made her way over to the figure, holding the saw in her hand. She reached down with her other hand and, like a blind person meeting their child for the first time, felt her hair and then moved down to her face. When she felt the rough tape over her mouth, she felt for the edge and then pulled it off as gently as she could. The woman started sobbing, but Ruby quieted her.

"Shh, I don't know how far the men are from here, and I don't want them to hear us."

"Ruby, is that you?" the woman asked incredulously. "It's me, Jacklyn Carter!"

"Jacklyn? I heard you were missing, but I never thought *I* would be the one to find you! What is going on? Have you been in here for two days? What do they want from us?"

"I'm not sure, but I'm afraid they are getting ready to kill us. We need to get out of here right now!"

Carefully feeling for Jacklyn's ankles, Ruby used the saw to cut her feet free and then worked her way up. She then made her way to the door of the shed and tried to force it open, but it was clear that someone had locked it from the outside.

"I wish I could see what we have to work with." Ruby made her way to the rear wall to feel for what else was hanging there. She felt the sharp prongs of a rake, the blades of a garden fork, and two shovels, one big and one small.

"Let's try to dig under the door and see if we can get out that way. Here, take this shovel."

She thought the floor of the shed was aluminum, but she hoped the ground it was sitting on could be dirt. They took the shovels and cantilevered an opening at the door by standing on the handles with all of their weight. After a few attempts, Ruby felt the aluminum siding of the door start to bend a little, and she slipped a few fingers underneath. She felt dirt! They kept working until they could wedge the blade of the shovel underneath the door until finally the hole was large enough for the two women to fit underneath.

At the last minute, Ruby ran back to the rear wall, grabbed the garden fork and, after listening for signs that the men were nearby and hearing nothing, the two women squeezed underneath the door. Jacklyn had trouble walking and moving as she had been stuck in the same position for a long time. After moving towards some tent structures, Ruby thought she knew where they were — the campground!

"Come on, let's go!" she whispered to Jacklyn. "There is a hiking trail nearby, and if we climb up, we can get to the interior of the island. There should be plenty of places to hide!"

As they made their way to the trailhead in the torrential rain, they heard the sound of a golf cart making its way toward them. They jumped behind some trees and tiptoed in the shadows towards the trailhead, moving as quickly as possible. They heard the men's angry shouts in Spanish when they discovered the damaged door and saw that the women were missing.

"We need to find them right now!" Pepe yelled. "David will have our balls if we let them get away!"

Once the women entered the trail, they made their way up the hill as quickly as possible given the slippery mud, knowing that their lead was small. Ruby had started out barefoot, having been dragged from her bed, and Jacklyn had lost a shoe in her haste.

"I doubt they headed into town. They would avoid the road. I bet they went further into the canyon. Let's go this way!"

"I hope you're right."

They jumped into the golf cart and headed uphill.

"Wait!" Ramón shouted. "Is that a shoe?"

They put the golf cart in reverse to get a better look and noticed the trailhead on the right.

"They must have gone up there. Let's follow them!"

Ramón tucked his gun into his waistband to keep it as dry as possible and then trotted up the hill. Pepe shoved his own gun into his jacket pocket and ran to catch up, slipping now and then as the rain came down harder.

Rain slicked the narrow path, turning dirt into treacherous mud. Ruby's bare feet slid with each step, her legs trembling from the climb. Behind her, Jacklyn panted, her breath ragged. Somewhere below, angry shouts in Spanish cut through the storm. A branch cracked under heavy footsteps. Their pursuers were close, too close. Ruby forced herself forward, biting back a cry as a sharp rock sliced her heel.

Ruby and Jacklyn climbed further up the hill as quickly as they could, knowing that the men were not far behind them now. They finally made it all the way up until they saw a solitary bison bull standing before them across the path. The movie poster hanging in her living room had not done the animal justice. The beast was even more terrifying up close with its muscular frame, horns, and massive head. Water dripped from his shaggy coat in rivulets. The bison's dark eyes gleamed aggressively, nostrils flaring as a snort burst through the rain. Ruby froze, her heart in her throat. The animal pawed the ground, its hooves sinking into the mud and head lowered like a coiled spring ready to explode.

"He must weigh an actual ton!" Jacklyn marveled. "I'm scared to go any closer."

"Let's go!" Ruby shouted. "At least the animal isn't packing heat! We need to take our chances."

The beast watched them closely, and they gave him a wide berth as they went around him. They got to the top of the hill and, looking down, they saw the men closing the distance between them. The men also noticed the women. When the men saw the bison ahead of them, they stopped in their tracks to confer.

"Okay, you distract him while I go around. If he gets close to you, just shoot him!" Ramón told Pepe.

"*N'hombre! You* distract him while *I* go around."

While the men argued, the bull became more agitated by the anger in their voices. Before they could decide, the animal charged toward them. Ramón shot his weapon at the bison but missed when he lost his footing in the mud. He leapt to his feet and ran into the brush but was too late. The sound of gunshots had made the beast angrier. The bison used its huge head as a battering ram, which knocked Ramón backward several feet. It then used its hind legs to viciously kick Ramón in the chest until the man lay still, and finally placidly sauntered off. Pepe ran up the hill away from the scene of carnage and toward the women.

David is never going to believe this! Pepe thought. *Attacked by a buffalo?! If I don't at least deliver the women to the boat, my life won't be worth a single* centavo.

Pepe got within fifty feet of Ruby and Jacklyn, and, appearing from out of the shadows, pointed his gun at Ruby's chest and ordered them to halt.

Ruby's feet faltered, the blade of the garden fork slipping from her grasp. With the gun pointed at her, there would be no hope of using it as a weapon, anyway. She barely felt the rain streaming down her face, her mind consumed by the muzzle of the gun aimed at her.

"Not one more step," Pepe growled, his voice cutting through the downpour. A deafening crack split the air as he fired a warning shot into the mud, the echo rattling their bones. The women knew they had been beaten. They slowly made their way back down to Pepe, who roughly pushed them downhill, marching single file down the path in front of him. When they got back to the campground, Pepe ordered them back into the shed.

"You tie her hands and feet," Pepe ordered Ruby. Once that was done, Pepe tied Ruby up and secured their mouths with duct tape. The three of them were sopping wet, muddy and exhausted.

"Now just wait until I come for you and don't make a sound." He scowled at both of them as he told them, "You have already caused me a lot of problems."

67

The Sea Ray Sundancer pitched and rolled as it made its way into Emerald Bay on the northwest side of the island, its prow slicing through the dark water. The three men scanned the sparsely populated shoreline, their eyes looking at the handful of boats anchored there. The harbor was quiet except for the howling wind scattering salt spray across the deck as Rico dropped the anchor. *No harbor patrol in sight. Good. Less scrutiny.*

Julio kept glancing toward the mouth of the bay as if expecting a patrol boat to appear any moment. "Let's get those fishing poles out," he muttered, his voice low but sharp with tension. Rico nodded, pulling out the fishing gear and quickly setting the lines into the water. The fishing rods stood as props, an excuse for their presence in the storm.

Waves slammed into the Sundancer's hull, each impact jolting the men inside. The wind shrieked, whipping through the rigging and sending icy needles of rain against the windows. The boat shuddered, its anchor rope straining as the storm tested its hold.

On land, David huddled beneath the beach club's awning

north of Avalon Harbor, his soaked hoodie plastered to his face. The rain came in sideways, driven by gusts that rattled the now empty barstools normally packed with tourists drinking margaritas on sunny days. He strained to hear over the storm, his ears catching the faint high-frequency whine of an outboard motor somewhere in the darkness. Relief flickered before the reality of the slippery rocks between him and the dinghy sank in.

David left the shelter of the awning and navigated the dark and wet rocks to reach the boat, the wind pushing him backwards. *One wrong step* … Once David reached the dinghy, he shouted to Julio over the roar of the wind, "Here, take the keys. Here's the pickup address and instructions."

Then David, with the wind whipping rain into his face, followed the deserted path back to the private heliport in Pebbly Beach on the south side of Avalon. He stopped on the way only long enough to remove a black *mano de azabache* necklace from deep in his pants pocket and fling it into the roiling black ocean. Julio and Mario jumped into the golf cart.

"*Jesús, María y José,* let's go get this done. I can't wait to get back on dry land," Mario shouted to Julio. Through the plastic windscreen of the golf cart, Avalon looked like a ghost town now, the streets deserted.

With Pepe already on board, David stepped into the aircraft that had been waiting for him and sat down.

"Where's Ramón?" David asked Pepe. "You are looking a little worse for wear."

"We ran into some trouble. The girls somehow cut themselves loose and made a run for it up into the hills. We were chasing after them when Ramón got into a fight with one of those giant buffaloes and lost."

David froze, his rain-soaked hair plastered to his forehead. "Wait, you're telling me Ramón got taken out by a buffalo? In the middle of a storm?" A laugh burst out of him, sharp and disbelieving. He doubled over, slapping his knee as he gasped for breath. "You can't make this shit up! A buffalo!" His laughter cut off when Pepe's glare pierced through the cabin's dim light.

"It wasn't funny if you were there," he said, irritated. "Poor Ramón. I had to leave his body there."

Against his better judgment, and under threat of death if he did not, the pilot immediately lifted the helicopter into the stormy air and flew them back to San Diego to a waiting black SUV, which drove them across the border back into Mexico.

Julio and Mario reached the shed at the deserted campground and unlocked the door. Ruby's breathing came in short, panicked bursts against the duct tape sealing her mouth. Her arms ached from being so tightly bound, and every muffled whimper from Jacklyn beside her only deepened the pit in her stomach. The shed door slid open, letting in a rush of cold, wet air. Ruby flinched as the men's shadows loomed over her.

"You grab one, I'll grab the other." Ruby's eyes were wide with fear when Julio grabbed her and hefted her under his arm and into the golf cart. Beneath the golf cart's plastic cover, the men gripped the women like cargo, their arms locked around them in mock embraces. The streets were deserted, and the rain blurred the few streetlights, obscuring their faces from any passing glance. To an outsider, it might have looked like a harmless, drunken joyride. Ruby could feel Julio's bony fingers digging into her side, a silent warning not to squirm.

At the beach club, Julio hefted Ruby over his shoulder; her muffled cries were drowned out by the wind. His boots slipped on the wet rocks, the added weight of her body throwing him off balance with every step. "Hold still, dammit," he hissed, adjusting his grip. Behind him, Mario cursed as his foot skidded on a rock, sending both him and Jacklyn's bound form teetering dangerously.

They unceremoniously threw the women into the dinghy, and then Julio and Mario stepped onto the rubber side of the boat lurching dangerously in the rough surf. Rico restarted the outboard motor, and the boat doubled back north to Emerald Bay. Everyone on board was waterlogged and shivering by the time they reached the cabin cruiser, and they moved Jacklyn and Ruby into the cabin.

The Sundancer groaned as Rico wrestled the anchor free, the boat pitching wildly in the storm-tossed waves. Dawn was still hours away, and the black water stretched endlessly in every direction. The wind screamed through the rigging, drowning out the women's muffled sobs from below deck. As the engines roared to life, the torrents of rain obscured the island, leaving only the churning sea and the faint hope of rescue behind.

68

Ricardo gripped the steering wheel as he pulled into the parking structure behind the clinic. His knuckles were white, and his stomach churned, a sour reminder of the hours he'd spent at the police station the night before. As he rolled down the window to greet the security guard, his voice cracked on the usual *"Buenos días"* greeting.

The guard's raised eyebrow didn't escape Ricardo's notice, but he managed a tight smile before parking his car. He sat there for a moment, his hands trembling on his lap. *They know too much.*

Ricardo strode into the New Me clinic, his footsteps echoing down the tiled hallway. He ignored the usual morning greetings from staff, his focus fixed on Marcelo's office door. He knocked twice before entering, shutting the door firmly behind him.

"Buenos días, jefe," Ricardo began, his voice barely above a whisper. He avoided Marcelo's eyes and sat down, his movements stiff and deliberate. "I need to talk to you about something."

Marcelo looked at Ricardo, his expression shifting from curiosity to concern. "Go on."

"On my way home from work yesterday, I was pulled over by the police and taken down to the station."

Marcelo's green eyes widened, and he rubbed his forehead. "What did they want?" His voice was calm, but Ricardo felt the concern underneath.

Ricardo licked his lips, his mouth dry. "They asked about the clinic, both upstairs and downstairs."

When Marcelo first told Ricardo about the secondary operation in the basement, Ricardo was shocked. He knew Marcelo was an aggressive businessman, and he had seen him cut some corners, as people sometimes had to do to circumvent the odious Mexican bureaucracy, but this was something else entirely. Ricardo was also uneasy about Marcelo getting in bed with the cartel. Yes, it was lucrative, but it was also dangerous, he knew. He felt ambivalent about this but wanted to be loyal to Marcelo and walk by his side as he had done over the years, and Marcelo had been good to him. Ricardo also did not want to risk his own income, which had grown exponentially since his days at the warehouse.

Marcelo stood up and paced. "And what did you tell them?"

"As little as I could," Ricardo said quickly, his words tumbling over each other. "I said we handle cosmetic surgeries for *gringos*. That's it. But, *jefe*, they know about the ambulances. They asked why planned elective surgeries would need an ambulance."

Marcelo's jaw tightened, and the room seemed to grow colder.

"I told them I didn't know, that I don't work downstairs. But *jefe*, the reason they let me go is that they want me to communicate with them about all activities in the clinic, to be a *soplón*," he told Marcelo, his voice quaking. "I told them under duress that I would, but obviously I will tell them the bare minimum. I think you should consider shutting down the downstairs operation, at least until this blows over."

"You're probably right, Ricardo, but I think our investors

would forbid this. Not only are they making a lot of money, but our operation is also helping them to move their product north. Our hands may be tied."

"Well, you're the boss," he said uncertainly, "but you know that the clinic is under surveillance. They interrogated me, and I also heard that they interrogated some nurses. You could be next! I think it's too risky to continue right now."

Marcelo immediately called Francisco to give him a sitrep, his hands shaking as he punched in the numbers. "Francisco, you have probably heard by now that the clinic is under surveillance. Can we pause our activities until this blows over?"

"No, that's out of the question!" Francisco fumed. He reached for his amulet out of habit, but of course it was no longer there. He cursed under his breath. "This operation has become a critical part of our business. I will handle it on my end."

Francisco paced the length of his office, his polished boots clicking against the tile floor. Finally, he grabbed his phone and dialed Enrique Cruz, Chief Inspector of the National Guard, his fingers pressing the buttons aggressively.

"Enrique," he said when the line connected. "It's Francisco."

A pause. "Francisco," Enrique replied cautiously, his tone wary. "What can I do for you?"

Francisco didn't bother with pleasantries. "There's surveillance at the New Me Clinic in Tijuana. I need it gone, immediately."

The pause on the other end stretched too long for Francisco's liking.

When the Federal Police was incorporated into the National Guard, Enrique had proved himself and quickly moved up the ranks, and La Familia had been investing in his success. Of course, he had taken the *mordida* like most of his colleagues, a little cash here and there since the police salaries in Mexico were pitiful. He had a family to support, after all. But this extra income didn't add up to a hill of beans compared to how much he earned once he started doing favors for Francisco.

"That might be difficult," Enrique said finally, his voice tight. "The Americans are involved, the FBI, I think. My hands aren't entirely free."

Francisco's grip on the phone tightened, his knuckles going white. "I don't want excuses, Enrique. I want results. Need I remind you of the favors we've done for you over the years?"

Enrique exhaled sharply. "I'll try, but the FBI—"

"Try?" Francisco's voice rose. "Try isn't good enough. Make it happen."

"I'll do my best," Enrique said, his voice barely audible.

Francisco's jaw clenched. "Get it done." He slammed the phone down and hurled it onto his desk, sighing in disgust and frustration.

69

Francisco paced the floor, the weight of La Familia's empire pressing down on his shoulders. His fingers hovered over the phone's keypad, trembling before he punched in the number for the Attorney General of the State of Baja California. La Familia had been investing in the Attorney General's office for just such a situation, and now it was time to call in the chits.

The call connected, and Salvador's smooth, practiced voice answered. "Francisco, good afternoon. I hope everything is well."

Salvador had spent years working his way up the chain of command. He no longer had any qualms about taking money from drug traffickers. There was so much money in circulation that he really couldn't refuse. He lived like a king and sent his children to high-quality universities in the U.S. *And if it weren't me,* he justified to himself, *it would just be someone else.* It was dangerous to say no to someone like Francisco. Salvador had his wife and kids to think about. *Besides, I'm only one person. How could I make the least bit of difference if I tried to stand up to the cartel?*

Francisco forced a tight smile, though no one could see it. "Salvador, my friend. I hope you and your family are doing well."

The Attorney General's relationship with La Familia had been mutually beneficial and lucrative. La Familia's money made its way in large quantities every month to the Attorney General and in return, as the money trickled down to the local law enforcement levels, the Attorney General instructed them to look the other way at drug trafficking operations in the state and assisted La Familia with violent enforcement of this hegemony when needed. He also instructed the officers to target rival drug traffickers by wiretapping their phones and arresting them as well as taking pains to release La Familia members and associates from prison if they were arrested for drug trafficking and related offenses. In much the same way, La Familia also had its tentacles embedded in the Mexican military.

Francisco glimpsed his reflection in the bathroom mirror across the room. Sunken eyes, disheveled hair, a shadow of the man who had once commanded fear and respect without effort. Now, he looked hunted. *This stress will kill me,* he thought grimly. *But not before I handle this.*

Salvador replied, "Everything's fine on my end," though he sounded apprehensive. He knew Francisco didn't make social calls. "What can I do for you?"

Francisco sank into the leather chair behind his desk, its cushions offering little comfort. "I'm in a bind," he admitted, his voice low and gravelly. "One of my businesses in Tijuana— the New Me Clinic— is under surveillance. The local cops, the National Guard and maybe even the *gringos* are there."

Salvador's silence on the other end stretched, the weight of the request settling like a stone in the pit of his stomach.

"The National Guard and the gringos?" Salvador finally said, his voice neutral. He had been in this game long enough to know the stakes. "That complicates things. Are you sure it's them?"

Francisco pinched the bridge of his nose, a dull throb building behind his eyes. "I'm not sure, but I need it handled immediately, and do it quietly."

Salvador leaned back in his chair, glancing at the family portrait on his desk. His wife's kind smile stared back at him, a reminder of why he could never refuse a man like Francisco. *It had been better to take the money than to risk their lives.*

"I'll look into it," Salvador said carefully. "Give me some time to figure out who's involved and what strings need pulling. But I'll warn you, if the Americans are involved, it could be messy."

Francisco's grip on the phone tightened. "Messy is not an option. I don't care how you do it. Make it stop."

The line clicked, and Francisco set the phone down with more force than he intended. He leaned back in his chair, exhaling shakily. His hand drifted to the chain around his neck, reaching for the smooth shape of his black amulet. When his fingers found nothing but air, a wave of unease rolled over him.

He lurched to his feet, pacing around his office again. His mind replayed the events of the previous night, the endless tossing and turning, the Virgin's serene gaze watching him from the ceiling. And then a rooster's crow.

Its crow had shattered the silence, its shrill call piercing through the darkness. At first, he thought it was a dream, but the sound had been unmistakable. His grandmother's words echoed in his mind: *"When a rooster crows at night, death is near."*

His chest tightened as the omen clawed at his thoughts. *Whose death was near? His own? Salvador's? A family member's? Someone else's?*

He glanced out the window at the backyard of the hacienda and the rolling hills below. La Familia's empire was vast, but it felt fragile tonight, like a castle built on sand.

70

Agent Robert Jones's phone buzzed on his nightstand, the ringtone slicing through the early morning quiet. He reached for it groggily, squinting at the screen.

"Sufuentes," Robert muttered, sitting up in bed.

"Agent Jones," came the sharp voice on the other end. "It's time. We're ready to bring Marcelo López in for interrogation and execute the search warrant on the *New Me Clínica Médica*. Do you want to be involved?"

Robert suddenly felt wide awake. His lips curled into a grin. "You're ready to bring them in and you want to know if I want to be involved? Is the Pope Catholic?" He was already swinging his legs out of bed, his adrenaline kicking in. "I'll head down to Tijuana."

"Good. Be here by early afternoon," Sufuentes said, then hung up without another word.

Robert immediately started dialing his team. As he paced his small apartment, the faint smell of last night's meal lingered in the air. "We move today," he barked into the phone, his voice sharp and no-nonsense. "Meet me in the parking lot by 10 a.m. Gear up, tell no one."

He paused before adding one final instruction. "And don't inform Agent Rojas."

The deliberate exclusion hung heavy in the air after he ended the call. Robert couldn't afford leaks, not now.

Agent Sufuentes sat in his cluttered office gathering files. His mind churned as he dialed the number for Chief Inspector Enrique Cruz.

"Cruz," came the curt response.

"We're moving on the New Me Clinic tomorrow morning. The Americans are already on their way."

The line was silent for a beat too long. "Do you have the search warrant in hand?" Cruz finally asked, his voice measured.

"No, not yet," Sufuentes admitted. "We'll finalize it later today. The last thing I need is word leaking out before we move."

Cruz exhaled, a low, irritated sound. "I think you're rushing this. Without the warrant, you risk—"

"We're not waiting," Sufuentes cut him off, his tone firm. "This is happening now. I'm only calling you as a courtesy."

Cruz rubbed his temple as he ended the call. He stepped outside, lighting a cigarette with trembling hands. The dread in his chest wouldn't lift.

He dialed another number.

"Francisco," he whispered when the line connected.

"What now, Enrique?" Francisco's voice was sharp, laced with impatience.

"The National Guard is raiding New Me tomorrow morning. The Americans are involved. There's nothing I can do to stop it."

A string of curses flew from Francisco's mouth. "What the hell am I even paying you for, Enrique?!"

Enrique gritted his teeth. "Listen, can you clear out the clinic tonight? Move the operation temporarily? There's still time."

"I'll handle it," Francisco snapped, ending the call abruptly.

The FBI SUVs rolled to a stop in the dusty parking lot of a non-descript Tijuana hotel just after 1 p.m. Robert stepped out first, scanning the surroundings with a practiced eye. The streets were busy with the sounds of traffic, street vendors calling out, and a faint whiff of roasted corn wafting in the air.

Inside the hotel, the team unpacked their gear in tense silence. They checked the rifles, tightened the vests, and tested the radios.

"Let's get this right," Robert said, his voice low but commanding.

By 3 p.m., Agent Sufuentes arrived in an unmarked truck, his face inscrutable, but Robert didn't miss the tightness in the man's jaw or the glances he threw over his shoulder as they loaded up.

In the staging area, Sufuentes unfolded a large map on the hood of a vehicle, tracing routes and exits with his finger. "We hit the clinic first," he explained. "After securing that location, we will move to the second location where we tracked López."

Robert studied him, noting the unease in his expression. "Are you good?" he asked, his tone sharp.

Sufuentes hesitated. "In this country, there are no secrets," he finally said, his voice barely above a whisper. "We need to move fast. Trust no one."

The weight of those words lingered as the team loaded into their vehicles.

By 4 p.m., the convoy rolled out. Dust billowed in their wake as the vehicles sped toward the clinic. Inside the lead SUV, Robert sat with his rifle across his lap, his heart pounding a steady rhythm.

In the distance, the outline of the New Me Clinic came into view. Its sterile white walls gleamed under the afternoon sun, an ironic facade for what they suspected lay beneath.

"Keep your eyes open," Sufuentes murmured into his radio.

They pulled to a stop just short of the clinic. The team slipped out, their movements rehearsed. From behind the building, a faint rustling sound caught Robert's attention. He froze, signaling for silence.

A man darted out from the rear exit, his face a blur of panic.

"Go, go, go!" Robert shouted, breaking the stillness.

The team surged forward, boots pounding against the pavement as the raid began in earnest.

71

The wind howled as the LA County Sheriff's Department SUV crawled up the winding hillside road toward Ruby's condo. Rain lashed against the windshield, and the wipers struggled to keep up. Inside the vehicle, Captain Morales gripped the wheel.

"It must be a full moon behind these clouds," he muttered. "First the Carter woman vanishes from that cruise ship, and now this. Avalon's usually quiet, some petty theft, maybe a drunk tourist, but two disappearances in a week?" He shook his head, glancing at his deputy. "I've never seen anything like it."

Deputy Anderson adjusted his flashlight in his lap, his face grim. "You think we've got a predator on the island?" he asked, almost whispering as if saying it too loudly would make it true.

Morales didn't answer right away. His eyes stayed fixed on the dark and slippery twisting road ahead. Finally, he said, "Let's hope this neighbor's just got an overactive imagination."

But when they stepped into Ruby's condo, the storm outside seemed to follow them in. The air was thick with the faint metallic scent of blood and the damp, musty odor of the rain-soaked carpet by the door.

The bedroom was a disaster. The bed was stripped bare, and the pillows were on the floor. Drawers hung open, their contents scattered across the floor. A shattered lamp lay near the nightstand, its bulb in pieces on the floor. A laptop and keyboard also lay on the ground where they had fallen from the desk.

Deputy Anderson crouched by the bedside table, picking up a small photo frame with a crack running through the glass and a birthday card with a drawing of a pirate on the front. "It looks like she put up a fight," he said softly.

Captain Morales scanned the room, his stomach tightening. "Yes, there was definitely a fight here. This is bad."

In the living room, Jaime, the neighbor who had called 911, fretted. His rain-soaked hoodie clung to his frame as he wrung his hands. "I heard screaming," he said, his voice trembling. "Then a banging noise, like something heavy hitting the floor. And then nothing."

Morales turned to Jaime, his tone sharp. "Did you see any-one? Did you hear a car, a boat, anything?"

"No, just the storm. And a golf cart," Jaime stammered, shaking his head.

Morales exchanged a look with Anderson. The captain reached for his radio. "We've got foul play here. Call the Harbor Patrol. Let's put out a BOLO. We need to lock the island down."

The harbor was alive with activity as the patrol boats pre-pared to deploy. Rain hammered the water, turning it into a churning, black expanse. The Harbor Master Kevin O'Sullivan barked orders over the roar of the storm.

"No boats leave this harbor until further notice!" he shouted. "I don't care if they're locals or tourists, no exceptions. We've got two missing women, and if they're still on this island, we're going to find them."

The search began with methodical precision. Patrol boats hugged the shoreline where the water was slightly calmer, their beams of light slicing through the darkness as the storm battered their hulls.

At Moonstone Cove, a Harbor Patrol officer leaned over the side of the boat, his flashlight scanning the rocky beach. He saw nothing but the pounding surf and shadows.

"There's not a soul here," he muttered. "No signs of life."

"Just keep moving," his supervisor ordered.

White's Landing and Buttonshell Cove were the same, empty and eerily still. The storm seemed to have driven everyone to shelter. But when they reached Emerald Bay, the beam of their searchlight illuminated a sailboat bobbing in the water.

"Kevin?" the officer called to his boss. "We've got movement."

As the patrol boat pulled alongside the sailboat, an older couple emerged from the cabin. The man shielded his eyes from the searchlight, shouting over the wind.

"What's going on?" he asked, his voice shaky.

O'Sullivan wasted no time. "Two women are missing. Have you seen anything suspicious? Any boats leaving in a hurry or anything out of place?"

The couple exchanged a glance. The woman nodded hesitantly. "There was a boat here earlier," she said, her voice barely audible over the wind. "There were three men, maybe Mexican. It looked like they were fishing."

"And?" O'Sullivan prompted, leaning closer to hear over the storm.

"They left in a hurry," the man added. "They packed up in the middle of the storm and headed toward the mainland. It didn't make any sense. No one in their right mind would leave a safe harbor in weather like this."

"Can you tell me what kind of boat?" O'Sullivan demanded. "Do you remember the size or make? Any markings?"

The woman furrowed her brow, clearly struggling to recall details. "Maybe thirty-five feet. It was a fishing boat, I think, with a blue hull. Sorry, I didn't catch the name."

O'Sullivan scribbled down the information, his handwriting barely legible on the rain-soaked notepad.

The Harbor Patrol wasted no time relaying the information to the Coast Guard. Within minutes, the larger search effort mobilized, and radio chatter filled the airwaves.

"This storm's going to make tracking them a nightmare," O'Sullivan muttered as he stared out at the dark expanse of ocean. "But we don't have a choice. If those women are on that boat, every minute counts."

<h1 style="text-align:center">72</h1>

Rico's knuckles whitened as he took the helm, his jaw set against the howling wind that rattled the Sundancer's cabin. The boat heaved and rolled, each wave slamming against the hull like a fist. Rain lashed at the windshield in relentless sheets, and the horizon disappeared into blackness.

"Keep your eyes sharp," Rico barked to Mario. "We can't afford any mistakes tonight."

Julio, hunched over near the stern, clung to the rail with trembling hands. His stomach roiled, but it wasn't just the violent seas that made the farm boy gag. "This weather is bad. Can't we just wait it out?"

"Wait it out?" Rico shot him a glare. "Do you think La Familia cares about your sea legs? Orders are orders."

The lights of Catalina Island were distant pinpricks now, swallowed up by the storm. Rico eyed his radar with worry as he kept the boat out of the shipping lanes. The last thing they needed was to be spotted by anyone.

Below deck, Ruby pressed her back against the cold wall of the cabin, her breath hitching and her stomach in knots with each lurch of the boat. Her wrists, bound with zip ties, ached against the hard edge of the bench. Beside her, Jacklyn shivered, her face pale and streaked with tears.

"Ruby," Jacklyn whispered, her voice barely audible over the roar of the storm. "What are they going to do to us?"

Ruby swallowed hard, forcing herself to meet Jacklyn's wide, terrified eyes. "They're just trying to scare us," she lied. "We'll be okay. I'm sorry I dragged you into this. I didn't know it would lead to this. Me and my nosy self. My mom always told me it would get me into trouble someday. I should have minded my own business, left this whole mess alone."

"It's not your fault," Jacklyn choked out the words. "This is Kevin's fault for getting involved with these animals." Jacklyn's lip quivered. "I don't want to die."

Ruby closed her eyes, steadying her breathing. Her mind raced, scrambling for a way out, but the zip ties around her wrists and ankles made every move impossible. The stale, humid air inside the cabin and the boat pitching back and forth sickened both women.

Miles away, Andy steadied himself against the pitching deck of the Coast Guard cutter, rescuing an idiotic boater who was fishing near Platform Edith and got caught in the storm, his eyes fixed on the stormy horizon. The call had come in twenty minutes ago about two hostages on a rogue cabin cruiser, a possibly armed crew, and dangerous seas. His pulse pounded in his ears.

The C-130 Hercules helicopter buzzed above, sent by the Coast Guard Rescue Coordination Center, its searchlights cutting through the dark. It flew in a tight search pattern, its heat-sensing forward-looking infrared cameras scanning the seas, hindered by the target boat's automatic identification system intentionally being unarmed. Over the radio, the pilot's voice crackled. "Target located. Cabin cruiser bearing north-northeast. Sending coordinates now." The aircraft stayed on the cabin cruiser, maintaining its distance and keeping its lights off to not spook the crew and keep the hostages safe.

Andy's gut twisted. Something about this mission gnawed at him, a prickling unease he couldn't shake. As the cutter powered through the swells, he scanned the horizon, his hand tightening on the rifle slung over his shoulder.

The Sundancer came into view, thrashing in the waves, its lights off. Andy's heart stopped when the binoculars caught a flicker of movement on the bow. He could make out two figures, bound and slumped, being dragged by their captors. One of them looked like...

"Ruby," he breathed, the name catching in his throat.

Mario braced himself against the railing, rain stinging his face as he pulled Ruby toward the bow. She kicked and twisted, but the slick deck offered no traction. "Don't make this harder than it has to be," he growled, wrapping the heavy anchor chain around her torso.

"No!" Ruby cried, her voice hoarse from screaming. "Please! You don't have to do this!"

Jacklyn sobbed as Julio hauled her forward. "I have children! Please don't—"

Neither man met their eyes. They worked quickly, securing the chains as the boat rocked violently beneath them. Mario's hands slipped, and he cursed under his breath. The cold metal of the chain dug into Ruby's ribs, making it hard to breathe. Her mind spiraled, every crashing wave echoing like a death knell. She knew it was illogical, definitely not the highest priority in this scenario, but she wondered if she would come face to face with any sharks on the way down.

"Hold steady!" Rico's voice cracked through the storm. Mario barely heard him. He fixed his eyes on the distant silhouette of a boat—no, two boats—when lightning suddenly flashed. His stomach dropped. "It's the Coast Guard..." he muttered, his words lost in the wind.

Ruby felt the impact of each torrential wave slamming into the Sundancer's hull rattling through her bones. Her eyes were clouded and stinging from the salty ocean water crashing over her continuously. The chain binding her to Jacklyn groaned with the weight of the anchor as Mario gave it a sharp tug, dragging her closer to the edge.

The C-130's spotlight suddenly blazed, flooding the Sundancer with harsh, white light. A booming voice cut through the storm. "Attention on the boat! This is the United States Coast Guard! Stop your vessel immediately and prepare to be boarded! Bring all of your crew to the back of the boat!"

Rico swore and reached for the handgun tucked into his waistband. "Get rid of them now!" he shouted to Mario, pointing towards the women. "They'll board us in minutes!" Rico hissed, his eyes darting between the approaching rescue boat and the C-130 hovering above.

Rico shot his weapon towards the Coast Guard rescue boat, which returned fire. Rico continued to shoot but wasn't hitting his mark as high waves were cresting and falling. Suddenly he shouted, "I'm hit!" and fell over the railing and into the roiling seas.

Ruby felt herself being dragged by one man toward the edge of the bow. She knew that this was the end. Her body would sink to the bottom like a torpedo with her hands and legs still bound, and the chain wrapped around her body. She glanced up and, to her utter shock and relief, saw Andy crouched in a rescue boat that was launched off the cutter's stern, hurtling towards them.

The rescue boat edged closer to the Sundancer's port side, the Coast Guard cutter providing cover behind them.

Ruby faintly heard Andy scream, "God, Ruby, hold on!" Gripping the rail of the cabin cruiser, Andy hoisted himself onto the deck, his boots slipping as he moved, an M16 rifle tight in his hands. Ruby struggled against her captor as she saw Andy pushing towards her. *Would he make it in time?*

"Back off, or I'll do it!" Mario shouted, using Ruby's chained body as a shield.

Andy leveled his rifle. "Let her go."

Behind him, a crack of gunfire exploded. Julio staggered, clutching his shoulder, and fell hard against the railing. Mario flinched, his grip faltering just long enough for Andy to surge forward.

Mario shoved Ruby towards the railing, her scream swallowed by the wind. "Don't!" Andy roared. Andy lunged at the chain around Ruby's body just as Mario heaved her overboard. Ruby felt herself falling towards the sea. For a split second, everything froze—the pounding rain, the roaring sea—and then Andy's adrenaline-fueled hand found the cold metal of the anchor chain, gripping it with every ounce of strength.

The weight of the chain and Ruby's body nearly dragged him over, but Andy dug his heels in, pulling Ruby back up inch by inch. Behind him, Mario scrambled to his feet, only to be struck by another shot from the rescue boat. He toppled backward, disappearing into the blackness of the sea.

Ruby's limp body fell into Andy's arms as he dragged her to the center of the deck. Her eyes opened wide with terror, and her breath came in shallow gasps.

"You're safe," Andy whispered, cradling her close. "I've got you. It's over."

On the rescue boat, medics worked frantically on Jacklyn, who had been pulled aboard moments earlier. Ruby coughed violently, seawater spilling from her lips, and Andy felt a rush of relief as her breathing steadied.

The helicopter hovered overhead, lowering a basket onto the deck. Ruby felt herself being placed into a basket and watched as Andy helped strap her in to be lifted into the helicopter. She felt his hands tremble as he caressed her face.

"I'm not letting go," he told her, his voice breaking. "Not ever."

Ruby's lips parted in a faint smile before the helicopter lifted the three injured victims away, disappearing into the stormy night.

73

ordon awoke to the shrill beep of his alarm clock that broke the early morning silence. He lay there for a moment, blinking into the darkness, his pulse quickening as he remembered. *Today's the day.* A smile curled across his lips.

The bathroom mirror reflected his restless night, dark circles under bloodshot eyes, a face taut with both anticipation and unease. After his routine of shit, shower, and shave, he put on a plain, worn-out hoodie and jeans. His *go-bag* sat by the door, packed meticulously the night before. He slung it over his shoulder and stepped outside, the morning air biting against his skin.

In the driveway, his less ostentatious Jeep Cherokee, a far cry from his shiny white Range Rover, waited for him like an accomplice. He entered the New Me Clinic address into the GPS and pulled out of his suburban neighborhood, glancing in the rearview mirror as though he half-expected to see someone following him.

By the time Gordon reached the border, the sun was just beginning to rise, casting a grayish hue over the sprawling San Ysidro checkpoint, where forty-eight million people crossed per year. The knot in his stomach tightened as he stopped to purchase Mexican car insurance.

There was no turning back now.

When he finally approached the Mexican side of the border crossing, the chaos of honking horns and shouting pedestrians jarred his already frayed nerves. The uniformed officer waved him to a stop.

"Pasaporte, por favor. What is the purpose of your visit to Mexico, *señor?"*

Gordon forced a smile, gripping the wheel tighter. "Medical treatment."

The officer scrutinized him for a moment longer than Gordon felt necessary. *"Muy bien. Enjoy your stay."*

The gate lifted, and Gordon's Jeep crawled into Tijuana.

The city unfolded around him in a disorienting blur of brightly colored signs, tangled power lines, and the smells of exhaust fumes and street food. Boulevard General Rodolfo Sánchez loomed ahead like a lifeline. His hands trembled as he navigated the wide streets to the clinic, the GPS softly chiming each turn.

The underground parking lot was dim, the lights casting long shadows across the stained concrete. He parked as far from the entrance as possible, the Jeep's metal groaning as he climbed out. His bag felt heavier now, his steps slower.

Presenting himself at the rear door as instructed, he pressed the buzzer. A crackling voice responded, and soon the door clicked open. A nurse, smiling too widely for his comfort, greeted him. *"Buenos días, Mr. Miller. This way, please."*

The air inside was cold and sterile. The nurse handed him a surgical gown and pointed him to a small room. "Please change into this. I'll be back shortly."

The minutes stretched endlessly. The hospital gown clung

awkwardly to his beer belly, and the thin blanket barely offered any warmth. He shivered, his nerves fraying with every passing second.

The nurse returned to insert his IV, her hands brisk but steady. The sharp sting of the needle made him flinch. *"Relax, señor. Soon you'll feel nothing at all,"* she said with a practiced smile, her heavily accented English oddly soothing and sinister.

Gordon nodded but said nothing. His heart hammered as the anesthesiologist entered, explaining the procedure, but his words barely registered.

When the surgeon finally appeared, Gordon sat up straighter. The man's face was expressionless, his voice calm and efficient as he outlined what would happen. But there was something in his eyes, a glint of concern, that made Gordon's mouth dry.

The whole preparation process took a few hours, but it was finally time. Gordon glanced at the clock on the wall as they were wheeling his gurney into the small, stark operating room. *Four o'clock already?* he noted with surprise. *They must be operating on Mexican Standard Time.* Gordon's pulse raced as his eyes caught on a table of gleaming metal instruments.

The anesthesiologist loomed above him, a mask in hand. "Take a few deep breaths and count down from ten, Mr. Miller."

"Ten..." His voice trembled. "Nine... eight..."

The room blurred at the edges, the hum of the spotlights merging with the rhythmic beep of the monitor. Just as darkness began to take him, a deafening boom shattered the air.

The doors burst open, slamming against the walls. Armed men in black stormed in, their rifles raised and laser sights cutting through the haze.

"*¡Alto!* Put the scalpel down and back away from the patient!" one of them barked.

Gordon struggled to open his eyes, but the drugs were pulling him under. The last thing he saw was the surgeon stepping back, his hands raised, as chaos erupted around him.

In the adjacent room, Robert burst in to find another patient, a gaunt young man lying unconscious on a gurney. His forearm displayed a tattoo of the flag of El Salvador, and his hand was missing the pinkie finger.

The second surgeon froze mid-motion, a scalpel glinting in his hand. Robert leveled his gun at him. "Drop it. Now."

The surgeon hesitated, then hurled the scalpel aside and bolted for the back door.

"Freeze!" Robert shouted, but the man was already gone. Outside, the sound of boots on wet pavement echoed as *Federales* swarmed the building. The surgeon stumbled into the parking lot only to find himself surrounded by law enforcement. He raised his hands slowly, his face pale and panicked.

Back in the operating room, Gordon's body sank further into the gurney as the propofol claimed him. He had blurred and disjointed thoughts, but one clear sentence formed in his mind before the void swallowed him.

Those fucking Mexicans—am I really not going to get my kidney today?

74

Francisco leaned back in his chair, watching Blanca fuss over their daughters as they ate. The warmth of the evening at home filled the room, a comforting aroma of mole and the girls giggling over some joke he hadn't caught. For a brief moment, he allowed himself to smile, though the weight in his chest never really eased.

His phone vibrated on the table, the screen lighting up with *David.* He stiffened.

"Cousin, I have some bad news," came David's voice, low and urgent.

Francisco's stomach tightened. He pushed back his chair; the legs scraping against the tile. "Sorry, *mi amor,*" he murmured to Blanca, standing and kissing her lightly on the head. "This is important. I won't be long."

Blanca gave him a questioning look but said nothing, turning back to the girls.

He hurried across the room, feeling a sense of dread. In his office, he shut the door and pressed his back against it, his pulse already pounding in his ears.

"What is it?" he demanded, his voice sharp. "I can't take

much more bad news." He reached up, feeling instinctively for the amulet that had hung there for years. His fingers met only the fabric of his shirt. *Shit. Where was it?*

David hesitated. "It's Tijuana."

Francisco's heart skipped. "The clinic?"

"The National Guard and the FBI raided it," David continued. "They're inside now, searching everything and arresting everyone."

The words hit like a gut punch. Francisco staggered to his desk and gripped the edge, his knuckles white. *"What the hell?!"* he hissed. His voice dropped, shaking with barely contained fury. "Enrique Cruz told me they weren't supposed to raid the clinic until *morning.* We were supposed to have time to clear the basement tonight."

"They moved early," David said, his voice tense. "One of the National Guard agents tipped me off."

"Enrique Cruz," Francisco spat. He slammed his hand down on the desk, the sound echoing in the small room. "That useless *cabrón.* He couldn't even stall them for a few hours?"

Francisco paced the room like a caged animal, his mind racing. "Did they get Marcelo?"

"Not yet," David said. "Apparently, he wasn't there when they raided the clinic. They're looking for him, but..."

Francisco stopped, gripping the back of his leather chair. "Marcelo better not talk," he said, his voice ice. "Do you hear me? If he mentions my name..." His hand clenched into a fist. "he's a dead man."

There was silence on the line for a moment, broken only by the sound of Francisco's heavy breathing.

"I'll make sure he knows," David finally said, his voice heavy.

Francisco let out a long breath and turned toward the window.

Outside, the night seemed darker than usual, as though the world itself knew what was coming. In the warm light of the dining room, where Blanca and the girls were eating, they were oblivious to the chaos unraveling in his mind.

"Keep me updated," he said, his voice colder now. "And find out who tipped them off. I want names."

He ended the call and stared at the phone in his hand. His chest felt tight, his thoughts a tangled mess of anger, fear, and desperation.

Through the thin walls, he could hear Blanca's laughter, soft and carefree. For a brief moment, he envied her innocence. Then he clenched his jaw, pushed the thought aside, and grabbed the family photo from Lola's party.

He couldn't shake the thought gnawing at the edge of his mind: *If Marcelo talks, it's all over.*

75

Marcelo sat in the fertility clinic's sterile waiting room, thumbing through his phone. His heart sank as a message from Ricardo popped up, stark and unforgiving on the screen:

"New Me has been attacked by *Federales*. Everyone is being taken into custody. RUN!"

Marcelo's breath caught in his throat. *Run?* His mind raced, scrambling for a plan. Where could he go? His wife and kids flashed in his mind, their laughter, their safety, but what could he do for them now? *If I stay, I'll lose everything. If I escape, maybe I can come back for them.*

He sprang to his feet, his legs unsteady beneath him. *La Familia was supposed to protect me. We were untouchable.* But now, as panic surged through his veins, Marcelo felt utterly alone.

Spotting a white lab coat hanging on a hook nearby, he grabbed it and slipped it on over his clothes. He adjusted the collar with trembling fingers, looking composed as he moved toward the back door. *If I drive north and cross the border, they'll never expect it.*

His pulse thundered in his ears as he cracked the door open. Cold rain lashed his face, and shadows flickered in the parking lot's dim security lights. He scanned the area and saw no one.

Clutching the lab coat tightly around him, Marcelo stepped out into the storm. His shoes splashed through puddles as he crossed to his car, keeping his head low. He fumbled with the keys, glancing nervously over his shoulder. *Just get in the car and drive.*

Sliding into the driver's seat, he pulled the door shut, exhaling shakily and gripping the steering wheel with clammy hands.

The roar came out of nowhere.

"¡POLICÍA! ¡BAJE DEL COCHE!"

Lights and shadows exploded around him. Figures swarmed the vehicle, their rifles leveled at his face. Shouts in Spanish and English overlapped, barking orders.

Marcelo froze, his chest tightening until it felt like he couldn't breathe. His bladder gave way as panic overtook him. *This is it.*

"Out of the car!" one officer yelled, yanking the door open. Another hand seized his arm, dragging him out and slamming him against the car. Pain shot through his cheek as it met the cold, wet metal.

"Take it easy!" Marcelo gasped. "I'm a businessman!"

A tall, broad-shouldered, dark-skinned man stepped forward, his face partially obscured by the rain. *"Mr. Businessman,"* the man said with a sneer, his voice thick with sarcasm. "Or should I say, *Mr. López?* We're going to have a nice little chat about your operations."

Marcelo tried to speak, but the words stuck in his throat.

Behind him, another agent jogged out of the clinic, his face pale and drawn. He gestured sharply to the other man.

"Robert," he said, his voice low but urgent. "There's something inside you need to see. Now."

Robert's gaze flicked to Marcelo, his eyes narrowing. Then he nodded and disappeared into the building.

Marcelo craned his neck toward the clinic, trying to see what was happening inside, but the rain blurred everything.

Robert emerged again, his jaw set, and his eyes blazing with anger. "There are young women in there," he said, his voice tight. "Sedated and unconscious. There's an exam table with stirrups and surgical equipment—" He struggled for control, shaking his head. "Whatever's going on in there, it's bad."

He turned back to Marcelo, his fists clenched at his sides. He had never wanted to punch someone in the face this much in his life, and he had grown up as a black man in the South, so that was saying something. *"You've been a very naughty boy,"* he said, his voice furious. "You'll be extradited to the U.S. soon enough."

They threw Marcelo into the back of a waiting police vehicle. His thoughts spun as the rain came down in torrents, his wet clothes clinging to his skin.

Through the window, he saw more ambulances pulling up to the clinic entrance. Gurneys rolled out, each carrying a drugged or unconscious woman.

One woman stirred, her eyes blinking open as the paramedics worked around her. Her voice cracked as she spoke, hoarse and raw.

"Valentina, Ximena, where are my daughters? *Mis princesas?!*"

The paramedic leaned closer and whispered in her ear. "*Señorita,* please try to relax. We're taking you to the hospital."

The woman's head rolled to the side, her confusion giving way to panic. Her weak sobs cut through the clamor of the rain.

"My daughters," she whispered again. Tears rolled down her face as her voice grew louder and more determined. *"My daughters."*

Marcelo turned away, his chest tightening as guilt and fear clawed at him. He didn't know who the woman was, but her voice haunted him.

"My daughters!" she screamed, a desperate sound that pierced the night.

76

Francisco lay in bed staring at the faint outline of the Blessed Mother painted on the ceiling. He clenched his jaw as he whispered a prayer to her for sleep. Just a few hours, he thought. That was all he needed to think clearly, to figure out his next move, but his mind refused to allow that.

The events of the past few weeks had gutted him. Losing the Tijuana operation was a blow he hadn't seen coming, a significant financial setback. His thoughts circled back to the moment everything unraveled. That damn doctor and his loose tongue had set off this chain of disasters.

He turned onto his side, fists grabbing the sheets in anger. *That idiot.* He could almost hear him spilling secrets to the FBI, his words dismantling the empire he'd spent years building. His body shook with pent-up rage. Sleep wasn't coming tonight; that much he knew. It was nearly dawn when he noiselessly slipped out of bed, careful not to wake Blanca.

In the dim light of his office, Francisco paced the floor. He examined the framed photo from Lola's *quinceañera* the previous year. The photo had captured a perfect night, Lola in her yellow ball gown looking like a princess and the rest of the happy family gathered around her smiling for the picture. Francisco stood tall, looking proud, commanding, like a man on top of the world.

He traced the edge of the picture frame with his thumb. *I'm not that scared little boy anymore. I'm a man people fear, respect, and obey.* And yet, here he was, undone by a nobody, an accountant, a *pinche* pencil pusher. His grip on the frame was so tight, the glass nearly shattered.

The phone's loud ring shattered the silence.

Francisco grabbed it, his voice tight and on edge. *"Bueno?"*

"Paco," David said, his voice tense. "It's me."

"What now?"

"I'm sorry, Cousin, but there's more bad news."

As David spoke, Francisco's heart hammered. Two of his men were dead, one more injured and captured. The U.S. Coast Guard had seized the boat. And worst of all, the accountant was still alive. The phone felt heavy in his hand as he hung up, the weight of David's words pressing on him.

Francisco's blood burned hot. He shoved the photo back onto the shelf and began pacing again, this time faster, his fists clenching and unclenching. *This cannot stand. That girl has humiliated me and La Familia.* If word got out, the other bosses would see him as weak, a laughingstock. *Un hazmerreír.*

He stopped pacing and took a deep breath, forcing himself to focus, although the last few weeks had taken a toll on his ability to think clearly. It was a risk, he knew, but if he wanted this done right, he'd have to handle it himself.

The wet hospital parking lot glistened, and the streetlights highlighted the curtains of falling rain. Francisco adjusted the green scrubs he'd changed into and clipped on the forged ID badge. His recent haircut and shaved mustache left his face sharper and less recognizable.

Keep your head down.

He entered through the employee entrance. No one looked at him twice as he took the elevator to the fifth floor. When the doors opened, the nurses' station came into view. Three nurses were stationed there. Two blonde women focused on their computers, and a male nurse spoke animatedly into the phone.

Francisco looked around and spied Room 515. *There were too many eyes.*

He ducked into Room 500 across the hall. An elderly man lay unconscious, his pale skin illuminated by the glow of the monitors. Without hesitation, Francisco began pulling cables from the machines, one by one, until alarms blared. He slipped back into the hallway, unnoticed amidst the commotion.

Seconds later, a nurse rushed into Room 500, calling out over her shoulder, "We've got an alarm! Room 500!"

Francisco slipped into the room across the hall. The old woman in the bed gasped, startled, and opened her mouth to scream.

"No, *señora,*" Francisco hissed, grabbing a pillow from the bed. Before she could make another sound, he clamped it over her face.

Her bony hands clawed at his, weak and trembling. He held firm, gritting his teeth as her struggles weakened. The alarms on her monitor joined the growing cacophony.

A nurse burst into the room, her face flushed from rushing. "What's going on in here?"

Francisco straightened, feigning calm. "I was servicing the monitor. I must have unplugged the wrong cable. My mistake."

The nurse glanced at the bed, frowning. "I'll check the patient. Thanks for catching it."

She turned to silence the alarm, and Francisco slipped out, heading toward Room 515.

The nurses' station was now empty, its occupants pulled away by the chaos. Francisco crept, heart pounding, towards the accountant's room.

He opened the door and stepped inside, shutting it softly behind him. The woman on the bed stirred, her eyelids fluttering. Her voice was groggy but suspicious.

"Who are you? Where's Andy?"

Francisco didn't answer. He lunged toward her, his voice a low growl. "I'm your worst nightmare."

Her eyes widened as she struggled to sit up, but Francisco was faster. He grabbed the syringe from his pocket and uncapped it. The liquid glinted in the faint light, a lethal dose of potassium chloride.

The accountant's voice broke as she whimpered, "Please—"

Francisco plunged the needle into her IV line, injecting the liquid in one swift motion. The monitors screamed as her body jerked once, then went still.

Francisco wiped the syringe on his scrubs and slipped it back into his pocket. He had left the room and had almost reached the elevators when the overhead intercom blared: "Code Blue, Room 515."

A small, satisfied smile curled his lips as he stepped into the elevator. By the time the doors closed, his mind was already on the next problem he needed to solve. As he headed outside to the waiting car and saw the moon poke out from behind the clouds for the first time in days, he took a deep breath of the clean post-rain air and felt some semblance of calmness restored in his heart.

The SUV sped south through the desert under a moonlit sky. Francisco stared out the window, the weight of recent events pressing heavily on his chest. His thoughts churned. The seized shipments. The heated plazas. The betrayals that sprung up everywhere.

And now, his amulet was gone.

Who knew how much the necklace meant to me? His mind raced, turning over names and faces. And then, like a punch to the gut, realization hit him.

"David," he whispered. Suddenly, he felt and heard the ground beneath him shift and rumble before an earthquake of thoughts began to rock his world. There was only one person in the world who had his finger on the pulse of all of the business operations and also knew the significance of his amulet, how it made him feel centered and safe in a dangerous world.

It made no sense. David was family, blood. They had grown up together. Francisco trusted him implicitly. But who else had the knowledge and the access?

His stomach twisted. His hands trembled as he reached instinctively for his amulet, only to remember again that it wasn't there.

"Chucho," he called to the driver, his voice shaking. "I need a drink."

Chucho handed him a flask. Francisco took a deep swig of the distilled agave plant of his Aztec ancestors, the mezcal burning its way down his throat as he looked out the window at the Mexican desert surrounding him.

David had flown back to San Diego by helicopter in the

storm and then made his way back to Mexico. That must have been a brutal helicopter ride, he thought. He would tease David about it later. But then he remembered David was lost to him. He already felt like an orphan. *No matter,* he told himself, I will take care of business like I always have. He closed his eyes, letting the fire of the mezcal anchor him.

When he opened them again, his mind was clear. *David must think he can outsmart me. But he'll learn.*

He texted his cousin: *Lunch tomorrow. My house. 1 p.m.*

David's response came quickly: a thumbs-up emoji.

Francisco's jaw tightened. As the SUV sped through the desert night, he leaned back, letting fury replace the ache of betrayal. Tomorrow, he thought. Tomorrow, he would settle this.

77

ndy's boots thudded against the hospital floor as he made his way to the basement cafeteria. His stomach growled, but his mind was on Ruby, pale and bruised but stable. He hadn't left her side since they'd brought her in. Now, as he picked through a row of sandwiches, he allowed himself the smallest flicker of relief. She was going to make it.

The buzz of the intercom overhead barely registered as he stopped at the cashier and set his tray on the counter. It crackled, and a garbled announcement filtered through.

"...515..."

Andy's ears pricked up at the familiar number. He froze, wallet in hand, and listened more carefully.

The intercom crackled again. This time, the message was clearer: "Code Blue, Room 515."

His heart stopped.

"That's Ruby's room!" His voice echoed in the cafeteria. His tray clattered to the floor, sending his water bottle rolling under a nearby table.

Andy bolted for the elevator bank, his breaths coming hard and fast. The display above the doors mocked him. Both elevators were stuck on upper floors. He spun on his heels, spotting the stairwell door.

He took the stairs two steps at a time, then three. His thighs burned, but adrenaline propelled him forward. The stairwell echoed with the thudding of his boots and the hammering of his heart. When he burst onto the fifth floor, his worst fear greeted him.

Ruby's room was swarming with clinicians. Nurses, doctors, and techs moved in a blur of scrubs and urgency.

Andy pushed forward, his voice breaking. "What happened? She was fine a few minutes ago when I left!"

A nurse stepped in his path, blocking him. "Sir, you need to step back. Let us work."

"Just tell me what's going on!"

She didn't answer. Her lips pressed tight as she focused on the room.

Andy stood helplessly in the hallway, his fists clenched at his sides. Through the gaps in the crowd, he saw them intubating Ruby. One nurse straddled the bed, pumping her chest with rhythmic compressions. Another grabbed a set of defibrillator pads.

Andy watched the monitor. The squiggling, chaotic lines of ventricular fibrillation confirmed what he feared. Ruby's heart wasn't beating, just quivering.

The nurse pressed the pads to Ruby's chest and shouted, "Clear!"

Andy flinched as the shock jolted Ruby's body, her limbs jerking unnaturally.

The monitor held steady for a breathless moment, then reverted to chaos.

Andy's legs felt like rubber, and he slumped against the

wall. He couldn't take his eyes off Ruby's still form as the team worked furiously, their voices overlapping.

"Another round of epi!"

"Compressions, let's go!"

"Clear!"

Another jolt with the paddles.

Andy watched them work on her, willing her to fight, to come back to him. His training told him what was happening, but nothing prepared him for the feeling of being the loved one who could only watch helplessly while they fought to keep her alive.

Minutes felt like hours until finally, a blip.

The rhythm on the monitor changed to a steadier one, weak but unmistakable. Ruby's heart was beating again.

A collective sigh of relief swept through the room. The doctor yelled, "We've got a pulse."

Andy felt his knees buckle as the tension he had been holding drained from his body.

A nurse waved him into the room. He ran to Ruby's side and took her hand, still cold but warm enough to prove she was alive. He pressed it to his cheek and let the tears come out, his shoulders shaking.

"I thought I lost you," he whispered, laying his head on her chest.

Ruby's face was pale against the white pillowcase, but the steady rise and fall of her chest told him all he needed to know in that moment.

78

David hesitated outside Francisco's office, his hand hovering over the doorknob. He could hear the maids chattering from deeper in the hacienda, but here at Francisco's office it was silent. He knew that Francisco would be angry at him, so he steeled himself, knocked, and then pushed the door open and stepped inside.

Francisco didn't rise to greet him as he normally did. Instead, he stared at his glass of mezcal, the amber liquid catching the light. He finally looked up at David, his eyes cold and unblinking, before he drained the glass and set it down with a deliberate *clink*.

"Cousin," David greeted him, forcing a smile as he leaned in for a hug. The embrace was brief and awkward. David took a seat on one of the hand-painted chairs, its bright colors in stark contrast with the tense atmosphere in the room.

"Let's take a walk," Francisco said flatly, rising to his feet.

David followed him out onto the veranda and then down the stone steps that led to the edge of the hacienda's backyard. The air smelled of wet earth from the recent rain, and the hills below stretched out across the valley.

Francisco stopped at the edge and crossed his arms. David

lingered a few steps behind, his hands shoved deep in his pockets, and neither man spoke.

"I know you're angry at me," David finally ventured. "About Avalon. I'm sorry, I fucked up. I take full responsibility for how it went down."

Francisco's expression was unreadable. He tilted his head slightly but said nothing.

"I did what I could to contain the damage," David continued, his voice faltering. "Julio's loyal. He won't talk, and there's nothing the Coast Guard can trace back to us, so we're good there."

Francisco turned to face him, anger burning in his eyes. "Do you think that makes it any better?"

David faltered. "You're right, Paco. I just—"

"I handled Long Beach," Francisco interrupted, his voice low but simmering with barely contained fury. "Because you failed to do it."

David's mouth went dry. "I know, Paco. I know I failed you. I'm sorry."

Francisco stepped closer, so close that David smelled the mezcal and the smoke on his breath. "I need you to swear something. Swear to me on your son's life you'll tell me the truth."

David's chest tightened. "Of course, *primo,* anything."

Francisco's voice dropped further until it was barely a whisper. "Did you take my *mano de azabache?*"

The question shocked David, although it shouldn't have. David flinched, his breath catching in his throat. "What? Paco, no! How can you even ask me that? I would never—"

"Don't lie to me," Francisco snapped, his voice rising. David took a step back, but Francisco's hands shot out, grabbing

David by the collar and yanking him closer. Tears brimmed in Francisco's eyes. "Don't you dare lie to my face!"

David froze, his hands hovering near Francisco's arms, but he didn't pull away. "I didn't—"

"You did!" Francisco roared, his voice cracking. His face twisted with anguish as tears streaked down his cheeks. "You were my brother, David! My *blood!* Everything I had, I shared with you! And this is how you repay me?"

Francisco's body shook with rage, his neck veins bulging. David's own eyes filled with tears, his lower lip trembling as he finally broke under the weight of his cousin's fury.

"Say it," Francisco snarled. "At least have the decency to admit it like a man!"

David closed his eyes, bowing his head. When he finally spoke, his voice was raw. "This life, Paco. It eats everything it touches. You didn't deserve this. I'm so sorry."

Francisco loosened his grip on David, all of the air seemingly gone out of him, and his hands fell to his sides. He stepped back, his chest heaving.

"Leave," Francisco said, his voice barely audible. "And don't come back. Don't let me see your face or hear your name again. Because if I do…" His voice broke, but his eyes were ice cold. "I'll kill you myself."

David hesitated, his face crumpling as he too choked back a sob. He nodded once, then turned and walked slowly toward the house.

Francisco stood frozen, watching his cousin walk away. For the first time in his life, he felt truly alone.

He reached for his amulet, his hand reaching up to his chest before he remembered again that it was gone. The void reminded him of everything he had lost.

Was it all worth it?

The question lingered as Francisco stared out over the hills, but he got no response.

79

r. Carter stepped out of the exam room, berating himself for not being able to concentrate on his patient and her needs. All he could think about was Jacklyn, the boys, the FBI, and all of his current troubles. It felt as if his entire life had been a game of Jenga, building a tall tower until it became so unsteady that it collapsed. He felt like he couldn't breathe.

"Dr. Carter." His physician's assistant intercepted him in the hallway, her voice low and serious. "The FBI is here. They want to talk to you."

Kevin froze. Since the Coast Guard had rescued Jacklyn, the FBI had been waiting for her to recover in the hospital so that they could interview her. Would she betray him? He wouldn't blame her if she did.

"Tell them to contact Jack Neufeld, my attorney," he replied, forcing a calmness into his voice he didn't feel.

"I did," she whispered, glancing nervously toward the waiting room. "They said they need to speak with you personally."

He knew what that meant. Kevin nodded, his throat dry, and hurried toward his office. Once inside, he closed the door behind him and sagged against it, his pulse hammering in his chest.

On the desk sat a framed photo of Jacklyn, smiling as she held their youngest son in her lap, his older brother standing beside them. They had taken it in Hawaii on their last family vacation. His fingers shook as he studied the photo. He could almost hear Jacklyn's reassuring voice calming the chaos in his mind.

But it wasn't her voice that filled his head now. It was that other voice, the one that had been in his head since childhood. *You'll never be good enough.*

Kevin rubbed his eyes and tried to take a deep breath. He couldn't go out there. Not now, with the FBI waiting to interrogate him, to pull out the final Jenga block of his fragile life.

He grabbed his wallet and keys, the photo forgotten on the desk, and slipped out the back door of the office. The hallway was quiet except for the ding of the elevator. He moved quickly, his footsteps soft against the carpet, his breath ragged.

The exit to the stairwell loomed ahead. He pushed the door open and ran down four flights, gripping the railing to steady himself. At the bottom, he paused, peering through the narrow window in the door to the street outside.

When he saw no sign of the FBI, he slipped through the door and into the open air, the late afternoon sun blinding him for a moment. Keeping his head down, he walked briskly to his Mercedes. His heart thundered as he slid into the driver's seat and started the engine.

The Pacific Coast Highway stretched before him. *Should I head north or south?* His hands gripped the wheel, indecision clawing at him. He turned south towards the border.

In the waiting room, the two FBI agents exchanged impatient glances. "Where is he? What's taking him so long?" one asked.

The nurse returned looking confused. "I'm sorry, but he's not in any of the exam rooms. I think he may have left."

The agents' expressions hardened. One of them pulled out his radio. "We have a runner. Notify Newport Beach PD. APB on Dr. Kevin Carter, white male, mid-forties, driving a silver Mercedes sedan. Possibly heading south on PCH."

Without waiting for the elevator, the agents bolted for the stairs, taking them two at a time.

Dr. Carter pulled into the Crystal Cove State Park parking lot and parked as far away from the other cars as possible. His hands were shaking as he cut the engine and stepped out. The ocean spread before him, a vast expanse of blue, the waves shimmering in the fading light of the setting sun.

He followed the steep trail down to the beach, his polished dress shoes slipping on the sandy path. At the bottom he paused, letting the ocean air fill his lungs. The rhythmic crash of the waves soothed him, if only for a moment, and he felt a pang of regret for his choices. A squadron of pelicans crossed the sky in front of him in a V-formation. He removed his shoes and socks, letting the cool sand shift beneath his toes. Button by button, he opened his dress shirt, letting it fall to the ground. The winter breeze chilled his bare chest, and he had goosebumps on his skin as he stepped toward the water.

The first wave lapped at his feet, cold and biting to his skin. *It was definitely not like the warm Hawaiian water from our family vacations.* He hesitated, glancing over his shoulder. The beach was almost completely empty now, the lifeguard tower a silent sentinel in the distance.

He waded deeper, the chill seeping into his bones, but he didn't stop. The ocean pushed him forward, pulling him further from shore with each step.

He swam out, his strokes sluggish against the water's resistance. He had been a runner, never a swimmer. The buoy marking the swimming limit bobbed ahead, but he kept going. His muscles burned, but still he pushed forward, the horizon stretching endlessly before him.

You'll never be good enough. Never special enough.

He swam past the buoy, its chain disappearing into the dark ocean depths. The lifeguard tower was barely a speck now, the beach a faint line on the edge of his vision. His arms felt like lead, and his breaths were shallow and labored.

Finally, he stopped swimming out, treading water as the sun dipped lower, its pink and orange hues painting the sky. Catalina Island loomed on the horizon, its silhouette dark against the fiery backdrop of the sunset.

For a moment, he floated, the salty water cradling him like Moses in the basket of reeds. Then, with a final exhale, he let himself sink.

The cold water enveloped him, and the last light of the sun slipped behind the island. His final thought was not of escape but of failure.

I'm not good enough.

80

R uby shifted her weight in the stiff hospital bed trying to get comfortable, the rhythmic beeping of the heart monitor filling the room like Muzak, annoying and unheard at the same time. Andy's warm hand felt comforting in hers. She closed her eyes, but although the seas had calmed, her own thoughts were still a maelstrom.

It felt like a lifetime ago that she had been lounging on her balcony in Avalon, watching pelicans dive for fish offshore and sipping iced tea. Back then, life had seemed manageable and routine. But that was in the distant past. It had all started with those damned bank statements.

She had tried to brush off the discrepancies, just as Dr. Carter had suggested. *"It's not worth the trouble,"* he'd said with a dismissive smile. But the numbers didn't sit right with her. They didn't add up and, as an accountant, she knew that numbers always told a story. Ruby had been curious enough (nosy enough?) to dig deeper, even though she knew it might lead somewhere dark.

"Andy, does the hospital have my personal effects? Maybe in the closet there?" she asked, pointing to the small cupboard in the hospital room.

Andy removed a plastic bag with Ruby's still damp clothing. When he reached into the bottom of the bag, he pulled out Ruby's charm bracelet.

"Is this what you're looking for, hun?" he asked, the heart charm dangling from his fingers.

Ruby felt tears of relief roll down her cheeks. Maybe, she realized, the heart had nothing to do with finding love again. Maybe instead it symbolized courage, and *that* was what had appealed to her all those months before on the Acapulco beach. She thought about Psalm 31:24: "Be strong and let your heart take courage," encouraging a person to have the spiritual fortitude to act even when they are afraid. She had certainly felt afraid over the past few weeks, but she had acted despite her fears, and that made her feel good about herself.

When Robert finally explained the full results of their investigation, including the abductions, the disappearances, the stolen organs and the murders, her stomach had turned. She remembered his words in the hospital room: *"Innocent people were being butchered, Ruby. All for a kidney or liver someone in the U.S. doesn't want to wait for,"* as if they were being spoken right now.

She had spent her career calculating profits and losses, but this? This was profit drenched in the blood of innocent victims. She had tried not to imagine the faces of those who'd been murdered, but they haunted her, anyway.

Andy's soft squeeze of her hand brought her back to the room. His hazel eyes were watching her with concern.

"The doctors say you'll need to stay in the hospital another night or two," he said, his voice gentle. "But then we can take you home."

"Good," Ruby murmured, her throat dry. "I just want to go

home and hug Abacus." Her voice cracked. "He must be traumatized, poor guy. I'll probably have to get him some dog Xanax."

Andy chuckled, the sound lightening the mood in the grim hospital room. "Your brother Jack called earlier to check in on you. And Robert stopped by, but you were out cold. He wanted me to tell you that Jaime's been taking care of Abacus. Oh, and get this, he said the FBI might never have cracked this case without you. He thinks they'll want to hire you for their financial crimes team. And," Andy grinned, "he said he's getting promoted."

Ruby smiled faintly but didn't respond right away. She looked out the window.

"I'm happy for him," she said finally, her voice distant. "But I can't think about work right now." Her chest ached as she looked back at Andy. "I want to sit on the balcony of my condo and watch the ocean." She closed her eyes, and when she opened them, she searched into his eyes and then asked, "Can you stay with me?"

Her question hung in the air, vulnerable and raw. The armor she had worn for years, against her mother, against men like Nick, against herself, had cracked, and she didn't want to patch it back together.

"Of course," Andy said without hesitation. "I've taken leave. I'll be there as long as you need me."

Ruby felt her shoulders relax for the first time in days. "Thank you," she whispered, her voice trembling.

The door opened, interrupting the moment. Janice swept in, Doris following like a loyal shadow.

"Hi, Mom. Hi Janice," Ruby said, forcing a smile.

Janice let out a long sigh, unraveling the scarf from around her neck. "The traffic was ridiculous. And parking? Don't even get me started. I'm absolutely exhausted." She waved a dismissive hand toward Ruby's bed. "But I had to see you."

Ruby swallowed down a barb forming at her lips. "Thanks for coming, Mom."

"I'm sure you're doing better," Janice continued, "but I'm not. I just came out of sheer willpower, you know. Ashley's coming to stay with me for a few days. Did I tell you her husband got promoted to VP? I'm so proud of him." Her gaze shifted to Andy. "And you must be the famous Andy. Careful with this one," she said, pointing at Ruby. "She's like a black hole; she'll pull you down with her."

Ruby closed her eyes, taking a deep breath to stop herself from rolling them. *"May you be happy... may you be free from suffering..."* she thought silently.

Janice's visit was mercifully short. Sensing Ruby's discomfort, Andy gently escorted her and Doris to the door, telling them that Ruby needed to rest.

"I get it," Janice huffed. "I come all this way, when I'm not feeling well myself, and now you just want me to leave? Fine." She turned sharply. "Let's go, Doris."

The door clicked shut, leaving the room blessedly quiet. Ruby sighed, her chest tight with both relief and heaviness.

Andy leaned closer, reaching out to wrap her hand in his. "You don't have to carry her weight anymore," he said.

Ruby nodded, though the ache remained. Her mother would never change, but Ruby could choose how much power she let Janice have over her.

For now, all she wanted was to go home, wrap herself in Abacus's unconditional love, and heal.

81

Sweeping in like an unexpected tide, the arrests washed through hospital corridors and private practices. The FBI took down the American doctors in Dr. Carter's network one by one except for Carter himself, who had slipped through their fingers. The doctors, shackled in suits that once commanded authority, maintained their innocence with trembling voices.

"We had no idea," they insisted. "We only referred patients for treatment."

But the patients told a different story. These were men and women with scars to show for the new organs beneath their skin. What could be taken from them now? They had nothing to lose, and their testimonies pointed directly at the shadowy New Me network.

The consequences were swift and brutal. Stripped of their medical licenses, the doctors faced indictment, their glossy careers reduced to ash.

The DEA fired Agent Miriam Rojas in disgrace, and she had numerous charges pending against her.

Farther south, the FBI turned its gaze toward the man behind the operation: Francisco Obregón. The mere mention of his name in Mexico was enough to still conversation. Layers of protection shielded him, corrupt officials, armed guards, and La Familia itself, bound by loyalty and fear.

Even so, the Mexican authorities were willing to try. La Familia had grown too bold, its crimes too visible. But Obregón didn't leave trails, and those who knew the truth, Marcelo López among them, kept their mouths shut. Not because of loyalty, but because they knew the price of betrayal.

La Familia didn't send messages; they left brutal examples for everyone to see.

And even if Obregón could be taken out, he could easily be replaced, and possibly by someone worse. A power vacuum could lead to increased violence, with rivals fighting each other for territory and markets. And the drugs would continue to flow north, because despite the U.S. government having spent trillions in the war on drugs, the demand for them was still as strong as ever.

At the hacienda, Francisco paced the path that lined the perimeter of his hacienda, his polished boots crunching against loose gravel. The valley below spread out like a painting, the golden light of the setting sun igniting the fields in fiery hues. But Francisco wasn't admiring the view.

He ran his hand along the wrought-iron fence, his gaze distant. David's betrayal had cut deeper than he cared to admit. For weeks now, his mind replayed the moment, the venom in David's voice, the crack in his own resolve as he'd ordered his cousin to leave. Yet what choice had he had? Betrayal wasn't something he could afford to ignore.

Still, the void left by David's absence lingered. He felt it like a physical ache. Francisco clenched his jaw. "You need to move forward," he muttered to himself. "Always forward."

Ahead of him, the backyard bustled with activity. Workers strung lanterns between the tall trees. The sounds of laughter and music drifted toward him, preparations for Esperanza's *compleañera*. It had been a year since Lola's grand celebration, but he remembered the joy on her face, the way the entire town had buzzed with life.

My daughters, my princesses, will never lack for anything, he thought.

Yet beneath his confidence was a gnawing unease. The FBI, the whispers in town, the tightening grip of law enforcement—it was all too close. But Francisco wasn't afraid. He'd faced worse threats before.

"I'm still the king," he said aloud, straightening his shoulders.

82

Janice tore a piece from her almond croissant, the flaky layers crumbling onto the white ceramic plate in front of her. She popped it into her mouth, closing her eyes as the buttery sweetness hit her tongue. "Mmm," she groaned, savoring the moment. "I swear, Doris, these are the best."

Doris, sitting across from her at the small marble-topped table in the French bakery, stirred her espresso, the small spoon clinking softly against the porcelain cup. "I'm glad you like it," she said, her tone dry.

Janice brushed a few rogue crumbs from her tropical-print Chico's blouse. "Did I tell you about Ashley?" she asked, her voice brightening. "She made this huge sale to a Saudi sheikh who's buying it as an investment property! She's really knocking it out of the park these days." A proud smile spread across her face as she leaned back in her chair.

"That's nice," Doris replied, the corners of her lips tugging downward. "Has she been to see you lately?"

Janice didn't catch the sting beneath the words. "Oh, she's been so busy with work," she said, waving a hand dismissively. "But I'm sure she'll stop by soon."

Doris raised an eyebrow, her spoon pausing mid-stir, but she didn't press the point.

As Janice finished off the last bite of her croissant, her phone rang, startling her. She wiped her fingers on a napkin, grabbed the phone, and answered it mid-chew, her voice muffled. "This is Janice Simon."

"Mrs. Simon," a man's voice said on the other end. "We have some good news. A liver match has become available for you. Please come to the hospital as soon as you can for evaluation."

Janice froze, the rest of her croissant forgotten. Her hand shook as she lowered the phone to her lap, her wide eyes looking to Doris. "It's finally time," she whispered, her voice cracking.

Doris sat up, setting her espresso aside. "Well, then," she said, more briskly than warmly, "let's not waste a minute."

Janice fumbled to call Ruby but could only leave a message. *She's never there for me when I need her.* "Ruby," she said, her words hurried, breathless. "Don't rush, but come to the hospital when you can. Doris and I are heading there now."

The drive to Janice's house was a blur, and neither woman spoke. Doris gripped the steering wheel as if she were navigating a minefield, her lips pressed into a tight line. Janice sat beside her, twisting her hands in her lap.

At home, Janice grabbed the small overnight duffel she'd kept packed for months, the same one she had packed for her visit to the New Me Clinic. The bag felt heavier, as if it sensed the moment's importance.

Back in the car, the 405 freeway stretched before them as they navigated to the hospital.

Doris glanced over. "Are you nervous?"

Janice nodded, her fingers clutching the strap of her bag. "Terrified," she admitted.

"Well," Doris said, her voice softening for the first time that day, "you've waited long enough. You're ready for this."

Janice turned to look out the window, the city lights blurring in the distance as they headed toward Cedars-Sinai Hospital. For the first time in years, she allowed herself to imagine what life might feel like without the weight of waiting hanging over her.

83

The woman with a long gray braid down her back tightened an orange bandana around her head. Her weathered hands, calloused from years of washing dishes, a small tin heart-shaped *milagro* pinned to her chest, gripped a white cross etched with her son Alejandro's name. She stood among a group of women, their faces relief maps of grief and defiance, each holding a cross or a faded photograph of the child they were still searching for. The air was thick with the scent of marigolds from nearby *Día de los Muertos* altars, their vibrant orange blooms contrasting with the stark white of the crosses.

The women called themselves *madres buscadoras,* the searching mothers. Their mission today, like so many others before, was a desperate one: to search the unmarked graves scattered across the Mexican land, to comb through morgues and prisons chasing the faintest shadow of hope. The odds were grim as only two percent of the missing were ever found, but hope was stubborn, and grief sharper than fear.

Each step they took could mean danger. The cartels and law enforcement didn't take kindly to their presence. Over the years, too many of the mothers had been silenced, murdered for asking questions nobody wanted to answer. But today, *Día de los Muertos,* the Day of the Dead when the boundary between the living and the dead was said to thin, the mothers' sorrow turned into a louder defiance.

In the main square, where families celebrated their loved ones with marigold-laden altars and painted sugar skulls, the mothers formed a line. Their chant broke through the festive music and laughter, their voices raw and demanding: *"¿Dónde están nuestros hijos?"* Where are our children?

Alejandro's mother's voice cracked with each shout. She gripped his cross, tears streaking her lined face. Beside her stood Noemi, Alejandro's girlfriend, holding up a large photo of him, his familiar smile looking back at her frozen in time. Noemi's throat burned with anger as she screamed his name, her grip on the photo trembling.

She remembered the last time she saw Alejandro, his easy laugh, the warmth in his dark eyes. It had been a lifetime ago, it seemed. Now, every day without him felt like a punishment, a reminder of the violence that had swallowed him whole.

Noemi's anger festered, her mind racing. She was tired of the fear that gripped her every time she left her home, tired of the violence controlling her every move, tired of a government that looked away while bodies disappeared and lives were shattered. She thought of the cartels, their thirst for power and blood, but her anger turned northward too toward the U.S. The demand of the buyers and their endless streams of money funded the carnage. Noemi clenched her fists. If there were no buyers, there would be no market. If there were no market, there would be no blood-soaked streets. But the buyers in the North remained invisible, their hands seemingly clean, while families like hers bore the weight of their addiction.

The mothers' chants rose above the noise of the square. Passersby stopped to watch, some bowing their heads in sympathy, others turning away uncomfortably.

Noemi didn't care who was watching. She stared at Alejandro's photo, her resolve hardening. The painted skulls and skeletons around her reminded everyone that death was an inevitable part of life, not something to be feared. But here in Mexico, death didn't wear the painted smile of a Day of the Dead skull, or offer the promise of a peaceful afterlife. Death here came with greed and violence, its hands stained red, leaving behind the cries of mothers and girlfriends.

The square grew quieter, the festive music subdued under the weight of the mothers' cries. Noemi held Alejandro's photo higher, her voice joining the others, raw and fierce: *"¿Dónde están nuestros hijos?"* Where are our children?

Even if no one answered, she vowed the question would never go silent.

84

uby's golf cart navigated the winding path down the hill, the sun casting long golden shadows over the island. She parked near the Casino and stepped out, the pavement warm beneath her sandals. The air smelled of brine and sun-dried seaweed, and a breeze ruffled with her hair, tangling the loose blond curls. She drew a deep breath, letting the salty air fill her lungs.

Ruby turned toward the water. The waves sparkled, and she heard the chatter of beachgoers drifting up from the Descanso Beach Club. She hesitated, glancing back toward the path that led to her condo, her safe and predictable home. But today wasn't about safety.

It's time.

Her palms were damp as she removed her visor and gripped her snorkel and fins. She stepped toward the dive park tentatively, like a man to the gallows, her legs trembling like a newborn deer as she approached the stairs leading down to the water. Each step was slow and deliberate, as if testing the resolve she wasn't sure she had.

The ocean shimmered in various shades of blue, so clear that she could make out the bright flashes of garibaldi fish darting between the kelp below. Ruby surveyed the water for shark fins above the surface. Some things never changed.

She tied her hair back with trembling fingers and slipped the rash guard over her bathing suit. She sat on the edge of the stairs leading down to the water. The rail felt cold and slick beneath her grip. She tugged the mask over her face, adjusted the strap, and took a deep breath.

The water lapped at her toes, then her calves, then her thighs. She flinched as the chill crept higher. *Okay,* she whispered to herself. *Just take one step at a time.*

When she finally jumped in, the shock of cold stole her breath, but as she resurfaced, gasping and laughing, she felt a thrill shoot through her chest. Floating on her back near the shore, she let the sun warm her face. The island's silhouette rose sharply behind her, framed by the sinking sun.

I'm doing it, Dad. For both of us.

The salty water cradled her, weightless and forgiving, as if to say, *Welcome back.*

That evening, Ruby sat curled in a patio chair on the balcony of the condo that in the end her mom had decided not to sell after all, a mug of tea cooling in her hands. She felt grateful to still be working on the island as a sole practitioner with private clients. The Board of Accountancy had investigated the claims against her and ruled that they had no merit.

The ocean stretched out before her, glowing orange and pink in the twilight, and the rhythmic crash of waves filled the silence. Abacus lay beside her, his tiny snores rising and falling in time with the surf.

How did I get here? she thought, as she looked out at the vastness of the Pacific Ocean towards the mainland.

She had spent most of her life locked in the pursuit of security, safety, and stability. It had been her shield against the
world, her armor against vulnerability. As an accountant, she
had prided herself on her ability to control the chaos around
her, the checks and balances, on ensuring that everything
added up. But in the last year, nothing had added up.

The moment she uncovered the trafficking network, everything she thought she knew about herself and her life had
crumbled.

Now, for the first time she could remember, Ruby realized
she wasn't just a witness to the world around her; she was
a participant. She had actively shaped her destiny, and in
doing so, she had reclaimed a piece of herself that she had
lost long ago.

She had learned, in the process, that fear didn't go away.
But it could be managed and used as fuel and motivation. She
realized that her need for control had been a defense mecha-
nism, a way to feel safe in a world that often felt unpredictable
and dangerous. But now, she understood that safety wasn't
about control but rather acceptance.

Acceptance that she was vulnerable. Acceptance that life
could change in an instant, and that was okay. *That only a
person who risks is free.*

Her eyes wandered to the mosaic project on her craft table
inside. Shards of iridescent blues and greens caught the dim
light, arranged in a pattern she hadn't known she could create.
It had taken weeks of painstaking effort and patience to fit the
broken pieces together. She traced the process in her mind,
selecting fragments, turning them over, and finding the spot
where they belonged.

She hadn't rushed. She had been careful but unafraid to

take risks. Now, with the design complete, all that remained was the grout to hold it together.

Much like her own life.

The last year had shattered her, left her in jagged pieces. The trafficking network, the danger, the fear, they had exposed her, stripped her down to nothing. But from the wreckage, she had started to rebuild, slowly and imperfectly, piece by piece.

As Ruby walked toward the sliding glass door to go back into her condo, the last rays of sunlight stretched across the sky. As she reached for the door handle, she paused, looking out at the ocean one last time. In the distance, the ferry made its way toward the mainland, its lights flickering in the darkening sky. She thought about Andy, who had become a steady presence in her life. She knew deep down that she couldn't push him away forever. He had been there when she needed him most, and he had never asked her to be anyone other than herself.

She walked in and stepped over to the craft table and looked down at the iridescent blue and green seashell mosaic project that she had finally completed last night. It had taken time and patience to create the design piece by broken piece, but she had done it. She was still recovering both physically and emotionally from the trauma of the past year. But she started to feel that her life, once in disparate broken pieces, was now pieced together into something coherent, colorful, and beautiful.

The world felt impossibly big, and its problems endless. But maybe it wasn't about fixing everything. Maybe it was about doing what you could, when you could, for the people you could. One life, one moment at a time, one broken piece at a time. *The Power of One.* And maybe that was enough.

She had no idea what the future held, or whether she would ever truly feel free of the shadows of the past. But for the first time, she wasn't afraid of the unknown. The horizon no longer seemed like an intimidating void. It felt like the promise of something new, of growth, and of embracing the possibilities ahead.

Acknowledgements

Dear Reader:

Thanks for taking a chance on my debut thriller. If the book resonated with you, I invite you to consider leaving a review on the platform where you acquired or encountered this book. This will help other readers discover and support my work as an author.

A 2021 *New York Times* article by Oscar López entitled, "GONE: Nearly 100,000 people have disappeared in Mexico. Their families now search for clues among the dead" inspired this project. Photos of clothing and personal effects of the victims discovered in clandestine graves accompanied López's article.

I thought I was reasonably well informed about global affairs, at least for an American, but the statistics shocked me. *How could I not have known about this?* I wrote this story—fictional and (hopefully) entertaining but based on actual news headlines—to educate and inform readers about the toll of the global narco-trafficking industry, which leaves innocent victims on both sides of the border in its penumbra.

I am immensely grateful to my early readers for their critiques of my work before it was ready for prime time: Barb Sims,

Annette Fineberg, Rebecca Gillman, Scott Menter, Lili Landman, Maureen Brown, Eric Brown, and Corey Nelson, as well as my daughters for their unwavering enthusiasm.

I would like to express my gratitude to subject experts, including Greg Wisner, a retired U.S. Coast Guard officer now running the local School of Sailing and Seamanship, who provided guidance on how the Coast Guard would intercept and board a vessel. Thanks also to the clever and devious Dr. D.P. Lyle, author of "Murder and Mayhem", who guided me in how to hypothetically poison someone in the hospital setting. My thanks go out as well to the indomitable Jerri Williams, a retired FBI agent, podcast hostess, and crime writer on a mission to "rep" the FBI organization. I also learned a lot from Ioan Grillo, a badass boots-on-the-ground journalist who has written extensively about narco-trafficking and gun running.

Finally, I am thankful for the support of my writing community. My fellow writers in the Sisters in Crime organization have inspired me, especially the Guppy Chapter classes for writers who are still learning the craft. I am especially grateful to the late Jean Ardell for being my first writing teacher at the Newport Beach Public Library, as well as Chris Epting, author extraordinaire and writing teacher at the same location.

In the time it has taken me to complete this book, the number of the disappeared in Mexico has risen to over 130,000.

About the Author

Deborah Siminou is a former CPA, fluent in Spanish and several other languages, who has conducted financial audits and criminal investigations while serving in the U.S. Foreign Service in Washington, DC and Latin America.

Now an executive in the medical devices industry, she lives behind the Orange Curtain in Orange County, California. In her spare time, when she isn't writing, Deborah volunteers to assist refugees and asylum seekers in her community. She enjoys reading, practicing Pilates, and traveling to exotic destinations.

Deborah is a member of Sisters in Crime. Some of her nonfiction writing is available at DeborahSiminou.substack.com and Medium.com/@dsiminou.

www.DeborahSiminouAuthor.com